SADDLE UP

VICTORIA VANE

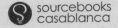

sourcebooks
casablanca

Published by Sourcebooks Casablanca, an imprint of Sourcebooks, Inc.
P.O. Box 4410, Naperville, Illinois 60567-4410
(630) 961-3900
Fax: (630) 961-2168
www.sourcebooks.com

Printed and bound in Canada.
MBP 10 9 8 7 6 5 4 3 2 1

For Annette

Chapter 1

WITH SPEAKERS BLASTING AEROSMITH'S "BACK IN THE Saddle," the buckskin-clad rider vaulted onto the horse's back. Squeezing moccasin-covered heels into the animal's flanks, he pierced the air with a war cry and entered the arena at a hand gallop, crouched low over the pinto stallion's neck.

Bareback and bridle-less, he performed an intricate series of maneuvers—flying lead changes, spins, and piaffes—before circling one last time and sliding to a stop in the center of the arena. Leaping to the ground, he strode the length of white-rail fence separating him from his enraptured spectators, leather fringe softly slapping long, muscular legs as his horse trailed closely behind.

His black eyes were piercing, his cheekbones prominent, and his features, chiseled perfection. His physique was equally mouthwatering, honed of lean, hard muscle. "I'm not here to teach you how to train a horse," he said, black eyes dancing over his captivated audience. "That's not what this is about. I'm here to tell you how you can forge a lifelong partnership, a spiritual bond that is virtually unbreakable." He paused, the connection with his spectators almost palpable.

"Just as in love," he continued, "there are three possible kinds of relationships you can have with your equine partner. The first is much like a stale marriage.

You barely tolerate one another. When you speak, he mostly ignores you. Like a passionless husband, this horse is completely indifferent to you."

He glanced over his shoulder.

Cued to his movement, the horse turned his hindquarters and walked off.

The audience snickered.

"Unless, of course, he wants something from you."

The horse came sauntering back to nudge his pocket, snatched a treat, and then promptly trotted away again with its head in the air.

"As you might guess, this one-way relationship can lead only to frustration and ultimate dissatisfaction."

He paused again, this time for effect.

"The second kind of relationship is confrontational and combative. You fight all the time, exchange harsh words, maybe even blows. You use the crop, and he reciprocates with his teeth. You are almost fearful of him. When you ride, he bucks and rears, employing any tactic to get you off his back. You beg and plead, becoming euphoric with the least crumb of cooperation."

He reached out tentatively toward the horse. It reared, baring its teeth, then kicked out and bolted across the arena.

"The third kind of relationship is what we all seek— the romance and passion. The magical relationship when your two souls become one. Like a good lover, he not only responds to your sounds, moods, and body cues, but even comes to anticipate your innermost thoughts and unspoken desires."

He looked over his shoulder with a smile. The horse came trotting up, offering his muzzle with a soft nicker. The man once more scanned the spellbound faces and his mouth stretched into a slow, seductive smile. "Now I ask, which kind of relationship do you want?"

Miranda glanced up from the video monitor as her roommate, Lexi, passed by. "Whoa, Nelly!" she exclaimed with a double take. "*Who. Is. That?*"

Miranda paused the video. "*That's* the guy I'm filming tomorrow. He calls himself Two Wolves. He's supposed to be some sort of equine behaviorist."

Leaning over Miranda's shoulder for a better look, Lexi gave a low whistle. "Man, just look at that ass."

Miranda rolled her eyes. "Don't drool all over my keyboard, Lex."

Lexi peered closer, clearly appreciating the glittering eyes, silky black hair, and delicious hard body. "Rawrrr." Lexi gave a throaty growl. "I'd do him in a heartbeat."

"By the look of it, so would half the women in his audience," Miranda replied dryly, not about to admit she was just as enthralled. She'd never seen anyone quite like him. From the top of his head to the tips of his beaded moccasins, everything about the guy oozed raw sensuality. One thing for certain: He sure knew how to work a crowd. No wonder he'd caught Bibi's eye.

Lexi popped the top of her Dr. Pepper. "Randa, honey," she chided in her native West Texas drawl, "just because you aren't gettin' any doesn't mean you have to begrudge the rest of the world."

"My love life, or lack thereof, is none of your business, Lex."

"Someone needs to make it their business, because you certainly aren't doing anything about it."

"I don't have time—"

"No time?" Lexi snorted, nearly choking on her

drink. "You have nothing *but* time. How many hours a week do you spend vegging in front of the tube, watching old movies?"

"It's work!" Miranda protested. "How can I learn anything if I don't study my craft?"

"All right, I'll bite, but why not take one lousy night off just to play? Go out and mingle with the other half, spread some pheromones."

"Like where?"

"I don't know." Lexi shrugged. "How about the beach?"

"Are you kidding?" Miranda snorted. "With this skin? I have to wear SPF 40 just to walk out to my car."

"Then go clubbing with me."

"No offense, but I'm really uncomfortable in those kinds of places. I don't have the right look or wear the right clothes. I don't fit in with all the 'beautiful' people here."

In four years she'd had no real dates to speak of. Not that she hadn't wanted to date, but she'd never been all that comfortable meeting new people, let alone Lexi's flamboyant crowd of actors and musicians. No matter how hard she'd tried, she always felt like a fish out of water. That was the one thing she hated most about L.A., feeling insecure. She knew she didn't fit here. Although she'd accepted that long ago, acceptance didn't alleviate loneliness. Lexi had just about given up on her. Then again, who had time for a real relationship anyway?

Lexi laughed. "Honey, this is Southern California. Anyone can be beautiful. All you need is a credit card. Do you think this nose came naturally?" She turned her head to display a pert, perfect profile. "So what's the story with this hottie horse whisperer, anyway?"

"I don't really know," Miranda said. "Bibi called a couple of hours ago, telling me to drop whatever I had going on this weekend to go down to Rancho Santa Fe. Marty was supposed to video for her, but he's in the ER with a kidney stone. She wants me to fill in for him."

Bibi was a big name in indie filmmaking and long accustomed to everyone jumping at her command—not that Miranda had any plans this weekend, or any other. She didn't care that Bibi was giving her the assignment only because her lead videographer had called in sick. The reason didn't matter. All that counted was that she'd finally have a chance to get behind a camera and prove herself.

"In Rancho Santa Fe?" Lexi's brows rose. "Not quite slumming it, are you?"

"It's only a promo video," Miranda said, "but I'm hoping she'll finally let me have some creative input."

"Don't get your hopes up too high," Lexi warned. "You know how tough this business is."

"I know." Miranda sighed. "But I can't help hoping for a chance. Hey, do you want to go with me? We haven't done anything together in ages. It could be really fun."

"Wish I could," Lexi answered. "I'd love the chance to get up close and personal with him." She nodded to the paused image. "But I got a callback yesterday on the new zombie flick. I have to memorize the script."

"You actually have lines in this one? I thought zombies didn't talk."

Lexi grimaced. "No lines exactly. But I plan to raise my grunts and groans to an art form."

"Good luck with that," Miranda remarked.

Lexi's brows met in a scowl. "Need I remind you that Jamie Lee Curtis got her big break by screaming?"

"I'm sorry, Lex. I didn't mean to sound disparaging," Miranda replied, adding with an apologetic smile, "Break a leg, okay?"

In truth, she couldn't help feeling a pang of envy. Like her aspiring-actress roommate, Miranda had arrived in Hollywood with stars in her eyes. Lexi was at least getting callbacks, but thus far, the closest Miranda had come to fulfilling her own dream was fetching lattes for the camera crew.

After Lexi disappeared into her room, Miranda went back to the video. She'd initially hoped this would be her chance to prove herself, but put little hope in a project featuring a man decked out in Native American regalia doing a bunch of circus tricks. It was unlikely to win her any professional accolades, no matter how smoking hot he was.

Determined not to go into the project blindly, she spent the rest of the afternoon researching her subject, but Google gave her almost nothing besides his appearance schedule and clinic videos. Other than a brief bio on his website, the man in the ass-hugging buckskin was a complete mystery.

―⁓―

The following morning, Miranda tossed her overnight bag in the back seat of her VW Jetta and rolled down all four windows before pulling out of the drive. The AC had quit working months ago, but rather than wallowing in misery, she chose to fantasize that she was behind the wheel of the shiny red Mustang convertible she'd promised herself once she got her big break. It was the car she'd vowed to drive in the entire length of the Pacific

Coast Highway—still another unfulfilled promise she'd made herself the day she'd arrived in L.A.

Everything about California had been so exotic and exciting back then, but over time, disappointment and disillusionment had begun to tarnish the glitter of Tinsel Town. Passing the historic Studio City Theatre on Ventura, she was vividly reminded of the dream that had driven her west in the first place—the chance to make movies. Would she ever get a break? Statistics weighed heavily against it. Only stubborn pride had kept her from hanging it all up and going back home to Ohio.

Hedged in by traffic on all sides, she crept along, lost in her thoughts, until finally merging onto the Hollywood Freeway. Although this assignment wasn't quite what she'd hoped for, she was determined to make the best of it. She consoled herself that it was at least a step up from the weddings and bar mitzvahs that normally filled her weekends. The drive would also give her the chance to escape the monotony of her real life for a few days.

Approaching the junction of Interstates 5 and 710 in East L.A., she suddenly felt like she'd come to a fork in her life. For five years she'd been too blinded by ambition to enjoy herself, and what had it gotten her? An overpriced apartment the size of a postage stamp and a lonely single bed.

Seconds passed.

Her hands tightened on the wheel.

A horn blasted as she swerved right into the lane leading to the Long Beach Freeway. The ocean route would add at least two hours to her drive, but she was determined to fulfill at least part of her dream.

Chapter 2

ARRIVING AHEAD OF SCHEDULE, MIRANDA PRESENTED HER employee ID to the security guard manning the entrance. "Hi. I'm Miranda Sutton with Starlight Productions. We're filming an event here." With Lexi's reminder of her neglected love life lingering in her mind, Miranda flashed her most disarming smile.

"Sutton?" He scanned a sheet for her name. "Go ahead." He nodded, and then opened the gate without even looking up.

"Thanks," she replied, disappointed in having wasted her best smile.

Pulling through the elaborate wrought iron entrance, Miranda found not one, but three full-size equestrian arenas and a parking lot dotted with high-priced cars. Pulling between a Lexus and a Mercedes convertible, she parked and climbed out of her car, camera bag slung over her shoulder. Finding no sign of Bibi, Miranda checked her watch. She was an hour early.

Miranda decided to scout the site. As she approached the main arena, she encountered a curvy brunette in tight-fitting white dressage breeches and glossy black boots leading a huge chestnut horse with a stud chain wrapped tightly around its nose. The horse was visibly agitated, with its ears pinned and nostrils flared.

Although Miranda hadn't been around horses in several years, she knew enough to recognize the signs of its distress. Any time he snorted or pulled his head away, the woman gave a hard jerk on the chain, which only seemed to increase the animal's agitation. Miranda was almost ready to speak out when a man appeared and snatched the lead from the woman's hands.

"What the hell are you doing?" the brunette demanded.

"Pain is only going to get resentment from him, not respect. Right now this animal is fighting you every step of the way—and this is why." To Miranda's amazement, he unsnapped the chain and then removed the animal's halter as well. The moment the horse realized it was free, it spun and bolted, bucking all the way to the far end of the arena. "Most horses will walk or trot over to the fence when released. Picasso ran like his tail was on fire. What does that tell you?" he asked the gaping woman.

"He's difficult to work with," the brunette snapped. "All the horses in his bloodline are high-strung."

"That's because high-dollar show horses like him spend way too much time confined in a stall. You need to let your horse just be a horse now and then."

The woman frowned at the chestnut that was now galloping laps around the arena. "How the hell am I supposed to control him now?" she demanded, hands on hips.

"You're going to get nowhere unless you give him some downtime. When he snorts, tosses his head, bucks, or kicks up his heels, he's not being bad, Steffi. He's just feeling good."

"I thought I was paying you to work with him," she said, still visibly miffed.

"I will. But first we need to teach him that work can be fun. Let him have it, and he'll start to relax. Once that happens, he'll concentrate better on what you want rather than trying to escape at every opportunity."

"I don't understand the point," the woman argued. "How is any of this going to improve his performance under saddle?"

"Performance is all about cooperation. Just give this guy a few minutes to release some pent-up energy and I promise he'll be a different animal. Time spent on this kind of activity will pay off in spades once you're in the saddle."

The cowboy tossed the lasso he held in his hands toward the horse. The startled animal changed course and began trotting in the other direction. The man's soft, sexy voice was as confident as his movements. "I don't care what gait he's in as long as he's moving in the direction I send him in. In essence, we're acting the way a dominant horse would in a herd situation."

Mesmerized, Miranda watched the interplay between man and horse. She uncapped her camera lens and began filming the cowboy and the horse. Within minutes, the animal was moving in a relaxed, floating gait. Although her personal experience with equines was limited to the working livestock on her grandparents' ranch, she recognized the expert skill with which this man directed the animal's movements.

After several more laps, it lowered its head and approached the cowboy. He stretched out his hand and caressed the animal's muzzle. "You see how little effort that took? Now he's willing to get to work."

The cowboy turned in Miranda's direction. It was

only then that she realized he was the man she was looking for. The long, loose hair he'd worn in the videos was
plaited in two long, neat braids covered by the cowboy
hat. In his jeans, faded denim shirt, hat, and boots, he'd
looked far more cowboy than Indian—until he'd faced
her. Their eyes met for the first time. His black brows
rose as his gaze dropped to her camera. "I didn't realize
we were being filmed."

The brunette speared Miranda with a haughty stare.
"Filming someone without permission. That's presump-
tuous, don't you think?"

"I'm sorry," Miranda said. "Maybe I should have
asked, but I hated to interrupt you." She lowered her
camera and climbed over the fence rail. "I'm Miranda
Sutton. I came to film the clinic." She stepped forward,
hand extended. He took her hand in his, flashing a smile
so dazzling it made her breath catch. She struggled not
to gape.

"I'm Two Wolves," he introduced himself.

"I kinda figured that out," Miranda said dryly.

"This is Steffi Hoffman," he said. "A…client of mine."

"A pleasure," Miranda replied, once more offering
her hand.

The brunette ignored her.

Shrugging off the snub, Miranda asked, "When you
finish here, do you think we could talk for a few minutes? I have some ideas on camera placement I'd like to
run by you."

"Sure thing," he replied. "But I'm on Steffi's dime at
present. Can you give us about fifteen more minutes?"

"No problem." Miranda perched on the fence
and continued to watch him work with a much more

cooperative Picasso. Although she'd found him attractive before, the amateur videos she'd watched didn't come close to doing him justice. No indeed-y.

"Since you don't like the longe whip," Steffi said, "could you show me how to throw your rope?"

The ploy was painfully obvious, but he didn't seem to notice.

He sidled up from behind and placed his hands over hers to demonstrate the motion of throwing the rope. Steffi shot Miranda a triumphant look. Her possessiveness hinted that there was more to the relationship than simple instruction. No surprise there. Miranda turned away with a pang of envy. Although she couldn't deny the instant attraction she felt toward him, rich and beautiful always won out over plain with brains.

———⁓———

"You worked magic with him," Steffi gushed after Keith handed the horse off to Steffi's groom, *without* the stud chain. "I didn't realize until I met you how much I need your...services. When can we do another session?"

Ignoring the innuendo in her tone, Keith forced a smile. "I'm a clinician, not a trainer."

"Maybe you don't understand," she insisted. "I can pay you whatever you like."

"It's not always about money, Steffi." Or meaningless sex. But it had taken him a long time to realize it. "I've already shown you what he needs. Now it's up to you to make it work."

"But what about what I need?" she asked, any pretense of subtlety now gone.

How many times had he heard lines like that from rich

women looking for a hired stud? He'd lost count. "I'm sorry, Steffi, but my time isn't my own." He nodded at the slim girl with the camera, whose name he'd already forgotten. Melissa? Melinda? Something with an *M*. He was glad she'd hung around.

Steffi gave the camera girl an icy look. "Another time then. You have my number?"

"Yes. I certainly do," Keith reassured her. In the beginning he'd been flattered by all the attention and had rarely turned down an attractive woman, but eventually he'd tired of the constant propositions.

After extricating himself from Steffi, Keith returned to find the camera girl leaning on the gleaming white PVC fence rail.

"I guess you must get that a lot," she said.

"Get what?" He cocked a brow, feigning ignorance.

"Nothing," she replied quickly, a blush tinting her cheeks. "I won't keep you long if you have another... er...engagement." She glanced in Steffi's direction.

"No engagements beyond my exhibition...unless you're free?" The words slipped out thoughtlessly.

Surprise flickered in her gray eyes. "Free for *what*?"

"Whatever you like." He gave her the slow, sexy smile that never failed him.

She stared back at him. "You're joking, right?"

"Am I laughing?"

Her eyes met his for only a millisecond before she looked away. Her face colored even deeper than before. Odd. California women didn't blush. She seemed so different from all the others he'd met here. Refreshingly different. He found her natural look and direct manner appealing after a steady diet of women like Steffi.

"I don't think so," she said. "I've got a lot of work to do."

"So do I, but we all need downtime now and then." He flashed a grin. "Just ask Picasso."

"You have quite a way with horses," she said. "It's an impressive talent."

"I have a number of other talents I'd like to impress you with," he quipped back.

Her brows came together in a puzzled look. "Are you flirting with me? You're wasting your time," she said.

She was rebuffing him? When was the last time that had happened? He couldn't even remember. It was a novel experience, and not one he particularly cared for.

She was gazing at him steadily. "Can we please talk about the cameras now?"

"Sure thing." Her rejection stung, but Keith shrugged it off. If he wanted company, there were hundreds of women coming to his clinic. He could take his pick.

"Keith, you had us all entranced," Bibi gushed after his performance. "You're such a natural. I know you came out here only to do your clinic, but have you thought about staying in Southern California?"

"Staying? For how long?" he asked.

"Indefinitely," she replied. "I'm talking about relocation."

"I really hadn't considered it before." It was a half-truth.

He'd thought for some time about making some changes and finally setting down roots somewhere. He'd accepted the invitation to come to Rancho Santa Fe, hoping to explore the opportunities here, but he already knew California wasn't for him.

"You really should," Bibi continued. "The camera absolutely loves you. I think we could get you into films. There are so few indigenous actors in L.A. The field is wide-open. All you need to do is enroll in some classes."

He'd been around long enough to know nothing came for free. It didn't make sense that someone with her reputation would want to make a promo video for him. He'd wondered from the start what strings were attached.

"You know, I think your looks are exotic enough to carry off several ethnicities." Her gaze swept slowly over him in a way that answered any lingering doubts about what she wanted. Her lips curved into that suggestive half smile he'd seen countless times. "Why don't we have dinner tonight and talk about it?"

The thought made him shudder. He wondered how many times her face had been lifted. Bibi was sixty if a day, but fighting the years tooth and nail. He forced a smile. "I'd love to, but I'm afraid I have plans tonight." Not exactly true. He'd only *hoped* to have plans with the camerawoman he'd met a few hours ago, but it was the first excuse that had come to mind.

"Tomorrow then," Bibi said. "I'll drive you to my beach house, and we'll review your tape together." Her smile tightened. "I won't take no for an answer. If you have other plans, change them."

Her message was clear. He wouldn't get another shot.

Chapter 3

STAB, SQUEEZE, LIFT, RELEASE. ANOTHER CLOD OF earth displaced. Ignoring his burning muscles and blistered hands, Keith continued the mindless mechanical rhythm under the burning sun, his body on autopilot while his mind raced. He just wished he could manage the direction of those thoughts, but they were as out of his control as the chinook winds. Scowling at the dirt, he raised his arms, jabbing the ground with another grunt.

Stab, squeeze, lift, release. He'd felt like king of the world only a year ago. Was this all he had to look forward to for the next thirty—digging holes, pulling barbwire, and shoveling horse shit? He could only guess that when he'd sold his soul to the devil spirits, it must have been insufficient payment.

Stab, squeeze, lift, release. It was because of *her* that he was starting over with nothing—his entire life and livelihood up in smoke. When he'd rejected her, she'd turned on him like a viper. *Hell hath no fury like a woman scorned*.

Stab, squeeze, lift, release. This was his sixth day of riding fence. The ranch was vast and remote. With nineteen thousand acres, he'd be out here for a couple more weeks at least. The isolation was the only blessing. It gave him time to think. He'd come to accept his fate, but that didn't mean he had to like it. He told himself it was all for the best. It was well past time to get his life back on track.

Grinding his teeth, he raised his arms and punched the ground even harder. *Crunch*. The jarring pain careened up his arms and into his shoulders before the crash of metal on solid bedrock registered in his ears.

"Sweet motherfucking son of a bitch!" His shrieked curse carried on the wind, but it wasn't enough. Spinning like a discus thrower, he flung the posthole digger as far as his numb arms would allow. Venting his frustration and rage was only a temporary relief. Once he cooled down, he'd have to retrieve his instrument of torture and dig another fucking hole.

At the sound of an approaching ATV, he shaded his eyes against the late afternoon sun, squinting at the horizon. His gaze tracked the trail of dust originating in the direction of the ranch. As the vehicle got closer, he recognized Tonya. He snatched up his discarded shirt and jerked his arms into the sleeves, not bothering with the buttons.

Moments later she put the brake on and dismounted. "Got some food, water, and supplies for you, Cuz. Thought you might be getting low." He hoped she'd brought something better than jerky and canned beans. "So how's it coming along?"

"It's coming," he grunted.

"Really? Don't you think you might need this? Or do you plan to use your bare hands?" She reached into the utility cart and tossed him the digger he'd thrown.

"Must have dropped it."

She gave him an appraising stare. "I know this has to be hard on you after living like some kind of movie star—"

He raised a hand to cut her off. "It's honest work." And, admittedly, more honest than what he'd been doing for the past eight years.

"I got wind of something that might suit you better," Tonya suggested.

"Oh yeah? Like what?"

"The BLM called the ranch last night, looking for wranglers for some emergency horse gathers. They're removing seven hundred head from the checkerboard, and then they have another emergency roundup scheduled out in Nevada."

He pushed his hat back. "Why you telling me?"

"C'mon, Cuz. Don't be ridiculous," she chided. "I can't believe you'd rather dig holes and pull wire."

He jutted his chin. "Someone has to do it."

"I don't get it. Why are you wasting yourself like this?"

Why? He stared down at the hard, unforgiving earth, as hard and unforgiving as his grandfather's heart. He'd come back seeking peace and anonymity, only to learn he'd lost what had once mattered most. He'd brought shame to his family and to his tribe; now he had to pay the price. His worst penance, however, was self-inflicted—he hadn't touched either a woman or a horse in almost a year.

"You know I don't believe in that program," he said. "Most of those horses are going to fall into the hands of idiots who don't know what the hell they're doing."

"At least the animals don't starve," Tonya argued.

"Maybe not in body, but what about the spirit, Ton? Captivity is no life for them. It's no better than prison."

"Look, Keith, it is what it is. We can't change the system, but we can try to make the best of it, right? So why don't you at least help? You know those mustangs better than anyone. This is a chance for you to make some money and also get first pick of the horses."

"I'm not doing anything with horses anymore. Haven't you heard?" He gave a bitter laugh. "I'm just a counterfeit, a con artist, the Native American gigolo."

"Don't look to me for pity. You brought all that on yourself by playing up to the Twinkies. You exploited our heritage. You know that's not our way."

He dropped down to the ground, resting his elbows on his knees, gazing off into the distance. "Is that what you think too, Ton? That I sold out?"

"Does it really matter what I think? You're the one who has to live with your conscience."

"I asked you, didn't I?"

"Look, Cuz," she replied, "I try not to judge because I live in the white world too, but the elders still follow the old ways. Huttsi calls you her apple child, red only on the outside but all white on the inside. You first came out here because you said you wanted to be one of us, but then you left, proving that deep down you aren't. So why did you come back?"

Keith dropped back onto his elbows to gaze up at the fast-moving clouds. "Because I had nowhere else to go." Only a couple of years ago, there were thousands of people who'd treated him like some kind of rock star, but those relationships were as shallow as a creek in drought. Now that he needed a home, some place to lick his wounds, he had no home. Huttsi and Kenu, who had once embraced their half-blood grandchild with open arms, now rejected him. They hadn't exactly told him to leave, but they hadn't welcomed him either.

After a long silence, he murmured half to himself, "They won't take me back, because I fed the wrong wolf."

Tonya's forehead wrinkled. "What? I don't understand you."

"Didn't I ever tell you how I got my Shoshone name?"

"No. You didn't." Tonya dropped down beside him, offering a beer that he waved away.

"When I first came to the rez, Kenu said he'd had a vision the night before I arrived of a black wolf and a white wolf fighting."

"So that's why he called you Two Wolves?"

"Yes, but there's more. He said the white wolf represented all of the good things I desired, and the black wolf represented all of the bad. When I asked him which of the wolves would win the fight, he said to me, 'The one you feed.' That's why he won't see me now, Ton," he said woodenly. "Because I fed the black wolf."

"They still love you, Keith," Tonya said. "They're just deeply disappointed. Until you find some way to make amends, you are as good as dead to them."

"But how am I supposed to do that?" he asked. "I've come back like a beaten dog. I work hard. I keep my nose to the ground and bring no attention to myself. I even cut off my hair! What more can I do? I feel like I have a gaping hole"—he brought his hand to his left breast—"right here."

"I don't know the answer. I wish I did, but until you figure it out, I think you should leave the rez. Take the job and get away for a while. Find what you've lost."

"And what's that?"

"Yourself, Cuz. You don't even know who you are anymore, and you won't belong anywhere until you do."

Chapter 4

"YOU'RE BACK ALREADY?" MIRANDA REMARKED IN SUR-prise. After several nonspeaking parts in low-budget horror flicks, Lexi had finally scored her first big role in a film called *Zombie Cheerleaders from Mars*.

"Yup. Low budget always means a lightning-fast shoot." Lexi dropped her bags on the kitchen floor and then reached into the fridge for a Dr. Pepper. "Want one?"

"No, thanks." Miranda hated even the smell of the sickly sweet stuff, but Texas-born Lexi had practically been bottle-fed on it. "So how was it?" she asked.

"Omigod," Lexi groaned. "Have you ever been to the Black Rock Desert? There is absolutely no sign of civilization for hundreds of miles. It's like being on the surface of the moon! On top of that, it was blistering during the day and freezing at night. There was only one motel for fifty miles and only one place to eat. Most of us had to camp out in tents and cook our own food, an experience I *never* want to repeat."

Miranda shuddered at the thought. Lexi's cooking skills were atrocious, even in the best of circumstances. The girl burned holes in boiled eggs.

"The only highlight was meeting this smoking-hot camera guy named Kent," Lexi said.

"Oh yeah? Did *he* cook?" Miranda asked.

"No." Lexi grinned. "But food was last on our minds."

"Oh." Miranda flushed.

"How was your week?" Lexi asked.

"I filmed a hemorrhoid commercial," Miranda replied dryly, dismayed that it was her greatest claim to fame since graduating film school.

"We all have to pay our dues," Lexi replied.

"I know." Miranda sighed. "But I came to L.A. to make *films*. I just wish Bibi would give me a chance."

"What about that horse-whisperer gig you did?" Lexi asked.

"You mean the one she took all the credit for?" The innovative camera work Miranda contributed to the short production had even garnered an award.

"I never dreamed I'd still be waiting tables after all this time, either, but the fact is, most of us never do get a break. If you could only bring yourself to compromise your ideals a little, maybe you could get more freelance work."

"But I hate all the commercial crap."

"Randa, honey, until we make it big, my tips and your commercial *crap* pays our bills."

"I know you're right," Miranda replied. "I just want a tiny bit of creative freedom. Maybe I should make a documentary. They don't cost much to produce. I'd just need to find the right subject."

Lexi chewed her lip pensively. "You know, if that's what you're looking for, I just might have a lead for you."

"A lead? What do you mean?" Miranda asked.

"I was hanging out with Kent on his break when this guy from the Bureau of Land Management pulls up, asking about hiring a cameraman for a wild-horse roundup a few miles north in the Calico Mountains."

"Wild horses?" Miranda instantly perked up. "Are you for real?"

"Sure am, but don't get too excited. It seems the company they contract with to gather the horses is involved in a court battle with animal rights activists. Long story short, the activists got a court mandate to video the roundup. Kent asked a few questions about the job, but then turned the guy down with a laugh when he heard the pay he was offering."

"How much?" Miranda asked, her interest piqued. The location alone would be a cinematographer's dream.

"The guy said he needed a camera for two days but offered only five hundred bucks for the entire job. Nonnegotiable. Said it's some government deal. Kent countered that he needed two hundred an hour plus expenses. If you're willing to work cheap, they might still be looking. He said there's a hold on the roundup until they've hired someone."

"Are you kidding me?" Miranda squealed. "I'm all over this. Please tell me you have a contact number for this guy."

"I don't," Lexi replied. "But I can call Kent and see if he got the name and number."

"Can you call now?" Miranda almost pleaded. "I'll owe you forever for this, Lexi. I'm giddy just thinking about the possibilities."

"Do you know anything about wild horses?" Lexi asked.

"Well…no. Not really," Miranda admitted. "But I do know a bit about domestic ones. My grandparents raised cattle in Montana. I used to spend all my summers with them. They are actually how I got interested in filmmaking. It was my grandpa who bought me my first camera. He and my Grandma, Jo-Jo, are the only people who ever encouraged my dream of filmmaking. I really want to do this job, Lex. I owe it to them as much as to myself. This is finally something worthwhile, and what's it really going to cost me but my time?"

"How about your job?" Lexi shot back. "What are you going to do about work? Call in sick?"

Miranda's stomach knotted—she hadn't even thought about that part. "I'd rather just ask for some personal time off."

"Without notice, Bibi might very well say no," Lexi countered.

"Then I'll have to take my chances. I may never get another opportunity like this."

"Think carefully, sweets. Bibi Newman has a ton of clout in this town. Cross her, and you might never find work again."

Miranda jutted her chin. "I don't care, Lex. Making films is what I came out here to do, and I'm damned well going to do it...or die trying." She just hoped it wouldn't be dying of dehydration in the middle of the Black Rock Desert.

———∿∿∿———

Calico Mountains, Northwestern Nevada

Driving out to Nevada a few days ahead of the crew, Keith sought out the local ranchers and inquired after the location of the horses and the water sources. After making camp on the Donnelly Flat, he set out on horseback to scale Donnelly Peak and get a better lay of the land.

Cresting the barren butte, he scanned the equally

desolate horizon, devoid of all vegetation but clusters of cactus and scattered thickets of sage. It had been years since he'd spent any time alone in the desert. He'd once loved it, but now the landscape felt as arid and bleak as his own soul.

Tonya had been right when she'd said he'd been "performing" for so long that he'd lost himself. If he was ever going to get his life back together, he needed to leave the rez. She was also right that his only true option was to try to salvage what little remained of his tattered reputation. At least there were people who knew him from before. Maybe Mitch and Beth West didn't approve of how he'd used his talents, but they still trusted his skills and judgment.

From his elevated position, Keith spotted half a dozen small family bands of mustangs. The knowledge of their fate pulled at his conscience. Tomorrow the wranglers would gather up hundreds of these horses, mainly for the crime of competing for the limited resources that had recently worsened with wildfires and drought.

Was it better to round them up and save them from death by keeping them in captivity? Or was there greater dignity in a quiet death? Which would the horses choose if they knew?

His own father had chosen death over life in a prison.

Suddenly he was thirteen again, standing on the top of Crow Heart Butte, the most famous landmark in all of the Wind River Valley. He and Grandfather had come to scatter his father's ashes. "This is the site of a great battle," Kenu said. "It was here that our people fought for hunting rights after the Fort Laramie Treaty granted the Crows the same privileges we'd been given in the

Fort Bridger Treaty. After four bloody days of battle, the two great warrior chiefs met in an attempt to end the bloodshed. Washakie of the Shoshone raised his fist to Big Robber of the Crow. 'You and I will fight to the death, and when I beat you, I will cut out your heart and eat it!'"

"Who won, Grandfather?" Keith asked.

"Chief Washakie was the victor. As promised, he cut out Big Robber's heart and displayed it proudly on the end of his spear. That is why this place is named Crow Heart."

"Did he really eat it?"

His grandfather replied with a secretive smile. "No one really knows. When questioned later in his life, Washakie said only that young men do foolish things." He laid a tremulous hand on Keith's shoulder. "Your father had the heart of such a warrior, but he let bitterness and hatred take root. That is how he earned his Shoshone name, Kills With Words."

Keith recalled with a sharp pang the look of desolation in Kenu's eyes and the tears that trickled down the old man's weathered face. Placing the urn in Keith's hands, he said, "Take this, my son. Cast the ashes to the four winds and we will pray that his troubled spirit will at last find peace."

Looking out over the vast desert plains, Kenu murmured a Shoshone prayer to the Great Spirit. Keith had never forgotten his grandfather's words. Now he uttered the same prayer for himself.

***

The highway became long, straight, and increasingly barren the farther north Miranda drove. Too weary to continue all the way to Gerlach, she'd opted to stop for the night in Fernley, which she later discovered was the last vestige of civilization.

Waking well before sunrise, she continued north through the Paiute Reservation and the tribal head-quarters of Nixon, a mere bump in the road. After that, she found herself alone on the highway for sixty miles. Not for the first time, Miranda felt the urge to turn back. She was still amazed that she'd committed herself to trekking into a desert wilderness to film wild horses. Maybe she should *be* committed. Surely she'd lost her mind.

The route, lined by treeless, grassy mountains that transformed into undulating hills, ran through a narrow valley formed by the dry bed of Winnemucca Lake. She passed through the forsaken mining town of Empire, almost ghostly now with its boarded-up general store and empty houses. A few miles farther up, the highway opened onto a narrow patch of desert leading into the tiny town of Gerlach.

True to his word, Mitch West was waiting for her when she pulled into Bruno's Country Club Motel. Even if his hat, boots, and faded denim hadn't identified him, the West Livestock emblem on the pickup truck behind him was a dead giveaway.

"Miz Sutton? We were wondering if you'd really show up. I'm Mitch." He extended his hand, closing heavily callused fingers around hers. "And this is my wife, Beth." He inclined his head to a smiling woman in her mid-fifties, dressed much the same as he was in hat, boots, and denim Sherpa jacket.

"Nice to meet you both," Miranda said.

"We're set up at the Donnelly Flat, at the western base of the Calicos," Mitch replied. "You can ride with us in the truck."

"Can't I just follow you?"

"Not in that." Mitch nodded to her Mustang convertible. "The roads are rough for the next few miles, and then there aren't any roads at all."

"No roads?" Miranda swallowed hard. "What am I going to do with my car?" She eyed it with misgivings. Although she'd bought it used, it was still her pride and joy. It was her gift to herself for the videography award. She knew she'd rightfully won it, even though Bibi had taken all the credit.

"It'll be safe right here," Mitch reassured her. "I've known Bruno for years."

"You might want to go ahead and make a pit stop before we head out," Beth advised. "There are no restrooms where we're going, and not much privacy either. It's pretty much open desert."

"Thanks for the advice. I'll be back in just a minute."

Mitch was talking on a satellite phone when she came back out. "We'd best head on out," he said. "The crew's already on site. Trey'll be ready to start scouting at sunrise."

"Trey?" Miranda asked.

"The chopper pilot," he explained. "He's also our oldest son. If you're ready, we'd best get rolling. He'll be taking off in about an hour, and we've got a good forty-mile drive ahead of us."

Miranda popped her trunk to collect her gear—her new Black Magic cinema camera, a case of bottled water, and a few other necessities she'd shoved into a backpack. She wasn't sure how long the shoot would take, but had prepared for several days.

Beth eyed Miranda's pack skeptically. "Is that all you have? Where's your video gear?"

"It's all right here." Miranda patted the outer compartment. "I have a mini cinema camera. It's perfect for this project." The camera was a videographer's dream come true, the latest technology and totally portable. She'd drooled over it for months until it went on sale at a price she could afford. Miranda closed her trunk with a shiver, wishing she'd packed a heavier jacket.

"If you're cold, I've got a thermos of coffee in the truck. It'll help warm you up," Beth offered.

"I'd love some." After Miranda climbed into the truck, Beth handed her a Styrofoam cup. Mitch joined them in the cab a moment later. "This place looks so familiar," Miranda remarked. "I feel almost as if I've seen it before. Is this the same desert where *The Misfits* was filmed?"

"Nope," Mitch said. "That was a couple of hours south, near Dayton."

"Is it an accurate portrayal?" Miranda asked. "Did they really capture horses that way and sell them for dog food?"

"Yes. It's sad but true," Beth replied. "They used to chase them down by airplane, rope them, and then make them drag tires until they dropped. It's why our practice of gathering by helicopter has such a stigma attached to it. The animal rights people think we're doing the same thing—running the horses to death. In truth, it's the most efficient and humane way to gather them."

"We're dealing with a real bad situation up here," Mitch said. "I can't stress enough that we need to get this thing done quickly. We have to finish this job before hundreds of horses die."

"I don't understand how it got to this point," Miranda said. "If drought is the problem, why not just bring in some water?"

"The group that's suing us already tried that," Mitch replied. "They brought in twenty thousand gallons of water, but the animals wouldn't go near the stock tanks. There's some that died of dehydration just yards away from the water. It just goes to show that these people might have good intentions, but they're clueless about how wild horses think."

"Incredible." Miranda shook her head in shock and dismay.

"Maybe our system isn't perfect," Mitch said, "but we've been doing this for almost thirty years and take great care in how we handle the animals."

"How did you get started?" Miranda asked.

"My family's homestead back in Wyoming abuts several hundred thousand acres of BLM land that's been home to wild mustangs for generations," he answered. "We started gathering the horses back in the very beginning, when the BLM first began the mustang adoption program. They needed wranglers to catch the horses. We already knew the geography and the animals. It seemed a good fit. Our family's been doing it ever since."

"I read about the last wild-horse gather up here a few years ago. Were you involved with that one too?" Miranda asked.

"Yes," Beth replied. "It was one of the largest removals we've ever done, over twelve hundred head. There were some that got hurt in the process, and some that died through no fault of ours, but we got accused of all manner of inhumane treatment toward the horses. We got several death threats over it. Even had to change our phone number."

"That's why we're happy to have you film this gather," Mitch said. "It's as much to protect our reputation as it is to satisfy the judge."

Approaching the mountains, Miranda directed her lens to the wide-open expanse of desert, slowly panning the landscape, hoping to capture the magical play of light and shadow as the first rays of dawn stretched out over the rocky outcroppings. She gasped at her first glimpse of the sun cresting the horizon, casting the multitoned Calicos in an awe-inspiring mosaic of pink, orange, and red.

Chapter 5

KEITH CLIMBED ON TOP OF THE CORRAL PANEL FOR A BETTER look at the horses. All of the ones they'd gathered had shown signs of severe dehydration. After being given food and water, four were later found dead, and six others were showing signs of water intoxication. The few horses that were stable enough had been transported to Palomino Valley, but none of this bunch had been up to the rigors of long-distance transport.

With their roundup operations suspended, he was growing restless and uneasy. Animals were dying because the government had waited too long to authorize the roundup, and now that some were dead, the courts had suspended operations while they investigated the dead horses. All of which was only going to lead to dozens, if not hundreds, more dead horses.

He gazed into the mountains with a heavy heart. With so many special-interest groups involved, the animals were getting caught in the middle. Would they *all* end up dead because of damned politics?

"How are they looking?" he asked Trey, who was doing his preflight check.

"Not too good. I've been watching two groups real close. The first is only about a mile away to the west, and the other is about eight miles northeast, heading toward Soldiers Meadow. I doubt they've wandered very far since last night."

Unable to contain his unease any longer, Keith determined to do some first-hand recon. Although the helicopter did an aerial flyover twice a day, there was no way to discern from the air what would be readily evident on the ground. "I'm going to ride out there and take a closer look," he told Trey. "Radio me when you're ready to lift off, and I'll head straight back to the trap."

<center>~~~</center>

After driving across seemingly endless desert, the trap site finally came into view, marked by scattered pickup trucks and several horse trailers. In addition to Mitch and Beth, Miranda counted eight wranglers, all male, of various ages. "We have a really great crew here," Mitch declared with obvious pride. "C'mon. I'll introduce you around." He scanned the group with a wrinkled brow. "Donny," he asked one of the young men, "where's Keith?"

"He's our head wrangler," Beth explained to Miranda.

"He rode out about an hour ago," Donny replied. "Said he wanted to check on the horses on the north ridge. He told Trey to radio him when he's ready to lift off."

After introducing Miranda to the rest of the roundup crew, Mitch led her to the helicopter where the pilot appeared busy with preflight preparations. "Miz Sutton, this is our son Trey."

"Ma'am." Trey acknowledged Miranda with a tip of his hat. He was good-looking in a rugged, slightly weathered kind of way. Although probably only about thirty, he looked older.

"Miz Sutton is here to film this gather," Mitch continued. "Think she could go up in the chopper with you?"

Trey pursed his lips. "I don't particularly like the flight

conditions right now." His voice was slow and even, but his brow was creased with concern. "Sorry, Miz Sutton, I don't feel comfortable taking a passenger. We've got some fog over there reducing visibility." He jerked his head toward the mountains. "On top of that, the wind's a bit iffy. If it picks up at all, I'm grounding the bird. Maybe I can take you up later if the conditions improve."

"I understand," Miranda said, barely hiding her disappointment. A few minutes later, she filmed the helicopter lifting off and disappearing into the fog-enshrouded mountains.

"This is the main grazing area," Beth said, "but as you can see, the water here is almost completely dried up." Miranda did a slow pan of the barren landscape and then zoomed in on the muddy creek bed. "Trey'll start moving the smaller family bands together into a larger herd, and then direct them toward the trap. He'll radio Mitch once they get close."

About fifteen minutes later, a squawk erupted from Mitch's radio. An incomprehensible buzz of words followed. "Roger that," Mitch replied and then holstered his radio. "Trey's only about half a mile out with the first group. Get ready, boys," Mitch shouted to the wranglers.

Beth pointed toward the mountains. "Just keep your eyes on that ridge over there. They're gonna come in from that direction. You might want to climb up on the rig." Beth nodded to the semi parked nearby.

"For a better view?" she asked.

"That too, but also to keep you out of harm's way. We wouldn't want you to get kicked or trampled."

With no further time for questions, Miranda paused her camera and climbed on top of the tractor trailer, where she panned the ridge. Within seconds, the Hughes 500 helicopter popped into view. She followed the maneuvering aircraft with her camera as it dipped behind the band of trotting horses. In fits and starts, the chopper coaxed the animals toward the trap, herding at their heels like an airborne border collie.

"Do you see those?" Beth pointed to a long V-shaped corridor fabricated of T-posts and brown jute. "We call that the wing. It acts as a funnel to guide the horses into the traps."

Nearing the wing, the chopper began to push more aggressively. Miranda's pulse raced with adrenaline as the herd approached. The rhythmic *whop-whop* of the rotor blades was soon joined by a thunderous echo of galloping hoofbeats as the horses picked up speed.

"Look over there." Beth pointed to the end of the wings. Miranda zoomed in tight on a horse that was stomping and tossing his head. "He's the Judas horse. His job is to bring them in."

Beth indicated four wranglers positioned in pairs behind the jute wings. "When the horses enter the trap, the wranglers'll jump out and shut the gates. Once the horses settle down, we'll sort and load them into the trailers. The whole process usually takes only a couple of hours if nothing goes wrong."

Breaking into a contagious canter, the horses produced a ground-quaking reverberation she could feel even from her perch on top of the truck, and raised a cloud of dust large enough to obscure her view of the mountains. As the front of the herd approached the wings, Mitch's radio squawked again, but Miranda couldn't make out the words over the stampede. A moment later, the high-pitched buzz of a twin engine plane joined the chaotic cacophony of galloping horses.

"Shit!" Mitch kicked the ground. "It's happening again."

"What's wrong?" Miranda asked.

"There's a Beechcraft Baron on Trey's ass. This is all about to go FUBAR."

Miranda zoomed in on a photographer leaning out the plane window, snapping pictures as it swooped down in front of the horses, a maneuver that effectively split the herd down the middle. She quickly panned back to the wrangler who'd released the Judas horse. The fretful animal bolted, charging to the front of the fractured herd in an attempt to lead it into the catch pens, but only half of the herd entered the trap, while the others galloped wildly past.

The plane dipped low to the ground and flew past the trap. The pilot flashed a triumphant smile and gave the crew the one-finger salute.

"Son of a bitch!" Mitch cursed. "I hope you got that on film."

"As a matter of fact I did," Miranda replied. "What are you going to do?"

Mitch gave a fatalistic shrug. "The damage is already done. There's nothing we can do now but report the license number."

The scene that followed was pure pandemonium. The captured horses reared and rammed themselves against the steel panels in an effort to join the runaways, and a few tried to climb over the top of the pen. One, a black stallion, even made it halfway up. Miranda cried out in alarm as he crashed backward onto another horse. "Can't you stop him?"

"There's nothing we can do," Mitch said. "That plane's interference has put their fight-or-flight instincts into high gear."

"Won't they hurt themselves?"

"Hopefully not," Mitch replied. "All we can do now is try to control the chaos."

The same horse made another attempt, this time with a running start that sent him soaring over the six-foot panel. "Holy crap!" Miranda cried, thrilled that she'd still had her camera going and had caught it all. "I can't believe he cleared it!"

Mitch sighed, watching the horse's dramatic escape with a bemused look. "Most of them don't want to run anymore, but there's always an outlaw that'll fight for his freedom."

"Will you go after him?" she asked.

Mitch shook his head. "No. That renegade's not worth all the trouble he'll cause. He's a fighter. He'll be okay out there on his own. As for the rest of this bunch, they'll calm down pretty quick once that plane's gone. Mustangs are smart. They usually figure things out fast. As a rule, they don't waste their energy once they know they can't escape. We just have to wait it out."

"What about the ones the plane chased off? Are you going after them?"

"We've got no choice," he replied. "There's almost no water left for at least fifty miles and very little forage remaining where the water is. It's going to be really hard on the oldest and youngest ones, because they're the weakest. We'll have to try and bring them all back in."

"What'll happen to them if you can't?"

"It's real simple, Miz Sutton," Mitch said. "If they don't come back, they'll die."

"Easy, brother," Keith soothed the restless animal. The agitated gelding tossed his head and jerked on the bit in his growing anxiety to join the galloping herd. The rising dust obscured Keith's vision, choking him as he watched everything fall apart. He shook his head on a curse as the horses began scattering helter-skelter. For a few seconds he debated joining the wranglers that were mounting up to flank the runaways, but it was just no good. At this point they'd only be able to catch up with the ones that were too weak to keep up with their herd mates. No, the only way to gain any control would be to take command as the leader.

"C'mon, little brother. I'm counting on you." Squeezing both heels into the horse's flanks, Keith urged his horse forward. The animal hesitated only a millisecond before diving straight down the near-vertical drop.

"I thought you said you didn't use any riders for the horse gather," Miranda remarked.

"We don't," Beth replied with a puzzled look. "We only use the Judas horse to lead the mustangs in."

"Then I guess your Judas horse has found himself a rider. Look up there." Miranda pointed to a lone horseman poised on the bluff overlooking the trap. Seconds later, he came charging straight down the cliff to join the runaway band, just like the iconic scene from *The Man from Snowy River*. "Oh. My. God. Do you see that?" she exclaimed. The rider was crouched low over his horse's withers and riding hell for leather after the runaways, eating yards of ground with every stride.

"I'll be damned," Mitch murmured from behind. "It's Keith."

Her pulse accelerated as he began to gain on the lead horse. She'd never seen anyone ride like that. Well, not quite. She'd seen only *one* person ever ride like that. Miranda zoomed in on the wrangler and did an instant double take. *It can't be*. Her racing heart skipped a beat. But it *had* to be. It'd been well over a year since she'd seen him, but she'd recognize *him* anywhere.

Chapter 6

AFTER TWO HOURS OF HARD RIDING, KEITH RETURNED AT the head of twenty-odd lathered and heaving horses. Even after claiming the lead, he'd still managed to bring in only about half of the runaways. He could only hope the chopper had gathered up the ones that had scattered into the mountains.

He'd no sooner dismounted than Mitch appeared, clapping him on the shoulder. "That was some damned fine riding. I've never seen anything like it."

"I was just the passenger." Keith shrugged. "The horse did the real work."

"Those mustangs were pretty spooked. Once frightened like that, they're damned hard to get control of."

Keith grinned. "Don't I know it."

"Trey brought in a few more while you were out chasing that bunch down," Mitch continued, to Keith's relief. "He says there are still about a half dozen older and weaker ones that he didn't dare push, but if we don't bring them back in, some aren't going to survive the night."

"They're also gonna be especially vulnerable to predators, as exhausted as they are," Keith said. "There're plenty of mountain lions in these parts to make a meal out of 'em."

"Are you willing to ride out again after the stragglers?" Mitch asked.

"Yeah. I'm willing," Keith said.

Mitch squinted at the sky. "We're losing daylight fast."

"They can't be too far," Keith reassured him, "but I'll make camp if I have to."

"I'll send Dave and Donny with you," Mitch said. "I'll leave a pen and a stock trailer behind. Round up what you can but, if we don't get them all by tomorrow, we'll just have to call it a loss."

Keith was tying his bedroll behind the cantle of his saddle when Mitch reappeared a few minutes later.

"I just thank God we got all this on video," Mitch said. "At least we have documentation that it wasn't our negligence or ineptitude that caused this cockup. Speaking of which, I don't think you've met Miranda Sutton yet."

It was only then that Keith noticed the woman standing in the background with a video camera. He noted the reddish-gold curls escaping from her ball cap and his pulse quickened. He'd seen very few women with hair like that. Of all people. *It can't be her*. She lowered the camera, and his gut churned. It was *her* all right. What the hell was she doing here? And what were the chances of running into Bibi's protégé in the middle of the desert? Was he cursed?

"Miranda." Mitch waved her over. "This is Keith Russo, one of the best horsemen you'll ever meet. That ride you saw down the cliff was proof that I don't exaggerate."

Their gazes locked. Keith said nothing, just speared her with a hard, unblinking stare. Her eyes widened in recognition. Then her face flushed. After a second or two, she licked her lips and tore her gaze away, a sure sign of a guilty conscience.

"Miss Sutton and I are already acquainted," Keith replied stiffly. "Why is she here?"

Mitch's puzzled gaze shifted from Keith to Miranda and back again. "Is there a problem, Keith?"

"There's a problem all right," Keith replied. "I don't trust her, and you shouldn't either."

"Why do you say that?" Mitch asked, deep lines creasing his brow.

Keith's jaw tightened. "She ruined my reputation."

"Really?" Mitch remarked. "How?"

"What are you talking about?" she rejoined. "All I did was shoot some video."

Keith gave a derisive laugh. "Your video completely destroyed my credibility."

"I don't like what you're insinuating," she said. "I was simply doing my job, just like you do with these horses. If you have issues, you need to take it up with Bibi. She was the producer and editor."

"I have objections all right."

"I'm truly sorry for that," Miranda said. "But it still has nothing to do with me or my job here."

"The hell it doesn't." Keith addressed Mitch again. "Ask her why she's really here, Mitch. Has she said what she intends to *do* with this video?"

Miranda jutted her chin. "I'm *here* on a federal judge's order to film the wild-horse gather. I'm also here because I saw an opportunity to make a worthwhile film. I don't have a political agenda, if that's what you're implying." She turned to Mitch. "I'm afraid this is going to be really awkward. Is there someone else I could ride with?"

"What is she talking about?" Keith demanded.

"She's riding out with you when you go after the strays," Mitch said.

"No way." Keith shook his head. "I'm not taking her, Mitch."

Mitch cocked his head. "'Scuse me?"

Keith glowered back in resentment. "Said I'm *not* taking her."

Mitch scratched his chin. "Sorry, Keith, but that's not your call. If those horses die, the public will crucify us. We need hard proof that we did all we could to save them."

"I've got enough on my hands without worrying about a clueless tenderfoot," Keith grumbled.

"I'm not clueless," she snapped.

"Yeah, right." Keith snorted. "I don't need you slowing us down. We're going out on horseback. We ride long and hard. And if we don't find all the horses right away, we're going to have to make overnight camp."

"I can handle it," she insisted. "I know how to ride a horse, and I've camped out before."

"In the middle of a desert?" he asked.

"Well, no," she confessed, "but it's not like I'm going alone."

"This isn't Girl Scout camp, Miz Sutton. There's no tent, no cot, and no bathroom facilities. It's gonna be a bedroll on the hard ground." Noting the uncertainty in her eyes, he continued, "There are also predators—coyotes, black bears, and mountain lions, not to mention Gila monsters and six species of rattlesnakes."

Miranda swallowed and turned to Mitch. "Gila monster? Is he making that up?"

"Nope," Mitch said. "It's a large venomous lizard that lives in the desert."

"The desert is a dangerous place, Miz Sutton," Keith continued. "People get lost out there. *People die*."

As obdurate as ever, she appealed once more to Mitch. "I still want to go. How can I show the reality of this situation if I don't get it all on film?"

Mitch sighed. "She's right, Keith. Our reputation is on the line here. I told her she could go, and I'm not going to renege. I don't know what all went down between the two of you, but I'm used to trusting a person until they give me good reason not to."

"I just did."

Keith spun away with his pulse roaring in his ears. He'd warned Mitch. There was nothing more to say. If he had any sense, he'd send her deceitful ass packing.

―∾∾―

Miranda watched Keith stalk off stiff-backed and fuming.

"Wanna tell me what that was all about?" Mitch asked.

She exhaled with a sigh. "It's a long story, but I'll give you an abbreviated version. I was a grad student when my boss, Bibi, sent me to film this…er…equine exhibition. After looking at my camera work on it, the producer thought it would make a good short film, but apparently Keith didn't like how the film portrayed him."

"Didn't he have any say in it?" Mitch asked.

"Not really," she said. "Once a release is signed, the producer has the right to use the film however they see fit. I promise you, all I did was the camera work. I had nothing to do with the editing or post production. That was all Bibi."

"Don't fret none about him," Mitch said. "Maybe he ain't happy about this whole situation, but he won't let any harm come to you out there. I can promise you that.

I've known Keith since he was the twins' age, and his family even longer than that. His mixed heritage got him a little confused for a while, but ain't nobody better with the horses. He's the best damn wrangler we've got."

His words were meant to reassure, but uncertainty suddenly knotted her stomach at the prospect of riding into the desert with a man who obviously despised her. "But what if an accident or something unexpected happens?"

"I'll be sending Dave and Donny along with you. They all carry rifles, and Keith has a satellite phone. If there's any real emergency, they'll call in the chopper."

The thought that Keith carried a rifle was hardly comforting. She glanced back at him watching her from a few yards away. If looks could kill, she'd already be lying dead on the ground. Maybe he'd just shoot her and dump her lifeless body in a canyon. She'd have to make certain to ride behind him.

"Part of the cowboy code is to trust the ones you ride with," Mitch said, correctly reading her concerns. "If you're having second thoughts, it might be better for you to go out with Trey in the chopper instead. He's going to do another flyover to see if he can account for the rest of the missing horses."

"Under the circumstances, that might be best," Miranda reluctantly agreed. "I wanted to get some aerial footage anyway."

"Good," Mitch replied, looking relieved. "I'm real glad we got that resolved."

After scarfing down some sandwiches washed down with Gatorade, Keith, Donny, and Dave rode out toward the mountains, but the trio hadn't gone more than a couple of miles before coming upon two old mares with heaving flanks and sweat-coated skin, guarding a foal that was in similar shape. Keith dismounted and handed his reins to Donny, hoping it wasn't too late to save them. The first mare, a palomino pinto, laid her ears back in warning at his approach, but she was too exhausted to put up any real fight. He crouched beside the weakened foal, a near clone of the mare, right down to its markings. The animal nickered to its mother and then struggled to gain its feet, but the effort was too much.

"Easy, little man," he softly crooned, pressing a flattened palm against its neck. With his other hand he pinched the layer of skin at the colt's shoulder between his thumb and forefinger. He lifted the skin away from the muscle and twisted, frowning as he mentally counted the seconds. *Damn*. The tented skin should have snapped back after a second or so. Keith rolled back its upper lip to reveal whitish-tinted gums. "Shit. This colt's in some serious trouble."

Dave rose with a grunt to pull his rifle out of its scabbard.

"No." Keith raised a hand. "We're not shooting him. Not yet."

"It's only humane," Dave protested. "There's nothing we can do for him out here."

"Doesn't Mitch keep IV fluids on hand?" Keith asked.

"I s'pose there's a coupla bags in our emergency vet kit, but that's all the way back at the camp. By the time we fetch the supplies, it'll be too late. It's a waste of time, Keith. He's too far gone. Just look at him. He can't even stand, let alone walk."

Keith set his jaw. "Then I guess we'll just have to find a way to carry him."

Dave regarded him incredulously. "And just how are we s'posed to do that? He's got to weigh over two hundred pounds."

"Simple." Keith stood and retrieved the satellite phone. "I'm calling the chopper in."

"To carry the horse?" Dave asked. "That's crazy."

"Why? They airlift people, don't they? This foal won't make it if we don't try," Keith said. "The bird's already in the air. All Trey needs is our GPS position to land it."

"Look, Keith, they use special helicopters for rescue operations. We don't have any of that. What do you expect Trey to do? Fly with a horse in that tiny cockpit?"

"It's a really small horse," Keith argued. He silenced Dave's next protest with a dark look as he dialed base camp. "Mitch, it's Keith. No, we're all okay, but we've got a foal that's in a real bad way. I need you to send the chopper."

Mitch groaned. "How big is it?"

"'Bout two hundred pounds. We need to transport him. He's gonna die if we don't get some fluids into him ASAP."

There was a long pause before Mitch answered. "This'll have to be Trey's call."

"I understand that," Keith replied. "You'll call him?"

"Yeah. It's crazy as hell," Mitch replied, "but I'll call him."

"Thanks. I owe you." Keith disconnected the call.

"He's really sending the chopper?" Dave asked.

Keith smiled for the first time in three days. "He's sending it."

Chapter 7

"I⟨T GETS REALLY COLD ON THAT CHOPPER⟩. T⟨HESE⟩'LL KEEP you warm." Beth handed Miranda a sheepskin-lined jacket and a pair of leather gloves.

"Thanks. I really appreciate it." Miranda accepted the jacket, donning it over her hoodie. Her heart raced with excitement as she buckled herself into the helicopter. A succinct safety briefing followed. Trey was terse, almost gruff. She wondered if he'd taken a dislike to her or if it was just his personality. Then again, it had been a pretty shitty day for everyone.

"You're gonna need these too." Trey handed her a set of noise-canceling headphones.

"Will I be able to hear you with them on?" she asked.

"Yes, and I can hear you too. There's a built-in mic."

As soon as she put them on, Trey started the engine, and the aircraft jolted almost violently to life. She held her breath in anticipation as the blades began to rotate. Within seconds, the rough, rocking motion transformed into a smooth vibration. Her stomach filled with frantic butterflies as they lifted vertically into the air.

"How long have you been doing this?" she asked, trying again to break the ice.

"Flying? Or wild-horse roundups?"

"Well, both," she replied.

"I started helping out with the roundups almost as soon as I could manage a horse by myself. I guess I was about six or seven. I fell in love with flying the first time I went up in one of these, but I had to wait twelve years before I could learn how to fly one."

"How did you get your training?"

"Uncle Sam."

"You were a military pilot?" she asked.

"U.S. Army. Flew the Kiowa Warrior, a light scout helicopter 'bout the size of this one."

"Where were you deployed?" she asked.

"Afghanistan. Three combat tours in terrain a lot like this." His jaw tightened as he nodded to the mountainous desert below. His body language suppressed further questions. Having almost forgotten her purpose, Miranda uncapped her camera lens and began recording as Trey scouted the mountains for horses. With bated breath, she gazed out at the seemingly limitless expanse of sage-peppered desert stretching out between craggy mountain peaks. "Wow. It's so vast. And so beautiful in a rough-hewn kinda way."

Trey merely grunted.

"Look"—he pointed below a moment later—"there's two down there. We'll try to get them moving, but if they show signs of distress, I'll have to back off and call a wrangler in."

He'd already begun his descent when Mitch called on the radio.

"Keith needs you," she heard Mitch say. "He's got a foal in a bad way. He wants you to fly it in to camp. Can you go and check it out?"

"You expect me to put a *foal* in here?"

"I expect you to use your best judgment. I know you won't do anything stupid," Mitch replied.

"Famous last words," Trey mumbled. After Mitch gave him the GPS coordinates, Trey turned to Miranda. "Looks like we have a change of plans."

Miranda regarded the cramped cockpit incredulously. "You aren't really going to try to fly a *horse* in here, are you?"

"Maybe. Maybe not," he replied. "It's not the craziest thing I've ever done."

She never got a chance to ask him to elaborate. The helicopter quickly regained altitude and changed direction. In a matter of minutes they spotted the small group of horses and riders. The helicopter landed nearby. The mustangs skittered away, white-eyed and trembling, but they didn't run very far.

As soon as the blades quit rotating, Trey hopped out. Miranda followed, ducking her head and hugging her camera. Her chest squeezed at the sight of Keith kneeling by a fragile-looking colt with its eyes half-shut, looking as if it held onto life by a thread.

"Took your sweet time, didn't you?" Keith looked up at them, his forehead wrinkling as his gaze darted from Trey to Miranda and back. "Mitch didn't tell me *she* was with you."

Trey made a scoffing sound. "You're damned lucky I came at all. I can't believe you talked him into this."

"It's the only chance this one has," Keith said.

Trey scowled. "It's a waste of time and fuel. This one is past his last chance already."

"C'mon, Trey," Keith urged. "What's it gonna hurt to try?"

"Just tellin' it the way I see it, Keith," Trey said. "I

appreciate your good intentions, but how do you even propose to do this?"

"Someone'll have to hold him on their lap. This little guy's not gonna fight."

"Maybe not, but it's still gonna put us damned close to the weight limit of that chopper when we add in another person to hold it."

"Are you refusing?" Keith asked.

"Don't be so heartless," Miranda blurted. "You have to try."

"I don't *have* to do anything," Trey bit back.

Miranda lifted her chin, ready to do battle. "I'll hold him," she volunteered. "I don't weigh much."

Trey shook his head. "You're not strong enough. If he panics, I need someone who's able to hold him tight. I don't need that horse kicking the controls and crashing us."

"Oh." She bit her lip. "I see your point."

"I'll go," Donny volunteered.

Trey eyed the mares. "What are we going to do about those others? They look like they're in pretty bad shape too."

"Dave and I'll handle the mares," Keith replied. "We're only a couple of miles out from camp. If we take it really slow, they've got a shot."

"But it doesn't make sense for us both to go when we still have more strays to gather and only a couple more hours of daylight left," Dave said. "We can't afford to lose any more time. I can handle the two of them if you can go after the rest."

"There's only one problem with that plan," Keith said.

"What's that?" Dave asked.

Keith eyed Miranda with barely concealed hostility. *"Her."*

Miranda bristled. "What about *her*?"

"She could always ride back with me," Dave said.

"Which leaves Keith alone," Trey said. "He can't gather the rest of the horses by himself."

Miranda swallowed hard. "If I stay, I can help gather them."

"What the hell would you know about gathering horses?" Keith snapped.

Would he ever give her a chance? It seemed he took pleasure in not just finding but seeking out her every fault. Although he'd made it abundantly clear that he resented her presence, the situation had changed. She wasn't about to give him a choice this time. She needed to record the rescues, or even the deaths, of these horses. Leaving now would defeat her purpose in coming.

Miranda swallowed hard at the prospect of being stuck alone with him. But it was too important to get cold feet. "I know how to ride, and I've moved cows plenty of times before. My grandparents have a cattle ranch. I used to spend summers there as a kid. Maybe it's been a few years, but I haven't forgotten how."

"Rounding up mustangs is *nothing* like driving cattle. Cows move slowly. Horses run flat out. You have to lead them. To do that, you have to be able to ride hard and think fast."

"But you've already said these horses are weak and old, ones that have to move slower," she argued. "I came out here to film this horse gather, and whether you all like it or not, I'm going to follow this through."

Dave's gaze darted from Keith to Miranda. "I'll meet

up with Donny back at camp and then the two of us will ride back out here with fresh horses. We could catch up with you in a few hours."

"That sounds like a plan," Trey said. He looked to Keith and Miranda with a twitch of his mouth. "If the two of you aren't back in two days, we'll send out a posse to look for your bodies. Time's a wastin'. Let's see if we can get that foal on board."

Miranda uncapped her camera and filmed the three men hobbling the colt's front legs together. As he'd said, the horse was too weak to struggle. Keith then produced a canvas tarp from his saddle pack, using it as a sling to carry the young horse to the chopper. A few minutes later, the helicopter lifted off with Donny holding the colt securely in his lap.

She prayed the foal would survive the ordeal. "Do you think he'll make it?" she asked, capping her lens after the helicopter disappeared from view.

Keith shook his head. "Maybe not, but we had to try."

"I'm glad you did," she said softly.

Their eyes met for a millisecond. His softened infinitesimally, only to harden again. "You can take Donny's horse." He led Miranda to a strawberry roan he introduced as Sadie. "She's smart and steady and even came from these parts. She'll take good care of you if you just stay out of her way."

"Thanks," Miranda replied, taking Sadie's bridle.

He grunted his reply then mounted his horse and turned his attention back to the mustangs. "Dave will lead while we push from behind," he said. "Once they're following him, we'll slowly drop back."

"Will they keep following him if we leave?" she asked.

"It's a horse's nature to follow, and this pair is in dire need of a leader," Keith explained. "Dave is claiming that position. They'll trust him as long as they don't perceive him as a threat."

"You really do understand them, don't you?"

"You thought I was all bullshit?" Mumbling a curse, he turned his horse and rode off ahead of her. Just as she'd suspected, he was going to ignore her as much as possible. They might not like each other, but she still couldn't help admiring Keith's tenacity in fighting for the foal.

After a quarter mile or so, Keith and Miranda parted ways with Dave, and then turned back toward the mountains in the direction where Trey had reported several strays. They rode for an hour in stone-cold silence, before picking up a trail of hoofprints and horse dung that led to an old mining camp.

Keith pulled up. "The sun'll be setting soon. We'll make camp here. It'll be warmer than it is up on the mountain. There's also an old well where we can water the horses, and trees to picket them." Keith turned his back, making no effort to help her, not that she'd expected any. He obviously didn't intend to make this any easier on her. She'd volunteered to help him, damn it! Why was he still giving her the cold shoulder?

Miranda groaned as she attempted to dismount. Her ass was beyond numb, and her knees so cramped she didn't know if she'd be able to stand once she dismounted—if she could get off. Taking a deep breath, she threw her leg over the back of the saddle and slid down the horse. As she'd feared, her knees nearly gave way the moment her feet hit the ground. She had to grab onto the saddle horn for support.

"You'll feel far worse tomorrow," he tossed carelessly over his shoulder.

She still couldn't comprehend his continued hostility. She questioned her decision to stay behind with him. Dave's promise that he and Donny would rejoin them was little comfort.

"Why are you being so mean to me?" she asked, fighting the burning behind her eyes.

"It was your decision to do this," he replied coldly. "I told you how it would be. I get paid to round up horses. Kowtowing to you isn't in my contract, Miz Sutton."

"That's not what I expected. I feel like you're trying to make it more unpleasant than it has to be."

"Is that what you think?"

"Yes," she replied.

His gaze met hers. "Then you think too much."

What did he mean? It was pointless to ask. She knew he wouldn't explain. "What are you doing?" she asked. He had a coil of rope he was stringing between two trees, clothesline style.

"Making a picket line for the horses." He knotted the rope and gave a tug before releasing it.

"Oh." She loosened her horse's cinch and led it over to him. He nodded curtly as she slipped off Sadie's bridle and tied the horse. "What can I do to help you?" she asked, determined to prove she wasn't as clueless as he seemed to think.

He eyed her, gaze narrowed. "You can pump water." He pointed out a rusty-looking hand pump near a collapsed building that must have once served as the well house. "The horses are going to need about ten gallons each. Hopefully that old well will produce enough for all of us."

"All right. I can do that." She approached the rusted pump with a dubious look. It took both hands, all her strength, and a grunt just to raise the handle. "You don't happen to have some WD-40, do you?" she quipped, trying again to break the tension.

Keith scowled back. "The only lube we have is elbow grease. I suggest you use it."

Miranda threw herself into the effort, bearing all her weight down on the handle, but failed to raise it again. She silently cursed that she'd have to ask him for help. "I'm sorry, Keith. I'm not sure I have the strength even to prime the pump."

Keith came to the well, muttering a stream of incomprehensible words. "Fine. I'll pump the water. You go gather firewood. Just watch out for snakes and scorpions."

"Wonderful," she grumbled back. "The only thing I hate worse than scorpions is snakes."

"And I'd rather deal with either of them than a whiner."

"I'm not whining," she protested. "I just don't like things that slither and creep, okay?"

His gaze met hers, his expression dark and cold as he raised the pump handle. "And I don't like people who lie and deceive, so I guess we'll both just have to deal with it."

"I didn't lie!" She stamped her foot in protest. "Damn it! How many times do I have to say it? Maybe you didn't like the spin Bibi put on it, but everything in that film was factual. The words were from your own mouth, and the rest was taken straight from public records."

"And just how would you know that?" he asked, driving the handle back down.

"Because I fact-checked everything."

Determined to prove her worth to Bibi, she'd spent days digging before finally solving the mystery of Keith Russo, a.k.a "Two Wolves." Bibi was so pleased, she'd rewarded her with a job.

"Fact is not always the same as truth," he countered, his breath coming shorter as he vigorously forced the handle up and down. "Facts can be twisted and distorted into falsehoods. But truth can't be spun or twisted." The pump gave a violent hiccup. "Truth is immutable." A sudden surge of rusty water sputtered and splashed into the bucket. "You didn't present *the truth*," he contended fiercely.

"Oh really?" She snorted. "If anything, deceit is your specialty. You presented yourself as a clinician, when you're really just a poser. A talented one, I'll give you that, but you don't really *teach* anything. It was all just a big show, wasn't it? You trained your horse to do tricks and then worked your seductive magic on your audience. That's fine if you're just an entertainer, but you touted yourself as more than that."

She'd been as enthralled as the rest of them after watching him work with Picasso at his clinic and felt inexplicably let down once she'd realized what he was really after—sex and money.

"How about you?" he threw back. "That film you made depicted me as a phony, but it was nothing but a series of half-truths. My people have a proverb, Miz Sutton. 'Do not wrong your neighbor, for it is not he that you wrong, but yourself.'"

"But I didn't *wrong* anyone," she insisted. "Maybe Bibi embellished the film for the sake of entertainment, but how can you fault her when you'd already sensationalized yourself?" She faced him, hands on hips. "Do you deny that you were born in New York? That you changed your name purely to promote your career?"

"Lots of people use a stage name," he retorted. "There's nothing dishonest in that. I never tricked or deceived anyone. Two Wolves is the Shoshone name my grandfather gave me. It's mine by right of heritage."

"Heritage?" She regarded him, perplexed. "I-I don't understand. Isn't your family from Long Island? I looked it all up, your birth date, even the hospital name. Your family—"

He glared back at her. "They *aren't* my real family. I *was* born in New York, but my father was full-blooded Shoshone. I am Shoshone through his blood and by tribal adoption."

"What you're saying isn't making any sense."

"Of course not," he said. "How could it when you have only half of the story? If you'd ever asked me, I would have told you the rest. But you never asked, did you?"

"That wasn't up to me," she replied defensively. "It was Bibi's project, not mine. I just did the job she told me to do."

Still, guilt gnawed at her insides. She'd always considered herself a good judge of character, but it seemed she'd been wrong about him. Maybe he wasn't *all* he'd presented himself to be, but he also wasn't quite the phony the film accused him of being. "Did Bibi know the truth?" she asked.

"She knew."

Her jaw went slack. "I don't understand. Why would she have purposely—"

He turned back to the pump. "I'll water the horses. You gather wood."

———

Still brooding, Keith kept Miranda in his peripheral vision while he tended the horses. There was no question in his mind that Bibi had set out to ruin him, but Miranda wasn't completely innocent. Maybe under different circumstances he would have enjoyed being alone with her, but he couldn't forget the part she'd played.

She returned with an armful of dead wood she'd gathered from around the two Joshua trees and dumped it on the ground. "How much more?"

"Two more loads," he replied refusing to look up.

He turned his attention to unpacking supplies but couldn't seem to keep his eyes from following every time she turned her back. As much as he wanted to, he couldn't ignore his body's awareness of her. He hadn't felt himself inside a woman in a long time. Far too long. He'd had no shortage of opportunities, but he'd steered clear of them. It was all part of the self-inflicted penance he'd undertaken to purify his spirit. It had taken months of prayer, meditation, and time spent in the heat and darkness of the sweat lodge to purge impure thoughts.

He'd finally managed to banish sex almost completely from his mind...until now. He might not like Miranda, but the male part of him still appreciated the female parts of her. As she squatted and gathered up the dead branches, he couldn't help noticing the long legs encased in tight jeans that also showcased a small but perfectly shaped behind. He briefly fantasized how those long legs would feel wrapped around his waist while his hands cupped that nicely rounded ass.

Her hoarse whisper called him back from the erotic abyss.

"Keith, do you hear that?"

A soft, ominous rattle echoed her words.

"Shit." He grabbed the hunting knife from his belt scabbard. He hadn't really expected her to encounter any snakes. They were usually hibernating this time of year. He'd mentioned them simply to torture her, but the danger was real enough now. "Where is it?" he asked.

"I don't know. I can't see over the wood." Her arms were loaded and her eyes wide with fear. "What should I do?"

"Don't move until I say so." He crept toward her, knife in hand, locating it quickly by sound—a Mojave rattler, the deadliest snake in North America. It was coiled and extremely agitated. "It's on the left about two feet away from you," he said.

He approached from the opposite side, gaze locked on the snake, knife hand poised.

"Wh-what are you going to do?" she whispered.

"Kill it." One flick of his wrist released the knife and impaled the blade in the snake's head.

She gasped, dropping the wood with a clatter, her face as pale as a full moon. "H-how did you learn to throw a knife like that?"

"My grandfather taught me. He believes knife throwing is one of many lost arts."

"Wait, it's not dead!" she shrieked.

Although the knife had gone straight through its head, the snake still lurched and writhed.

"Yes it is," Keith replied matter-of-factly. "It'll just take a while for him to figure it out." Taking up a branch, he broke off the ends to form a short fork. "They're a lot like chickens that way. They can move around for up to an hour after you kill them, and they can still bite, even when the head is severed."

"They can poison you even after they're dead?" She shuddered. "One more reason to hate them."

"You can hate the live ones all you like, but this one is dinner." Using the forked stick, he immobilized the snake to remove his knife.

She regarded him with brows furrowed. "You're kidding, right?"

He ignored her question. "I'm going to skin and clean it now. If you're squeamish, you might want to look away, or better yet, go and start the cooking fire."

"You're *really* planning to *eat* that thing?"

His lips curved into a smirk. "Waste not, want not, Miz Sutton."

Chapter 8

Miranda ate her MRE in silence as Keith prepared a fire to roast his snake—once it finally stopped moving. She was edgy and acutely aware of him watching her. More than once she caught herself staring back. Her fascination had exponentially magnified with the knife throw, making him seem like some kind of larger-than-life adventure hero—her very own Jack T. Colton. A chuckle rose up in her throat as she recalled the snake scene from *Romancing the Stone*. Perhaps it was a case of delayed shock, but what began as a benign gurgle soon transformed into almost maniacal laughter.

"What is so damned hilarious?" he asked with a dark look.

"You." She gasped for air. "Cooking that snake. I guess life really does imitate art." She let out another chortle. "Are you certain it wasn't a bushmaster?"

"Bushmaster?" His gaze narrowed. "We don't have those here. They live in the jungle."

"C'mon, don't you get it?" Here she was almost dying of laughter, and he hadn't even cracked a smile. "It was a joke. You don't watch many movies, do you?"

"'Fraid not," he said. "I never had much interest in movies. 'Sides that, the nearest cinema was almost two hours from my home."

"What about cable TV?"

"No cable."

"Satellite?"

"Nope."

"No Internet either?"

He shook his head.

"Are you serious?" she asked, incredulous. "How did you ever survive?"

"Where I come from, there was always something more interesting to do outside."

"And where was that?" she asked. "Mars?"

She was happy to see his lips twitch. Maybe he had a sense of humor after all. He'd given hints of it, but she'd yet to see it surface. She'd seen him before as a charming and seductive showman, and now as a brooding, standoffish wrangler. She wondered which version was the real Keith.

"Wyoming," he replied after a moment.

"But your birth and school records were all in Long Island, New York. At least all I could find."

"I left Long Island when I was thirteen."

"To go to Wyoming? Why would you do that?"

"I had my reasons."

"What kind of reasons?" she asked.

He shook his head with a derisive laugh. "So *now* you want the real story?" He then turned his attention to building a fire. He was quiet for several more minutes, long enough for her to think he didn't intend to answer, but then he surprisingly broke his silence. "I grew up feeling like an outsider in my own family. I never understood why until the day this scary-looking dude with long hair, tattoos, and scars showed up claiming to be my father." He spoke slowly, watching her warily. "I had no idea who he was and freaked out, but I didn't tell anyone. A week later he came back, wanting to take me away with him. This time my mom was home. They got into it, and she called the cops and had him taken away. After that I started asking questions. Demanding answers."

"Was it true? Was he your real father?" she asked, trying to imagine the shock and fear he must have felt.

"Yup. It turns out my mom was quite a rebel in her college days. She got involved with this Shoshone guy who was a leader in the American Indian Movement. He was bad news. He eventually went to prison for a murder up in Pine Ridge, South Dakota. That's where he was when she found out she was pregnant, so she quietly married an accountant from New Jersey. They never told me anything about my real dad until he showed up. After I found out about all this, I couldn't let it go. I tracked my father down. We exchanged some letters and phone calls. Then, one day, he sent me a ticket to Wyoming. So I went."

"Your mother let you go? Just like that?"

"I didn't tell her. When I got to my grandparents' ranch, I called and told her I wasn't coming back."

"She didn't care?" Miranda asked, her heart wrenching at what he must have suffered to have been so desperate to leave.

"I didn't give her any choice," he replied with a careless shrug. "Once I knew where I wanted to be, she never could have kept me away. I was finally home. I had a new family, my grandparents, lots of cousins, and more freedom than I'd ever known. Maybe I wasn't born there, but I never felt I belonged anywhere else."

"I can't believe you weren't bored to tears after living in the city."

"It was a working horse ranch," he said. "There wasn't any time to be bored. There were always animals to take care of and things to fix. We also hunted a lot. Our freezer was always full of game. It was a completely different life—almost like stepping back in time."

"Sounds like an awful lot of work to me," she remarked. "What did you do for fun?"

"When the work was through, we liked to practice stuff—roping, riding, archery, shooting…knife throwing. My cousins and I were always very competitive about everything, always trying to one-up each other, especially when it came to the horses." For the first time, he chuckled, a low, soft sound. "We did some crazy-ass things with the horses."

"Like what?" she prompted, her curiosity growing.

"Reckless shit," he replied, adding more wood to the kindling beneath his makeshift grill. "You know, like hanging off the side of a galloping horse like the 'Injuns' in the old Westerns. Or jumping from one horse to another. My grandfather always encouraged us in all of the old ways. He also gave me my first horse, a yearling colt named Little Bear. I knew nothing about horses then, but he told me the horse would teach me all I needed to know. All I had to do was learn how to listen. So I did. For two years we were inseparable. Where I would go, the horse would follow. That horse became my brother. When he was finally old enough to ride, I rode him."

"Just like that?" she asked. "You just got on and rode?"

"Yes." He smiled. "Training a horse is not difficult if you exercise patience."

"Was he the horse you rode in that exhibition? That routine of yours was pretty amazing. It's like you and he read each other's minds."

"Body language," he replied. "Horses are masters of it. By mastering his, I gained his complete trust. He even let me ride him with a blindfold. In fact, that's how I got started performing. I roped a calf with the horse blindfolded to impress a girl. A rodeo promoter saw it and offered me a job."

"That's how you got started?" Miranda laughed. "By trying to impress a girl?"

"Teenage hormones." His face split into a grin, revealing perfect, pearly white teeth. "At first it was just local rodeos, but after a couple of years, I left the rez to tour full-time with a big rodeo producer. I taught Little Bear more tricks and began wearing feathers, buckskin, and war paint. When the whole horse-whispering craze came along, I decided to become a clinician. It was a great gig..." He added bitterly, "While it lasted."

She snorted. "Am I supposed to feel sorry for you? From what I saw, you used all this Native American mystique of yours just to exploit women. It seems to me you got what you deserved."

His eyes met hers and hardened again. "You got all that backward, sister. From the very beginning, *they* came to *me*. Just like that boss of yours. How is that exploitive? I just gave them what they wanted."

"You mean Bibi?" Miranda asked. "Are you saying she *propositioned* you?" She'd heard rumors, of course, but had never quite believed that men were also victims of the casting couch.

"After my clinic, she asked if I wanted to get into

films and even offered to pay for acting classes. She even tried to entice me with her Malibu beach house. How else was I to take that?"

"She's an influential woman. It couldn't have been easy to turn her down."

"It wasn't nearly as hard as you think." He gave a shudder. "Even if she'd been twenty years younger, I wouldn't have reacted any differently. You look surprised. Do you really have such a low opinion of me?"

"It's not that," she said. "I'm just trying to figure you out. I guess I didn't think men had the same kind of scruples about these things as women do."

"So you think I'm the kinda man who'd be kept as some rich woman's pet?"

"No." She shook her head. "Not when you put it *that* way. I can't picture any woman controlling you like that."

She knew now that he wasn't the type. He had too much pride and self-respect. He'd seduce women on *his* terms. She wondered how many had succumbed. Probably more than he could remember. "So I guess the whole Hollywood idea didn't live up to your expectations?"

"Hardly," he said. "How about you?"

"Not exactly," she admitted. "Or at least not yet. It all seemed so much more exciting and glamorous when I was on the outside looking in. Now, not so much. Then again, I had pie-in-the-sky expectations."

He looked up from tending his meal. "What do you mean?"

"I was clueless about the real world. I grew up in a small town, the kind of place where everyone knows everyone and no one ever leaves, but I always wanted more. After graduation I headed out to the West Coast, but L.A. was almost a culture shock for me. Where I grew up, most people didn't lock their houses or their cars. Out in L.A., we not only lock, but alarm everything. I never feel completely safe, even at home, but then again," she added dryly, "I don't live in the best of neighborhoods."

"So why filmmaking?" he asked.

"I don't know exactly. I've always loved movies and photography, so I guess filmmaking seemed like a good fit for me. But I've spent more time fetching Starbucks than making movies. In fact, that short of yours for Bibi was the only thing that even qualifies as a real film. The rest of my work has been mostly commercials and corporate promo crap that I hate. I suppose that's better than videotaping weddings, but it's still a far cry from what I want to do. I'd like to take on worthy projects, tell stories that others in this industry ignore. I'd like to be successful, but I'm not doing it to get rich and famous."

One corner of his mouth lifted. "Are you saying you're only interested in satisfying your creative muse?"

"Well, not at the expense of starving," she confessed with a laugh. "Speaking of which, are you *really* going to eat that snake?"

"Yes." Keith flashed a full-toothed smile for the first time. The effect almost knocked her on her ass. "My people have consumed them for centuries."

"But it's venomous," she argued.

"All of the venom is in the head. We don't eat that part. Want to try it?" He came toward her, offering his plate.

"No, thank you." She waved it away, her lips curled back in revulsion.

"The meat of this snake has got to be better than that

shit on a shingle you're having with God knows what in it."

She shuddered. "At least my meal never slithered on the ground."

"You don't know that. How can you be certain what's really in it? Or do you actually trust those government labels?"

"To be honest, I'd rather not know." She gave a dry laugh. "As they say, 'Ignorance is bliss.'"

His reserve had begun to melt, and the scowl had lifted from his brow. His black eyes taunted her as he took another hunk of meat off the stick he'd used as a skewer and popped a piece into his mouth. "Tastes just like chicken. Are you always afraid to try new things?"

"I am daring about *some* things," she insisted. "Just not my food."

"Oh yeah?" he challenged. "Ever gone skinny-dipping?" His gaze drifted slowly over her in a way that made her feel naked.

"Not since the kiddie pool in the backyard, but that was well before puberty."

"What about zip-lining? Ever done that?"

"Nope," she confessed. "I don't really like heights."

"I would have thought the girl who came out here in the middle of the desert would be much more adventurous."

"Are you implying that I'm dull? Am I boring you, Keith?" She didn't know why his opinion mattered. Maybe she wasn't the most exciting person in the world, but who would be, compared to this Indiana Jones? Although Indiana would certainly have sided with her about the snake.

"Don't put words in my mouth," he said. "I don't

know you well enough to imply anything. I'm just trying to get to know you better."

"Why?" she asked, wondering at his sudden interest, when only a couple of hours ago he wanted nothing to do with her.

"Might as well, since we're stuck here together," he replied.

Miranda felt another stab of disappointment. It wasn't real interest in her that prompted the questions but only a desire to pass the time. If that was the case, he'd get the *Reader's Digest Condensed* version.

"There's not much to tell beyond what you already know. I grew up in central Ohio, went to community college, and then came to California to learn cinematography. I finished my internship last year, and now I'm trying to get into films. I haven't had much luck yet, but I'm hoping to make something of this opportunity."

"Since you don't like unusual foods, I guess you haven't traveled much," he said.

"No, I haven't traveled," she admitted. "Other than summers with my grandparents in Montana and then moving to L.A., I haven't seen much of this country or any other for that matter. What about you?" she asked. "How adventurous are you?"

His mouth curved suggestively. "Depends on what we're discussing."

Was she imagining the innuendo? She couldn't ignore her response to him but refused to acknowledge it. She was already too physically aware of him to be encouraging *those* kinds of thoughts. "Other foods, other cultures," she said.

"I like to think I'm open-minded." He popped

another piece of roasted rattlesnake into his mouth. "I've lived on the road for the past eight years and spent two of those abroad."

"Really? Where did you go?" She hated that his life was so much more interesting than hers. In comparison, she really *was* dull and boring.

"I've been to every state in the Continental U.S. and have also seen a good bit of Europe. I spent a lot of time in different parts of Germany. They have a weird fascination with Native American culture over there that goes back to a German author of Western dime novels named Karl May."

"What did you do when you were there?" she asked.

A hint of humor softened his eyes and relaxed the lines around his mouth. "The same thing I did here: presented clinics on horse behavior and seduced countless women."

Chapter 9

KEITH WATCHED WITH INTEREST AS MIRANDA SCRAMBLED on all fours up a steep embankment, camera around her neck, to film the sunset. As much as he'd wanted to, he couldn't dislike her. She'd kept her composure during the snake incident and afterward had even shown a sense of humor when most women would have gone into hysterics. She'd been reasonably stoic, given the hard ride and rough conditions. She also had tenacity, which earned his grudging respect.

"Be careful," he called out. "I don't want to have to call the chopper when you break your neck."

She heaved herself up onto the biggest rock and uncapped her lens. "You worry like an old woman."

The barb struck home. "An *old woman*?"

She smirked. "You sure sound like one."

The second taunt was too much for his ego to bear. Taking a running start, he bounded up the rocky incline with as much ease as a mountain goat. She startled when he laid a hand on her shoulder and spun her around to face him. "What are you doing up here?" she asked, sounding a bit breathless.

"Take it back," he demanded.

Her forehead wrinkled. "Take what back?"

He jerked his chin. "The insult you just made."

She laughed. "It was a joke. You can't really be *that* sensitive."

"In my culture, men have two roles—hunter or warrior."

"A *warrior*? Aren't you a little late to that party? I think the cowboy and Indian wars ended well over a century ago."

"The identity remains," he returned staunchly. "It's who we are. Who *I* am." Or at least who he'd always wanted to be. "Comparing me to an old woman is no joke. It is an insult." His tone was calm and controlled, yet fire simmered in his veins.

"Are you for real? You honestly expect me to retract what I said?"

"Yes." Her careless laugh only stoked the flame.

Her laughter died. Her hands landed on her hips. She raised her chin a notch to meet his gaze, her smoky eyes challenging. "And if I don't take it back?"

"Then I will *make* you."

"Make me? Just how do you propose to do that?"

"Do you *really* want to go there?"

He stepped into her space.

She backed away, nervously licking her lips.

"Why did you come with me, Miranda? You knew I didn't want to bring you, yet you insisted. You would have been safe at camp, but you came even after I warned you of all the dangers."

"But we weren't supposed to be alone. Dave and Donny said they were going to join us."

"But they aren't here yet, are they?" *She could have gone back. She should have gone back.* "Why did you come?" he asked again, softly.

"I told you why." Her gray eyes flickered and then flitted away. "I-I wanted to help find the stray horses, and Mitch needs proof of what happened."

He advanced again until they stood thigh to thigh. "I had nothing to do with it?"

She gave another nervous laugh. "Is that what you think, Keith? That you're so irresistible that every woman you meet wants to jump your bones?"

"Not all," he replied with a shrug. "But I have enough experience to recognize the ones who do."

"You're mistaken this time."

"Am I? I don't think so. Your need speaks to me. It shines in your eyes."

Those wide, fawn-like eyes made him feel far too much like a ravenous beast emerging from hibernation. She squeezed them shut, a move that was as effective as an ostrich hiding its head in the sand. He inched in until he was close enough to feel her soft soughs of breath caressing his face, close enough for the subtle essence of honeysuckle to tease his nostrils. Her scent struck him hard, firing a primal need to touch…to taste. He looped a stray reddish-gold curl—the color of a desert sunrise—around his finger. She stared at his hand, swallowed hard, but didn't pull away. He slowly released the curl and grazed his thumb down her cheek to stroke across her bottom lip.

~~~

Finding herself between a rock and a hard place—specifically the boulder at her back and Keith at her front—Miranda recognized that she was in way over her head. Her gut had warned her where all this was heading, but she hadn't listened. Maybe she'd subconsciously asked for it, but now that he'd taken notice of her, her pulse pounded in panic.

"Do you deny that you want me, Miranda?" he whispered seductively. His gaze dropped to her mouth. Was he going to kiss her? Her nerves coiled tighter, her anticipation ramping up another notch. "Isn't that the real reason you came out here with me?" His mouth hovered inches from hers, his hot, humid breath inciting tiny ripples down her spine. "If I can't hear it from your lips, I'll make your body speak."

He dipped his head, but instead of the kiss she'd anticipated, he nuzzled her throat. His scorching mouth blazed a trail of liquid fire up her neck. Her breaths came short in almost painful rasps at the searing sensation of his tongue licking the tender hollow behind her ear. She shut her eyes on a shudder of pleasure. She'd never experienced a man touching her in such a sensual way. She'd also never been so quickly aroused. It was all she could do to keep her hands off him.

She gasped as he shifted his hips against her. He was aroused and wanted to be sure she knew it. She knew she should pull away but couldn't quite bring herself to comply. Her body jolted with a shock of pleasure, as pelvis to pelvis, he began a slow, rhythmic rocking. It was primal and erotic.

"Just say the word," he murmured, "and I'll give you what you want."

The single syllable was about to escape her lips when his words jolted her back to her senses. Her eyes snapped open. "What *I* want?" She shoved hard against his chest. "You egotistical prick! You're deluded if you think I'm going to become another notch on your…your…totem pole."

"Wrong tribe." A hint of a smirk curled his sensuous lips. "The plains Indians didn't carve totems."

"You get my gist!" she snapped. How could she have been such an idiot to let him lead her on like that? She knew what he was, and he sure as hell knew what he was doing. She'd seen him work his magic on an entire crowd of women. It was all just a game to him.

Miranda snatched up her camera and scuttled back down the embankment, mostly on her butt. Returning to the campsite, she tossed a few more thick branches on the fire. Hurt and humiliated, she stared into the flickering flames, refusing to look up even when the toes of his boots came into view.

"You forgot this." Keith offered her ball cap, his dark eyes dancing with amusement. Was he laughing at her? She tore her cap from his hands and shoved it back on her head, but he didn't take the hint and leave. Instead, he stood watching her, hands in his pockets, rocking back on his heels.

"It's getting dark," he remarked after a while. "I'm guessing Dave and Donny found more horses along the way and had to turn back again."

"Can you call them and find out?" she asked, wishing she was anyplace but out here with him.

"Can't. Mitch has the other satellite phone."

Her stomach sank. "So we're here alone together for the whole night?"

"Looks that way." He shrugged, the mocking look still lingering in his eyes. "I warned you how it would be."

Yes, he had. He'd cautioned her from the outset about snakes, scorpions, and even Gila monsters, but she never could have imagined that he'd be the greatest danger. Coming out here alone with him was foolhardy in the extreme. She watched covertly as he collected his saddlebag and rifle, and then cleared a space by the fire where he went to work laying out a bedroll. "Only one?" she remarked.

"It's all we need."

She glared at the bedroll. "I'm *not* sharing your bed, Keith. I thought I made myself clear about that."

"Now look who's being egotistical. I didn't ask you to. This is for you."

"Oh." Her face burned with embarrassment. "Thanks. But what about you? Where are you sleeping?"

"I'm not. I'll be keeping watch over the horses."

"What do you mean 'keeping watch'?"

"There are predators out here that make tied horses vulnerable to attack. If Donny and Dave were here, we'd take shifts, but since they aren't, I'll have to stand guard."

"All night?" she asked with a sudden pang of guilt. "That makes no sense when I can help. Why don't you and I take shifts?"

"Do you know how to use a rifle?" he asked.

"No." She shook her head. "I don't like guns."

"Then what are you going to do if you see a coyote, bear, or mountain lion? Wave your hands and try to shoo it away?"

"No." She scowled back at him. "I'll just scream and wake you up."

His lips curved into a half smile. "I guess that would work."

"Then we have a plan." She stood and brushed the dirt from her hands on her even dirtier jeans. "Who takes first watch?"

"You will," he said. "It's safer. Most predators prefer the darkest hours before dawn."

He went to his saddlebag and produced a battery-operated Coleman lantern that he suspended at the near end of the picket line. "Unfortunately, there's almost no moon tonight. This light and the campfire will discourage them, but don't grow complacent." His eyes grew dark and predatory, reminding her once more of her own very real peril. "A hungry beast is always dangerous."

———⁓———

After laying out a tarp as a moisture barrier, Keith arranged the makeshift bed. If he were back in Wyoming, he'd have used it to create a shelter, but there was little chance of getting caught in the rain out here in the desert. Dew from the ground, however, was another matter. After pulling off his boots, he sprawled out full length on the bedroll, pillowing his head on his crossed arms. Once more, he watched Miranda watching him.

"Aren't you concerned about snakes?" she asked.

"No. They aren't as active at night. It's too cold."

The cooler temperature also magnified the beauty of the night. There was almost nothing he appreciated more than staring up at a canopy of shimmering lights. Tonight, the cloudless, moonless sky, showcased the full brilliance of a million stars.

"Do you do this often?" she asked. "Camping out under the stars?"

"I've done it often enough. When I was fourteen, I spent a few days alone in a place a lot like this."

"Why were you alone?" she asked.

"It was a vision quest."

"What is that exactly?" she asked. "I've heard the term, of course, but I don't really understand the purpose of it. There's a film I like called *Vision Quest* in which one of the main characters pretends to be an Indian, but it never explains what a real vision quest is."

He stared into the fire. "It's a rite of passage. When a young man reaches warrior age, he must go away to a secret place until he finds his *boo-ha-gant*, a kind of talisman to help him through life."

On his own quest, he'd gone to Crow Heart Butte, the same peak he'd scaled with his grandfather the year before when they'd scattered his father's ashes to the four winds. He'd remained for three days, immersed in fervent prayer, but no vision had come to him.

"Did it work?" she asked. "Did you find your *boo-ha-gant*?"

"No." He recalled his profound disappointment that the Great Spirit had deemed him unworthy. Was it due to his mixed blood, or was it a character flaw? He'd never know. Either way, he was determined that no one would learn of his failure. "I said I had a vision, but I lied."

"Why would you do that?" she asked.

"For acceptance. I'd been with my adopted family for over a year, but many on the rez still regarded me as an outsider. I was desperate to fit in. In the beginning, I suffered many black eyes and bloody noses, mostly from my own cousins. Although I had lots of practice fighting back home, the rules were different on the rez. I lost often but never backed down. That's what finally won their respect. My cousin Tonya was the first to come around, deciding that even mixed blood was thicker than water. Eventually, my male cousins followed. After that, they accepted me as family—at least until my decision to leave."

"Why did you leave?" she asked.

"In the beginning, I was enthralled by my native roots and embraced Indian culture as warmly as my grandparents embraced me, but as I grew older, I began to miss the material things I'd known before. Perhaps the novelty of the native life had worn off. I started to resent rather than revere the old traditions. I found them superstitious and oppressive; so when the opportunity was presented, I left."

"I can understand wanting to fit in," she said. "I lied about a lot of things too when I was young."

"What kinds of things?"

"I don't even remember now. Just a lot of stupid things that don't even matter. Wanting to belong can be a painful, sometimes damaging thing. Did you ever see the movie *Heathers*?" she asked.

"No. Told you I haven't seen many movies."

"It's a totally over-the-top dark comedy about this girl who wants to run with the 'in crowd' but gets involved with this cool new guy who starts killing the most popular kids. It won several independent film awards."

"You seem to spend a lot of time watching movies. Movies are only an imitation of life, Miranda."

Her lips compressed. "Are you implying that I have no life?"

"I'm wondering why you would prefer to watch other people's lives than living your own. Why do you hide behind your camera? What are you afraid of?"

"You're wrong! I'm not hiding, and I'm not afraid of anything…besides maybe snakes and other creepy things," she confessed. "But I even braved all that to come out here."

"Why?" he pressed again, suddenly wanting to understand her better. "Why is this so important to you?"

"I don't know how to explain it," she said. "I guess my camera is my view of the world. It's my eyes and ears and my voice."

"You think you're blind, deaf, and mute without it?" he asked, growing even more puzzled.

"No." She glanced up at him with a shake of her head. "It's just that I've always felt like I don't matter, as if I mean nothing to this world. Like I'm no more significant than a grain of sand in this desert. I guess someone like *you* could never understand that."

The remark irked him. "What do you mean someone *like me*? You seem to make a lot of assumptions about me." That fact annoyed him even more.

"I only meant you aren't like me," she said. "You're the kind of person people instantly notice. I'm usually invisible."

"Maybe because that's what you secretly want," he suggested.

"Why would you think that? I'm just stating facts here. I'm not beautiful or brilliant or even funny. I have no athletic ability. I can't read music or even carry a tune. There's nothing special about me." She tilted her head up to the sky, continuing wistfully. "But I *want* to be special. I want to matter, or at least feel like I do. That's why I want to tell stories that matter."

He took a moment to digest her words. "If you look to others for validation, Miranda, you look in the wrong place. They'll never give you what you need. What you seek can come only from within." At least that was what he told himself.

She visibly bristled, telling him he'd touched a sore spot. "Easy for *you* to say."

"I speak from experience, Miranda. I know it's true." It was the goal he'd been working toward for months—to find the inner peace and contentment that had always eluded him. He'd left the rez at twenty with stars in his eyes, but his success in the outside world had done nothing to soothe his restlessness or fill the emptiness.

"Shouldn't you get some sleep now?" she asked.

"I doubt I can," he replied. "I'll be far too worried about you alone and shivering." The temperature had already dropped at least twenty degrees from when they'd first set out.

"I'm fine." She jutted her chin, hugging herself tighter. "Beth loaned me her jacket."

He studied her. She looked cold and defiant sitting on a rock near the fire, arms wrapped around herself, but like the desert cacti, he recognized her prickliness as purely a defense mechanism.

"It's going to get a lot colder before morning," he warned. "There's a blanket in the other saddlebag…or… better yet"—he patted the place beside him—"you're always welcome to come here and share mine." He grinned. "I promise we'd both wake up warmer and happier."

"Or," she replied, "they'd find our dead carcasses, half-eaten by a mountain lion."

"Or that." He laughed and rolled onto his back, where he continued to watch her through hooded lids. Although he'd allow himself to doze, his protective instincts wouldn't let him fall into a deep sleep. He was also far too aware of *her* for comfort. His body was still coiled tight with unresolved sexual tension. Despite her viper tongue, her restless fidgeting and glances in his direction suggested that she felt the same. "Don't wander off," he mumbled. "If nature calls, wake me."

It was too dark now to see her face, but he chuckled at the snark in her reply. "Yes, *old woman*. I'll wake you."

Chapter 10

ONCE SHE THOUGHT HIM ASLEEP, MIRANDA PLOPPED DOWN cross-legged closer to the fire, staring thoughtfully into the flames. Though she'd rather have her toenails yanked out than admit it, Keith was right that she had no life. In truth, it sometimes felt as if she lived hiding in plain sight with no one ever really seeing her.

She'd given up almost everything to pursue her dream, but L.A. was expensive, loud, dirty, and very far from home and family. She had few friends beyond her roommate, Lexi, but hardly fit in with her crowd. So Miranda filled her waking hours with work, usually alone in her tiny apartment with a bag of Orville Redenbacher extra butter. She wondered now if the path she'd taken would eventually lead to happiness, or at least to the end of dissatisfaction with her life…with herself.

A coyote howl echoed her melancholy thoughts, breaking the silence with a long and lonesome cry. Another one answered. Was it a mating call?

She glanced again at Keith. Although his expression was relaxed, his face seemed sharper and more angular in the flickering firelight. She didn't know what devil made her continue to taunt him. He looked very much the warrior, the kind of man who wouldn't hesitate to take what he wanted. Her feelings about Keith were mixed and confused. He'd made her realize just how lonely and disconnected she was. Although she was more attracted to him than she'd ever been to anyone, she suspected he was just playing with her.

The fire popped, making her start. What was she doing here? She'd had a single purpose in coming out to the desert, but the whole situation seemed suddenly surreal, as if she'd been transported back in time. She almost wanted to laugh.

She shivered and hugged herself tighter. She could see her breath now. Maybe it was time to scrounge for that blanket. Keith had left a flashlight beside his rifle. She took it with her and scanned the ground as she walked, just in case he was wrong about the snakes. The horses stirred and nickered at her approach, suddenly restless…or were they nervous?

"What's wrong, Sadie?" she asked the mare, whose ears were flicking in all directions. Their sense of hearing was acute, functioning much like radar. She shined the light into the darkness. Was something out there? She could see nothing. Her skin prickled.

She tried to shrug off her feeling of unease as a case of the heebie-jeebies, just like she always got after watching a horror movie. Unfortunately, that last thought only reminded her of *The Hills Have Eyes*, a horror flick set in the desert that had given her nightmares for months.

Perhaps it was just the coyotes' cries that had the horses agitated? She found the blanket and clutched it around her shoulders with her free hand. She shivered again, but this time as much from nerves as cold. When she returned to the fire, Keith was sitting up, scowling at her.

"I told you not to wander off."

"I didn't wander. I only went to fetch a blanket and check on the horses. They seem jumpy."

"So do you," he observed.

"Maybe I am, a little. I think the coyotes spooked me. I'm not used to all this." She added a dry laugh. "The closest I've come to experiencing wildlife in the past four years was a visit to Venice Beach."

"Coyotes are harmless enough," he said. "They prey on mice and rabbits and rarely bother humans." He rose and shouldered his rifle, reminding her all too much of Daniel Day Lewis's Hawkeye in *The Last of the Mohicans*, her favorite epic romance. In that moment it was far too easy to cast herself as Cora Munro. She shook off the ludicrous thought.

"Where are you going?" she asked.

"To check on the horses."

"But it's not your turn yet," she said.

"Doesn't matter. I'm awake."

She eyed the bedroll covetously, wondering if it would still be warm from his body.

"Go ahead," he urged with a tilt of his head.

"But it's technically still my watch," she replied.

His brows furrowed. "Are you always so stubborn?"

"Not always," she said.

"Then you just like to argue with *me*."

"That's not true!" she argued.

Their eyes met. He cocked a brow.

Caught in the act, she couldn't suppress a chuckle.

He walked off, shaking his head and mumbling something she couldn't understand.

⁓

Miranda was right about the horses. They were jumpy as hell, but after scouting the area twice, Keith found nothing.

Damning the moonless night, he returned to the fire, laying the rifle within close reach. True to her stubborn nature, Miranda hadn't taken his place but sat before the fire, cocooned in the blanket. So be it. Let the little fool freeze.

He sank back into his bedroll, turning onto his side to better see into the darkness. He watched her with a growing mix of fascination and frustration. Tall, pale, and slender, Miranda Sutton was nothing like the women he normally went for, but her earthy innocence called out to his carnal nature. His brows contracted. "What are you afraid of? Me or yourself?"

"Neither," she snapped. "I'm not *afraid* of anything."

He made a scoffing sound. "Liar. You'd rather freeze your ass off than share this bed with me. You make no sense, Miranda. I want you, and I believe you want me too. There's no shame in a man and woman pleasuring each other. Making love is one of the most genuine acts of human nature."

"You have a silver tongue, Keith, but that's not what it would be. *Making love* is what you do with someone you have feelings for. Or at the least with someone you like and respect. Anything else is just a *fuck*. I'm not your next fuck."

"Did you know that there are no vulgar words pertaining to sex in any of the native tongues?"

"Is that true?" she asked.

"Yes. We don't defile the act with dirty words. In fact, we have no swearwords at all."

"Yet you think it's perfectly fine to randomly hop from partner to partner and bed to bed?"

"I didn't say we accept promiscuity. We don't. We call those kinds of people tepee creepers."

"Tepee creepers?" She laughed. "Really?"

"Yes. Just because we view sex differently doesn't imply that it's meaningless. We believe just the opposite: that the joining of two bodies forges a deeper connection between their souls. There are no walls in the moment of release, Miranda." He didn't add that his walls always came back up following the afterglow.

"You really believe that?" she scoffed.

"Yes. Sometimes words are inadequate between a man and a woman. They obstruct the essential truth. Sex is honesty. Pleasure *is* truth." Yet sex was really only a transitory escape from loneliness.

"Don't play with me," she whispered. "I don't like games—or being the brunt of jokes."

"You think I'm playing games?"

"I think I'm *convenient*. If we were anyplace else, you wouldn't look twice at me."

She was wrong. He *had* noticed her before, and *she'd* rebuffed *him*. The rejection had surprised as much as stung him.

"That's not true," he said. "Maybe you don't remember the first time we met?"

"Yes, I remember all of it," she answered.

"And?" he prompted.

"I didn't trust you."

"Why not? You thought I only wanted to use you?"

"Yes."

"And now?" he asked.

She hesitated. "I don't know. You made it obvious from the start that you didn't want me around. I don't understand the sudden turnabout. I'm not sure what I think."

"As I said before, you think too much."

Miranda was freezing cold, but she was also terrified. Of him. Of the feelings he'd roused in her.

He reached out his hand, beckoning softly. "Don't be foolish, Miranda. Come and get warm."

Tamping down her trepidations, she rose and settled herself lengthwise beside him. His arm came around her, wrapping her in his blanket, and instantly cocooning her in his body heat. He pulled her closer against him and nuzzled into her hair. "I don't understand you at all, Miranda…but I like how you smell."

She relaxed. "You do?"

"Yes. I do." He burrowed into her neck, his breath hot and his lips soft. "Very much."

She whispered back, "If we're making confessions, I like how you feel."

"Is that so?" He rolled her onto her back so that his body lay on top of hers. His mouth stretched into a slow smile. "Is there a particular *part* of me you like?"

Her face heated. If she'd had any doubt his desire was real, the proof was palpable through two layers of thick denim. "Um…maybe that didn't come out quite right. I meant that you make me feel safe."

"Safe?" His thumb skirted softly over her lips. "Maybe you aren't as safe as you think." He added in a tone that made her shiver with anticipation, "I think perhaps Goldilocks is about to discover that the old woman is really a big bad wolf."

"You're mixing up the stories, Keith. Goldilocks was with the three bears. Little Red Riding Hood was with the wolf."

"You make films your way, and let me tell the stories," he said. "Storytelling is in my blood, after all."

"All right, then. Have it your way. Tell me this story about Goldilocks and the Big Bad Wolf."

He flashed a big, bad lupine grin. "My version begins much the same as what you have heard before, but when Goldilocks enters her grandmother's tepee, she exclaims, *'Huttsi, what large hands you have!'*

'All the better to touch you with, my child,' the wolf replies.

'Huttsi, what a big mouth you have!'

'All the better to kiss you with, my dear!'

'Huttsi, what a long tongue you have!'

'All the better to lick every inch of you, my sweet.'"

His eyes gleamed mischievously. Miranda suspected she knew what was coming next.

"*'But, Huttsi, what an enormous—'*"

"Don't say it!" She covered his mouth. His chuckle warmed both her hand and her ears.

"Don't you want to know how it ends?" he asked.

"I'm not certain I do."

"I'll tell you anyway. He devours her bite by delectable bite." He flashed another very wolfish smile. "You see?" His smile disappeared. "You are never safe with a wolf."

His lips were soft, smooth, and so very knowing as his mouth melded with hers with slow, toe-curling deliberation. There was nothing hurried or clumsy, none of the typical hesitancy, nose bumping, or teeth clashing of a first kiss. Taking her face in his hands, he deepened the kiss by tiny degrees, increasing pressure, adding licks and nips, teasing and torturing her until his hot tongue breached her mouth. Their tongues met, sliding and tangling—both a prelude and promise of so much more. She'd never been kissed by a man who knew how to give her everything she wanted, but Keith did.

Shutting her eyes, she recalled a night spent in another desert when she'd driven down to Baja California for a project in time-lapse videography. After hours of scouting, she'd located a small growth of thin, inconspicuous, dead-looking branches hidden among a patch of scrub—a night-blooming cereus. After setting up cameras, she'd spent the night vigilantly watching for the desert queen to unfurl for its single night of glory. When the flower finally opened, it had perfumed the air with a sweet and delicate scent. She sat watching the flower until it had wilted and withered away with the first light of dawn. Watching that bloom come to life had been one her most memorable experiences.

Keith made her feel very much like that desert flower waiting to bloom. She yearned to be touched… to be loved…and her resistance to him was fading fast. The kiss intensified, blinding her with blissful sensation. Nothing compared to the taste of his mouth, of his musky scent, of the feel of his warm hands on her skin. It was everything she'd hoped for and more. Any lingering doubts vaporized like a puff of breath in the cold night air.

Her hands crept up to his chest, the heat of his skin permeating through the cotton of his shirt into her fingertips. She swallowed hard. A low growl broke the quiet of the night. Miranda froze. "What was that?"

He tensed. "What was *what*?"

"That sound."

Another growl was echoed by bloodcurdling shrieks from the two horses. Keith was instantly on his feet and shouldering his rifle. He took off running toward the horses while Miranda fumbled in the dark for the flashlight. She arrived at the scene just as a great shadow leaped through the air. She drew in a breath to scream but, paralyzed with terror, no sound emerged. The panic-stricken horses frantically kicked, reared, and hauled back on the picket line in their urgency to flee. The line snapped. The lamp crashed to the ground, casting the scene into darkness.

"I can't see anything!" Keith hissed. "Shine the light out there."

The narrow beam of her flashlight pierced the darkness, but not enough to help.

"Where is it?" she asked.

"I don't know. Shit!" Keith fired a shot into the air, cocked the rifle again, and fired another.

Miranda then shone the light on the ground beneath the picket line, where puddles of blood soaked the earth, trailing into the blackness beyond. She covered her mouth in horror. "Oh my God! What was it?"

"A mountain lion," he answered grimly. "With the way it leapt, it couldn't be anything else."

"What are we going to do?" she asked.

"Nothing. He's already made the kill."

"How do you know? How can you be certain the animal isn't just wounded?"

"Mountain lions never wound, Miranda. They are masters of the surgical strike. It's almost always a clean, fast kill. At least the other two got away."

Miranda's throat closed on a choked sob. "It's all my fault! It happened on *my* watch."

"There's nothing you could have done," he consoled her.

"Wh-what about us?" she asked. "What if it comes back? What if there are more of them out there?" Her hands flew to her neck at a sudden vision of a lion with fangs bared lunging at her throat.

"There won't be others," Keith replied. "Mountain lions are territorial. They always hunt alone. And that one is unlikely to strike twice, but my rifle's loaded just in case." Looping a strong arm around her waist, he guided her into motion. "Let's get away from here. You'll be safer by the fire."

~~~

Miranda's teeth chattered, and her body still racked with aftershocks as they settled back under the blanket together. She was close enough to be a second skin, but he knew it wasn't a sexual invitation. She sought only warmth and comfort, but he still couldn't help the surge of blood to his dick. Danger, especially close encounters with death, often incited sexual desire. The danger had been real, and so was his lingering lust, but the moment for acting on it had passed.

"Cold or frightened?" he asked, pulling her closer still.

"Both," she answered with a shaky laugh. "You really don't think it'll come back?" she whispered.

"It won't. It's probably gorging itself right now."

She shuddered. "I didn't need that visual. Which one did it get?"

"I'm not sure."

"What are we going to do out here with no horses?" she asked.

"I have the sat phone, remember? I can call for help

if need be, but we'll probably find the horses once the sun rises. After that adventure, they'll be as happy to go home as we'll be."

In reality, Keith would be more relieved than happy to take Miranda back. Although his first priority was to keep her safe, he wouldn't have minded more time alone with her.

"I can't believe this whole experience," she said. "It's like a weird dream. Do people really live like this? With poisonous snakes and horse-eating lions?"

"Where I come from they do. We coexist with many predators, including wolves and grizzlies. I thought you said your grandparents have a ranch. Didn't you ever encounter any wildlife there?"

"It's actually just my grandma's now. We rode horses and played around with the cattle, but I never experienced anything like this before."

He chuckled. "You aren't in Kansas anymore, Dorothy."

"Funny you said that. *The Wizard of Oz* is my favorite film. I've watched it thirteen times, part of which was a twenty-four-hour marathon."

"I don't understand you." He shook his head with a wry smile. "How can you watch the same film over and over when you already know what's going to happen?"

"Because every time I watch it I focus on a different character and try to experience the events through his or her eyes. It's all about the journey, not the destination."

"Which character do you best identify with?" he asked.

"Well, usually it's Dorothy, given that we're both country girls and my experience in L.A. was all too much like hers in Oz, but I have to admit that tonight I'm identifying a lot more with the cowardly lion."

"If that's so, I have something that might help." He reached beneath his shirt for a leather cord that he pulled over his head.

"What is it?" she asked, fingering the object that hung from the necklace.

"A grizzly tooth. It was my *boo-ha-gant*." He slipped it over her head. "Now it's yours." He smiled into her eyes. "It will give you courage, but you must keep it secret, or it'll lose its powers."

"Courage? So this is really how you killed that snake? Won't you lose your superpowers without it?"

"No." He stroked a finger along her collarbone above where the tooth lay nestled between her breasts. "For the record, you have yet to know my true superpowers. We were interrupted before I could demonstrate them to you."

Her face flushed. "You do think a lot of yourself, don't you?"

He brought his finger back up to her mouth to trace her lips. "Let's just say I wouldn't have disappointed you."

But disappointment reflected in her eyes. "Well, I guess we'll never know now, will we?"

"No," he replied, regretfully. "We never will." He wasn't likely ever to see her again, but in their short time together he'd opened up more with her than he had with anyone else in years. "Are you sorry you came?" he asked.

She exhaled a soft sigh. "No. Even with all that happened, I'm still glad I came."

Maybe her answer shouldn't have surprised him, but it did. This day had put her mettle to the test, revealing a strength she probably didn't even know she possessed.

She still had so much to learn about herself. He would have enjoyed the chance to watch her journey, but it wasn't meant to be. There was no point in dwelling on it. The opportunity was lost. Tomorrow they'd find the missing horses and part ways.

He pulled her head onto his chest and stroked her hair. "Sleep now, *Aiwattsi*. I'll keep you safe."

Chapter 11

SURPRISED THAT SHE'D EVER SHUT HER EYES, MIRANDA awoke to find herself alone beside a barely smoldering fire. Where was Keith? His rifle was gone and the campsite packed up, all but the canvas bedroll she'd slept on. She sat up, rubbing her bleary eyes with panic blooming in her chest as the events of last night replayed in her mind. She reached up to touch the bear tooth necklace and felt instantly at ease. Was it a psychosomatic response, or did her new talisman really have some kind of supernatural power?

Laughing at herself, she reached for her boots, but then remembered Keith's warning to check them first. She shook them upside down and shrieked at the two scorpions that tumbled out. She frantically smashed one with her boot heel but the other managed to scurry away. Her cry must have alerted Keith. He appeared a moment later, a frown etching his brow.

"I heard a scream. Are you okay?"

"Yes." She gave an embarrassed laugh. "Just scorpions."

"You didn't get stung, did you?"

"No. I'm fine," she replied. His show of concern warmed her.

"Good," he replied, the lines of apprehension slowly easing from his face. "That would be the last thing we need right now."

"Yes," she reassured him. "Where were you? I was afraid you'd left me."

"I was looking for the horses and gathering breakfast."

"Breakfast?" She glanced down to notice his hands full of something she didn't recognize. They were elongated, almost pear shape, and reddish in color, somewhat resembling mangos but with spines. "What are they?"

"You're kidding right? You've never had them?"

"No. I don't even know what they are."

"Prickly pear fruit. It's really good," he insisted.

She eyed them suspiciously. "If I recall, that's what you said about the rattlesnake."

"C'mon," he cajoled. "Have an open mind." His black eyes glittered with mocking humor. "Here's your chance to be adventurous, Miranda."

Accepting the challenge, she snatched one from his hands, only to be pricked by a spine. "Ouch!" She dropped the fruit with a curse to examine her injury. "Damn it! You didn't tell me they were dangerous."

"It's how they protect themselves," he replied. "The prickliest ones are always the sweetest. One must proceed with caution, but it's usually worth it in the end."

"Is it really worth all the trouble?" she asked.

"I guess that remains to be seen, doesn't it?" His gaze held hers, making her wonder if they were still talking about the fruit.

"How do you get around the spines?" she asked.

"Easy. Like this." He picked up her dropped fruit with his gloved hand and impaled it on the end of his knife. Squatting by the fire, he rolled it in the smoldering ashes. "See? It burns the spines off. Then you just peel and eat it like any other fruit." He proceeded to do exactly that. Slicing through the skin of the fruit, he peeled it back and offered it to her.

She hesitated. "You're sure it's safe?"

"Yes. Almost all cacti are edible. Of course, you're always welcome to the beef jerky instead."

She curled her lip. "I hate that stuff. It's like salty shoe leather." She sniffed and then committed herself to a tiny nibble. It was both sweet and tart, cucumber-ish in consistency, with tiny seeds like a kiwi. Not too bad, actually.

"Well?" He cocked a brow, urging her to take more.

"It's all right," she admitted. Accepting it from his hands, she took a bigger bite. "Did you see any sign of our horses?"

"Yes. I found the carcass and our horses' tracks."

"How do you know they were ours?" she asked.

He eyed her levelly. "Wild horses don't wear shoes, Miranda."

"Duh." She gave an embarrassed laugh. "I guess that *was* a really stupid question."

"They were headed back in the direction of the base camp," he continued. "If I'd been riding Little Bear, he would have come back to me, but this was only a bor-rowed horse."

"Little Bear? Was he the one you were riding in California?" she asked.

"Yes. He served me well for many years, so I finally retired him. He now has the job of pleasuring the mares on my grandfather's ranch."

She laughed. "I can think of a worse life. Don't you miss him?"

"Every day. But he has a new life now, as do I." He

began burning the spines off another cactus fruit. "The lion will be back," he said. "They usually take several days to devour a kill. I'd recommend we don't hang around here any longer than we have to."

"What should we do?" she asked.

"We can either wait a couple of hours to see if Dave and Donny show up or set out by foot."

"I'd rather not stay anywhere near that lion," she said. "And I have perfectly good legs last I checked."

He looked up with a slow, suggestive smile. "I noticed."

A flare of heat invaded her face. She hadn't forgotten what almost came to pass last night, but it was much harder to acknowledge what happened in the dark of night when it was now full light of day. "So what now?" she asked.

"We eat, and then we walk."

～～～

Two hours later, Miranda plopped down on a boulder with a groan. "These boots *weren't* made for walking. How much farther do you think we have?"

"Probably five miles or so, which equates to about two more hours."

"I'm sorry, Keith, but I don't think I can do it. It's these damned boots." She grimaced. The insides had rubbed her feet raw. "They were brand new."

"Let me see." Keith dropped the heavy pack he was carrying and squatted down beside her.

She hissed in pain as he tugged off her boot. Sure enough, they'd worn the hide right off the back of her heel. "I guess I'm a tenderfoot after all."

He shook his head. "I don't think you're going any farther. You'll have to wait for me here."

"You're going to leave me?" she asked with a surge of panic.

"Do you want me to call in the helicopter instead?"

"For blistered heels?" She considered it, and then discarded the option for fear that Keith would think her a total wimp. "It does seem like overkill, I suppose."

"Considering the cost of fuel, it does. I won't be long," he reassured her. "Traveling alone, I'll make better time. I should be able to get there and back again with a horse in about two hours."

"Two hours?" She sank her teeth into her lip. "I *guess* I'll survive."

"Yes." He flashed his startling white teeth. "You'll survive. But I'll leave my rifle with you just in case of trouble."

She scowled at the rifle. "You know how I feel about guns."

"Don't argue, *Aiwattsi*. It's only for your protection. I'll show you how to use it."

"Why do you keep calling me that?" she asked. "What does *Aiwattsi* mean?"

He shook his head with a secretive smile. "That's for you to figure out." He unsheathed his rifle. "Let me show you how to use this." He flipped the safety, cocked, and shouldered it. "Hold the stock firm to your shoulder like this, or the recoil will knock you on your ass, or worse, hit you in the face. You try it."

Miranda's palms were sweaty as she took the rifle from his hands. She hated guns, but he was right. She needed some protection if she was going to be out here alone with rattlesnakes and mountain lions and God knows what else. She shouldered and aimed it, but held back from firing a shot.

"Go ahead and shoot it," he urged. "You need to know how it feels."

She licked her lips and exhaled, instinctively shutting her eyes as she squeezed the trigger. The stock jammed into her shoulder as the sound of the gunshot exploded in her ears.

"Good." Keith gave a nod. "But keep your eyes open next time."

"I hope there won't *be* a next time."

He pulled a canteen from his pack. "I'll take this one, but there's more water in here and some salty shoe leather if you get hungry enough." Another grin stretched his mouth. His gaze then met hers, and his smile faded. "I promise I won't be long."

Leaving his pack behind, Keith took off at a jog. His look and words were meant to reassure, but Miranda still couldn't suppress a dull feeling of abandonment as she watched him slowly fade into the horizon.

⁓

Hoping to kill time, Miranda scouted the vicinity for the opportunity to take a few stills, but the barren, sage-dotted landscape in the noonday sun provided little inspiration. Seeking relief from the sun, Miranda pulled a blanket from the pack and then climbed on top of a boulder to hang it over the branches of a Joshua tree. Having created a shelter, she stretched out against the tree, her cap pulled down over her eyes, only to be startled a few minutes later by a soft nicker.

She opened her eyes to discover one of the stray foals they'd sought. Lying perfectly still, she was filled with a thrilling sense of wonder when the horse approached.

Seemingly fascinated, it sniffed her and then moved down her body until the whiskers of its muzzle tickled her hand.

Miranda suppressed a giggle at the sensation of moist, hot air fanning her skin. She opened her palm, whispering, "Hello, little horse."

It snorted and jumped back, wide-eyed. After a moment it recovered its courage and returned, but this time her hat seemed to have caught its interest. It sniffed, then experimentally lipped the visor. She noticed a second foal, a strawberry roan, standing a short distant away, watching them as the braver one continued smelling and chewing on her hat. After a time, he became bored and moved on to nose her pack, likely attracted to the smell of the fruit inside it. He proceeded to nudge it until he knocked it onto the ground, spilling the contents. Once more, he shied. A louder snort ensued, but then he returned to poke at the spineless prickly pears, eventually taking a bite.

Moving very slowly, she uncapped the camera around her neck and began to film them. The horse froze, watching her with front legs braced and ears flicking back and forth in uncertainty. But after a while, it seemed to lose both fear and interest as it wandered a few feet away and began cropping a patch of brome grass.

Watching her more warily, the second foal eventually joined the first. She sat there filming their every movement, filled with an incredible sense of awe.

Suddenly the horses startled. They gazed into the distance, ears pricked, looking as if they were about to bolt. Reflexively, Miranda reached out for the rifle as she squinted into the distance, but she could see nothing. Taking up her camera, she zoomed in the direction where the horses were focused. At first she made out only a dust cloud, but then shapes emerged: three men on horseback—her much anticipated rescue posse. Exhaling in relief, she released the rifle, hoping and praying the two young horses would stay put. Thankfully, they didn't stray far.

The riders soon approached. Keith eyed her with a look of surprise. "You found them?"

"They found me." She laughed. "What happens now? How do we get them back?"

"They'll follow us as long as we're on horseback," Dave answered.

"But there are only three horses," she remarked. "Where's Sadie?"

"She made it back to camp late last night, but she's hurt pretty bad," Donny said.

"Was it the lion?" Miranda asked.

"Nope, just rope burns and a leg sprain. She'll recover, but she can't carry any weight for a while."

Donny gathered up the spilled pack while Keith rode up beside the rock where Miranda was still perched. He stretched out his hand. "C'mon. You can ride with me."

Throwing her leg over the horse, she mounted behind his saddle, wrapping her arms tightly around his waist. All her senses immediately fired at the close contact. On the surface they might seem completely incompatible, but under it all, their chemistry was off the charts. She wondered what would have happened had the lion not attacked. How far would it have gone? She shut her eyes and breathed him in, hoping to etch it all on her brain. Once they returned with the foals, her adventure would be over, and even more regretfully, her time with Keith.

—∿∿—

Arriving back at camp, Miranda immediately accosted Mitch. "How is the foal? The one we put on the helicopter. Is he going to make it?"

"That one's back with his mama now." Mitch indicated a pen containing several mares and babies. "It's still a bit touch and go," he said, "but I think he's gonna pull through."

"Thank God." Miranda's heart squeezed at the sight of the pinto foal nursing his mother. She didn't even know how it had happened, but the fate of the foal suddenly meant a great deal to her. For the first time in her life she felt part of something important. Something that mattered. The last twenty-four hours had changed her, intrinsically and irrevocably, and Keith had been an integral part of that. She watched him wistfully as they completed the process of loading the last of the horses into the stock trailers.

"What happens to them now?" she asked as the steel door slammed shut for the final time.

"We're taking them all to join the others at the Palomino Valley processing center," Mitch replied. "That's where they'll get vet care and freeze branding for identification. After that, the younger ones will be shipped out to adoption centers."

Miranda gaped. "That baby's going to be taken from his mother after all this?"

"Not right away," Mitch replied. "But he will be as soon as he's weaned."

"Why?"

"Because younger horses are easier to adopt out," Mitch explained.

"What about the older ones? What happens to them?" She suddenly recalled the horror stories she'd read about the hundreds of thousands that were slaughtered for dog food decades earlier.

"They don't kill 'em, if that's what you fear," Mitch reassured her. "It's illegal—in this country anyway. Most'll be shipped out to long-term federal holding facilities. You're welcome to follow us to Palomino Valley. It's only three hours south of here, just outside Reno, which won't even be out of your way."

Keith suddenly glanced her way. "I'll drive you back to Bruno's," he volunteered. "You can just follow us from there."

"Are you sure you don't mind?" Miranda asked.

He shrugged. "Not at all."

"Great." Mitch tipped his hat. "I guess we'll see you both in a few hours."

After Mitch pulled out with his last load of horses, Miranda followed Keith to his truck.

"So what happens after this job is done?" she asked. "Are you all heading back to Wyoming?"

"No. Mitch is doing a nuisance gather in Tuscarora."

"What's a nuisance gather?"

"It's usually removing horses that push over fences and invade private property. Sometimes they present a hazard in residential areas as well, wandering onto highways and such. Mitch and his boys can handle it without me. I'm going to be busy hauling a load of horses to the Warm Springs Correctional Facility in Carson City."

"Correctional facility? Why are you taking horses to a prison?"

"It's a special program," he explained. "There are several prisons around the country that let the inmates work with the horses, gentling them for easier adoption, but the prisons can take only a handful of horses at a time. In the meantime, the BLM keeps culling the herds, even though they've run out of places to put them."

"What do you mean 'run out of places'?"

"At last report, they have about fifty thousand mustangs they're managing, and there's at least three more gathers scheduled over the next month in Nevada alone."

"Did you say *fifty thousand*?" she repeated incredulously. "That isn't management. It's insanity!"

Keith shook his head ruefully. "That's government bureaucracy at work."

"What's going to happen to them all?" she asked.

"Who knows? The BLM is so desperate, they've even begun turning to private ranchers for help."

"That's got to be less expensive than keeping them at holding facilities, and better for the horses too," she said.

"It still doesn't fix the problem," Keith said. "The entire mustang program is a total fuck up—a waste of time, money, and resources."

Keith opened her door, and she climbed into the cab. They drove in a strained silence, with Miranda casting him only occasional sidelong glances. His cynicism about the horse gathering surprised and disappointed her. Until now, she'd even begun to see him as the romantic lead in her own Wild West adventure, but his bitterness had tarnished some of the hero gleam.

"Something on your mind?" he prompted once they reached the end of the road where her car was parked.

"Yes. There is. I don't understand you, Keith. If you don't believe in this, why are you doing it?"

He cut off the engine and turned to face her. "Do you comprehend the term 'necessary evil'?" he asked.

"I suppose so."

"That's what this is. Most of those horses back there would have died if we hadn't gathered them."

"So you've saved them," she said. "Isn't that a good thing?"

"Yes, we saved them," he replied. "But that doesn't mean they'll have a good life."

"Why would you say that?"

"Because the ones that were gathered will be separated and never live as families again. Wild horses don't live in large herds, but in small family bands—usually one stallion with a few mares and their offspring. They have very strong bonds. These horses are much like us. They are not dumb animals. They feel emotions. They get pissed off just like we do. They fear. They show affection. They even mourn. It's a cruel practice to tear them apart."

"So you really do care," she said softly.

"Of course I care!" he exclaimed. "And I see far too many parallels between how the government is handling mustangs and how they 'managed' the Native American population."

"I never would have thought of it like that," she remarked.

"Because you have no connection to it. I do. Much like these horses, my father's people were taken from their homes, families fractured, gathered up and trekked across the country to their 'long-term pastures.' Have you ever been to a reservation, Miranda?"

"No, I haven't."

"The rez is a depressing and dispiriting place. The people have mostly lost hope. Abject poverty has broken many of them. Drugs and alcohol are rampant, and life expectancy is less than fifty years. So you see, our designated 'pastures' didn't turn out to be so green."

"If you feel so strongly about the mustangs, why don't you try to do something about it?"

"Do something? Like what?" he asked. "Look, Miranda. I learned a long time ago that some problems can't be solved. And there's no fixing this one. None of us here like the system, but there's not a damned thing we can about it."

"That's not true," she insisted. "You *could* do something. You just told me there are thousands of mustangs that need gentling, and you have a God-given talent with these animals. Why aren't you using it for the greater good?"

"Simple," he replied. "Because I've been around long enough to know that the 'greater good' rarely pays off."

Chapter 12

"Looks like we're about done here," Mitch said after they'd freeze branded and immunized all of the gathered horses. Watching the crew, Miranda had been impressed by the speed and efficiency of the process. "Did you get everything to satisfy the court order?" he asked her.

"I got everything I came for," Miranda answered. "But I'd really like to hang around with you a little bit longer."

"Are you staying in Reno tonight, or heading back to L.A.?" Mitch asked.

"I hadn't really decided yet," Miranda replied. "It's a really long drive, and I'm pretty whipped."

"If you're thinking about staying in Reno tonight, we get a special rate at JA's Nugget," Mitch said. "It's the only place the boys ever want to stay."

Beth looked to Mitch with a snort. "And it isn't for the buffet."

"Then why?" Miranda asked, glancing from one to the other. "I'm afraid I don't get the joke."

"They have bikini bull riding every weekend," Mitch explained.

"It's nothing but a shameful exhibitionist display, if you ask me," Beth added with a shake of her head.

"There ain't no harm in just lookin'," Mitch teased.

Beth flashed her husband the evil eye. "Oh yeah? I

promise you'll suffer plenty of harm if *you* go lookin', ol' man."

He wrapped his arms around her and nuzzled her neck. "You should know by now that I only have eyes for you, 'Lizbeth."

"Don't you dare try to cozy up to me now, Mitchell West." She batted his hands away with a mock glower. "I'll have you know we'll be getting two double beds tonight."

Miranda watched them with a vague feeling of wistfulness. Beth and Mitch had been together at least thirty years and had a comfortable, playful, and obviously passionate relationship. She wondered what it would be like to have that with someone.

Her mother and stepdad mostly ignored each other. They rarely conversed and hadn't even kissed in years. It was sad to see a couple living together in isolation— people who shared their lives but never their hearts. Maybe that's why she hadn't been able to commit to Jason. He was a great guy, but he hadn't shared her dreams and aspirations. She wondered if she'd ever find that—someone she could share her dreams with.

Though she and Keith were worlds apart in so many ways, somehow they'd shared a connection. Was it only transitory lust? Or could it have been something more. She wished they could have had a chance to find out.

"What about you, Keith?" Beth inquired, darting a sly look from Keith to Miranda. Had she picked up on the vibe between the two of them? "Are you staying in Reno tonight too?"

Keith tipped his hat back to glance at Miranda. "I was planning to drive down to Warm Springs today, but by the time we get another load on the trailer, it'll be near dark. I don't suppose that's the best time to deliver a load of wild horses to a prison. Maybe it'd be better to wait and go tomorrow."

"Probably would be best," Mitch agreed with a sly look.

So he'd be staying in Reno tonight too? Miranda's gaze riveted back to Keith. Was he thinking what she was thinking? His casual tone and blank expression gave nothing away.

"If that's the case, would you mind if I went also?" Miranda asked, looking from Keith to Mitch.

"To the prison?" Mitch asked.

"Yes," she said. "If we left early in the morning, maybe I could spend a couple of hours there and still get back to L.A. at a reasonable time."

Keith shrugged. "I don't mind as long as Mitch can arrange it."

He had hardly spoken to her from the time they'd arrived at the processing facility. Although he'd been busy sorting and loading horses, it felt like he was intentionally keeping his distance from her. She wondered why.

Mitch scratched his chin. "Don't see why not. You'll need authorization from the warden, but we've been working with that facility for years. I 'magine you'll be barraged with forms to sign, but I'll make the call if you want to go."

"Yes. I would." She beamed.

"If you're going to stay in town tonight, I hope you'll join us for some supper," Beth said.

"Thanks for the invitation," Miranda replied. "But to be honest, after sleeping on the ground last night, I'm seriously craving room service, a long, hot bath, and a nice soft bed."

———

With me. Keith wanted to blurt. He hadn't planned to overnight in Reno, but her decision to stay had changed everything. If they had a second chance to be together, he wasn't about to pass it up. "If you're ready to go, I'll give you a ride back to your car," he offered.

"Thanks," Miranda replied, but her smile held an uncertain edge as she packed up her gear.

He placed his hand on the small of her back, noting the slight shiver even at this light contact. There was a new tension between them now, an uneasy and unspoken anticipation. They drove in silence until reaching the end of the gravel road that marked the entrance to the Palomino Valley Wild Horse Adoption Center. Pulling up to her car, Keith put the truck in park. "Are you going to call the hotel for a room…or are you going to stay with me?"

"Stay with you?" She looked up in surprise. "That sounds a lot like a proposition."

"Is that what you'd call it?" He asked with a grin. "I thought it sounded like a really good idea."

"Or a really bad one," she blurted. "I don't get you. You were almost chilly toward me all day. Why this sudden about-face?"

"I was trying to make it easier on both of us, but it wasn't easy," he said. For the past few hours he'd tried to keep his mind focused on work, but couldn't get the thought of her out of his mind—or ignore the ball-aching frustration he still felt every time he looked at her. "I couldn't stop thinking about you, about last night."

"Last night was one thing," she replied, her expression wary. "But this is something else."

"Last night was different for me too," he said. "*You* are different."

"Different how?" she asked, her gaze searching his.

He paused, not knowing exactly how to answer her. "I don't deny I've been with a lot of women, Miranda, but I haven't wanted anyone like this in a long time." His eyes shuttered. "Too long. I still want you, and I think you still want me."

"Last night the circumstances drew us together. In the heat of passion it's always easy to throw good sense to the wind, but things tend to change in the light of day."

"So what are you saying?"

"That I know this thing between us can't go anywhere."

"Does that really matter?" he asked.

"I don't want to be another conquest, Keith. I told you before that I don't do hookups. I dated my last boyfriend for almost a year before we were ever intimate, and here you and I met only two days ago."

"Not true," he said. "We first met over a year ago."

"But we're still virtually strangers," she insisted.

"Time and intimacy are irrelevant, *Aiwattsi*. There are people who spend a lifetime together as strangers, and others who connect as if they'd known each other in another life. Why do you think it's wrong to be with me?"

"Wrong? No, I don't really feel that way." Her gaze darted away. "Maybe I should, but I don't."

"We all have a need to be touched," he said. "It's in our very nature. I want to be with you, *Aiwattsi*. Tell me you want this too." He ached to touch her, to be inside her, but the attraction was more than just strong sexual chemistry. He hoped she felt it too.

Desire and hesitation mingled in her eyes. "Part of

me does, but the other part just doesn't know if I can do this," she said.

"Then I think the second part of you needs a little convincing." Palming the back of her head, he claimed her mouth in a long, hungry kiss. Her arms came around his neck as she melted into it with a little moan. He drew her in deeper, kissing her hot and fierce, invading her mouth with his tongue, before reluctantly breaking away. His body screamed for release, but his truck wasn't the right place, especially when a comfortable room waited.

Keith held his breath, his gaze silently probing hers.

Her eyes met his, soft with desire. "Yes, Keith," she whispered. "I want to be with you too."

Chapter 13

STEPPING OUT OF THE SHOWER, MIRANDA PULLED ON HER cotton sleep shorts and a tank top, and then proceeded to dry her hair. Her jitters were growing by the second. Out in the desert, it was easy to fall victim to heat-of-the-moment passion. Danger and desire made an addictive cocktail, especially to someone who'd always lived vicariously through films, but spending the night with Keith in a hotel was very much a conscious decision.

She froze at the sound of a light knock on the door, fraught with nervous anticipation. She'd almost decided to back out, until she peered through the peephole and found Keith standing there with an overnight bag slung over his shoulder and bearing two very full trays of food.

"Room service." He grinned as she cracked the door.

Her anxiety eased by his playful tone, Miranda fumbled to release the chain and then stepped away to let him in.

"Hungry?" he asked.

Her stomach answered with an embarrassing growl.

"I'll take that as a yes." He chuckled. "What are you in the mood for? We've got a double decker club with fries, a Monte Cristo with onion rings, and a four-cheese pizza." He set the food on the table beside the queen-size bed and uncovered the trays with a scowl. "Maybe I should have ordered more."

"More?" She laughed. "There's enough food there for a small army. How much do you normally eat?"

His gaze raked slowly over her, heating her skin. "The kind of activity I have in mind burns many calories." He fed her a fry with a grin then offered her half a sandwich and a slice of pizza. "We're going to need our strength, so you'd better eat up."

She accepted the plate with a smile. Sitting on the edge of the bed, she took a bite of the sandwich, rolling her eyes in appreciation. He sat down beside her, sneaking an onion ring from her plate with a guilty look. For the next few minutes they ate in silence, Keith devouring his food with gusto while Miranda picked at hers. She was famished but too nervous to fully appreciate the meal.

"Second thoughts?" he asked.

She hesitated for a couple of seconds, weighing her feelings. "I just don't have any experience with this kind of thing. To be honest, I haven't a clue what to think... about you and me." Except that he read her better than anyone she'd ever met.

"Then don't think," he replied. "Just eat." His gaze traveled slowly over her, making her insides quiver. "And quickly."

Swallowing his last bite, he tossed his plate down and then took hers away. Slowly leaning in, he kissed her, just a light brush of his lips. Holding his body inches from hers, enough for her to feel his heat but not his flesh, he teased and enticed. Sucking her lower lip between his teeth, he gently nipped and then slowly released. "Any better now?" he asked.

"A little," she whispered back.

"Come." Taking her hand, he led her into the large,

tiled bathroom with its oversized Jacuzzi tub. He turned on the tap. "Earlier you mentioned a desire for a hot bath."

"But I already showered," she said.

"Showering doesn't sooth aching muscles like a hot soak does. You're tense. You need to relax." His smile faded. "And I want to undress you," he added with a dark look that made her pulse race.

"Arms up." He drew the thin white tank top over her head to reveal her small breasts and painfully erect nipples. She wished she'd worn one of those sexy pushup bras, but she only owned one and wore it only on special occasions. She realized with a pang that maybe seduction by one of the hottest men alive qualified as one. She fought the urge to cross her arms over her breasts.

His gaze locked on hers, and he slowly drew back. As if reading her mind, he brought her hands to her sides. His eyes not leaving hers, he cupped her breasts and stroked the peaks of her nipples with his thumbs. "I love your natural beauty, *Aiwattsi*. So slender and graceful. You remind me of a doe."

"Is that what it means?" she asked. "Doe?"

"Close," he replied. "*Aiwattsi* is a little fawn. Your eyes are innocent like one."

"But don't wolves eat fawns?" she asked.

"Yes," he replied, giving her a lupine flash of incisors. "I find fawns very tasty indeed."

She gave a tiny gasp as he planted his lips at the sensitive junction of her shoulder and neck. Sliding his hands down her back, he clasped her ass and then lowered his head. Kissing and licking, he worked his way down to claim her breasts with his hungry mouth. "Perfect. Beautiful. Delicious."

His words made her feel once more like an exotic desert flower. She arched her back and released a blissful sigh. He suckled her breasts as his hands mapped her body. Her fingers tangled in his thick, silky hair. She shut her eyes, throwing her head back with a moan, abandoning herself to the drugging pleasure of his mouth. Just like the wolf in his story, he devoured her by inches as he moved down her body with lips, teeth, and tongue.

A quiver raced over her skin as he caressed the curls of her mound through her shorts. She tensed again as he began to peel them off her hips. Her heart pounded in her chest at the realization that they were approaching the point of no return. He looked up with a grin as he bared her short nest of curls.

"Your down matches your hair. I want to bury my face in its softness."

His meaning made her throat go dry. "Um…" She swallowed. "You aren't planning to…do *things* down there…are you?"

"Things down there?" His chuckle warmed her exposed belly with a blast of moist, hot air. "I'd planned to do lots of *things*, but not if you can't even say it. Haven't you had lovers before, Miranda?"

"Only one," she confessed. "We were supposed to get married when I graduated college."

"And this guy you were going to marry didn't go down on you?"

"Um. He did once or twice, but I didn't like it." Jason had *tried* to please her sexually, but there was just no excitement, no passion between them. She'd never regretted breaking it off with him, but now she understood why. At the time, she hadn't even known what she was missing. Now she did.

"You will this time," he said. "If there's one thing I take pride in, it's pleasing my woman."

"*Your woman*?" she repeated, both irritated and flattered by the possessiveness of the statement. "Is that what you think I am?"

"You will be the moment I put my tongue in your—"

"Please don't say it, Keith. I don't like dirty talk."

"All right. I won't say it…but *you* will. Tell me you want it, Miranda. Tell me you want me to bury my nose in your soft down."

"But I don—" She gasped as he nuzzled her with his face.

"Oh, yes, you do," he insisted darkly. He kissed a slow path from one hip bone toward the other. "Tell me you want my lips and tongue inside your lips." He worked his way back to her navel, tracing it slowly with his tongue. Her inner walls responded, shuddering with a wave of intense want. "You want me to drink your salty sweetness while I kiss and suck the little pearl that hides within your womanhood. These are just a few of the *things* I wish to do *down there*, and all you have to do is tell me you want it."

She shut her eyes on another hard swallow.

"I'll make this good for you," he promised. "You won't regret it."

Her desire once more waged battle with her conscience. Knowing that he wanted her made her feel beautiful and desirable. Why shouldn't she feel those things? She didn't care if it was only for one night. "No. I won't regret it," she whispered as much to herself. "But what about that bath?" she suggested shyly.

"You distracted me, *Aiwattsi*." He chuckled and then began stripping, toeing off his boots and peeling off his T-shirt. She drank him in with thirsty eyes, from chest and shoulders down his torso to his low-slung jeans. She hadn't had a good look at him before, but now she could hardly tear her eyes away. His entire body was honed of lean, hard muscle under his sun-bronzed skin. In her eyes, Keith was physical perfection.

"Like what you see, *Aiwattsi*?" he asked softly.

"Yes." She tracked back up to his face. "I like it very much."

His gaze probed hers as he released his belt. Their eyes still locked, he took her hand, guiding it to his fly. Miranda lowered his zipper with trembling hands. She felt his abdominal muscles tighten as she reached inside, discovering hot, hard, *naked* flesh pulsing under her fingers.

"Commando?" she asked, surprised.

He shrugged. "I'm a free spirit."

Closing her hand around him, she caressed up and down his length. "I love how you feel."

His hand came over hers, guiding her with more aggressive strokes. "And I love that you do. I'm eager to know what else you enjoy."

Emboldened, Miranda kissed down his body while continuing to stroke and fondle him. His breaths grew heavier as she came face-level with his erection. He sounded a low growl as she freed him from his jeans. His erection grew bigger, pulsing hotly in her hand. She bit her lip and continued stroking him.

He released her hand from him with a growl. "Keep that up, and you can forget the bath."

He quickly shed the jeans and pulled her into the tub

with him, settling her between his legs. She was suddenly all too aware of his turgid shaft pressing against her ass. He drew her back against his chest. She sank into the steamy water, immersing herself to the chin with a long, sultry sigh. He murmured another warning in her ear, "You'd be wise not to make sounds like that either, *Aiwattsi*."

"I can't help myself. It feels so good."

"I can make it even better."

He reached for the soap, lathered his hands, and began massaging her shoulders, working his fingers into her muscles. She slumped deeper in the water, dropping her head forward with a helpless moan. "Oh. My. God. Please. Don't. Stop."

"You'd better save those kinds of words for later," he said darkly.

He grew gentler as he worked his hands around her, cupping her breasts and caressing her nipples with his thumbs. While one hand continued to play with her breasts, he glided the other down her belly, slowly exploring her inch by soap-slickened inch, as he licked and sucked her earlobe. "Open your legs."

She resisted at first and then jumped at the sharp nip of his teeth. "I told you to open your legs." Although they trembled uncontrollably, she obeyed. Taking her hands in his, he brought them up to her breasts. "I want you to touch yourself here, while I touch you there," he said. "I want to learn what you like. Then I'm going to make you come."

"Here? Now?" she asked in surprise.

"Yes. Here, now. And then I'll do it again with my mouth and yet again with my—"

"Don't say it," she replied. "I want to hear *your* word for it."

"*Pakan*," he answered. "Aptly, it can also mean arrow. And I intend to pierce you with my arrow. *After* I have made you come with my hands and my mouth."

"Three times?" She gave a nervous laugh. "That's certainly an ambitious plan."

He grinned. "I've spent many hours since last night plotting my strategy."

"What about me? Don't I have any say in this?"

"No," he replied sternly. "The only thing you get to say is, 'You're a god, Keith, don't ever stop.' We're done talking about it now. I need to concentrate."

"But—"

"No talking. Shut your eyes."

She leaned back with closed eyes, biting her lip and then inhaling a tiny gasp as he slid his hands between her legs. His mouth continued its play on her neck, licking and sucking. With his arms wrapped around her body, he located the hood of her clitoris. Circling and teasing the sensitive bud with one hand, the gently probing fingers of his other traced the folds to her entrance. Inserting two long and knowing fingers inside her, he worked them in and out. Strumming her clitoris, he played her body like an instrument, creating an ebb and flow that quickly had her undulating in pleasure.

"Please," she whimpered, her body trembling as her climax clawed for release.

Responding to her plea, he sucked harder on her neck, increasing the tempo of his fingers plunging in and out, harder and faster until she tensed, crying out a muffled sob as her orgasm broke free. Her climax hit hard, overwhelming her with tremors until she fell back against him, limp and lifeless. Keith clasped her snug against him until she stirred back to life.

Sitting up, she turned around to face him. "Why did you do that?"

He smiled smugly. "Because I wanted to. Because I could. Because I wanted you to *know* I could."

She frowned. "Is this some kind of kinky control thing?"

"Maybe a little." He shrugged. "Almost every man gets off watching a woman orgasm. Or better yet, *making* her come. Are you ready to get out yet? My fingers are pruning, and so is my *pakan*."

He pulled the plug and then stood, but before he could step out of the tub, she wrapped her hands around him. "It doesn't look shriveled at all to me." She cocked her head. "Quite the contrary."

"I thought I warned you about touching me like that."

"But, Keith"—she rose on her knees with a devilish look—"don't you know that almost every woman gets off watching a man orgasm…or better yet, *making* him come."

"Don't play this game with me, *Aiwattsi*," Keith warned. "Not unless you intend to finish it."

She licked her lips, her mouth watering in anticipation. Her voice emerged, husky with lust. "What makes you think I won't?"

"And I thought you would be shy about these things." His mouth stretched into a full-blown grin. "Every time I think I'm beginning to figure you out, you surprise me again."

———

Anticipation already had Keith hard as a post, but her suggestion engorged him with a fresh surge of hot blood that ramped his excitement to a whole a new level. Her initiative had taken him by surprise, after seeming so timid, but she wasn't so timid now.

Watching his eyes, Miranda made a long, slow swipe of her tongue. The first velvety rasp up his shaft had his knees nearly buckling. Almost knocked him on his ass, actually. Not that he minded. *Hell no*. It had been too damned long since he'd been sucked off. Nothing made a man feel more like a god than a beautiful woman worshipping his cock—stroking, sucking, and massaging his sac.

Drawing in a breath, he braced his hands on the tiled wall behind him. His heart thrummed a frantic tempo as she took him into her mouth. Although she began tentatively, she soon made up for it with enthusiasm. His chest tightened as he watched her through half-closed lids. The vision alone pushed him to the brink.

So good. So fucking good.

She took him deeper, sucking harder, flicking his underside with her tongue on every release 'til he thought he'd lose his mind. His balls reacted, tightening, drawing up. Shit, she'd hardly started, and he was about to blow like a volcano. He reached out to her, grinding his words through his teeth. "You'd best stop if you don't want me exploding in your mouth."

She slid her hands up to grip his ass with a look that shredded any remnant of self-control. His chest constricted with her sounds of pleasure, with the look of ecstasy etching her face. Hissing a long stream of Shoshoni, he threw his head back against the wall, his lungs burning and hips bucking as he pumped to a raw and raging release.

Chapter 14

MIRANDA'S GROWLING STOMACH WOKE HER FROM A DEEP, sexually sated sleep. After the hot bath and bout of mutual gratification, they'd crashed together in bed, falling almost instantly asleep. She opened her eyes, filled with a sense of perfect contentment, outside of ravenous hunger.

Keith was propped on an elbow, watching her. "Hungry again?"

"Yeah." She gave an embarrassed laugh. "I was too nervous to eat much before."

"Maybe I can give you something else to think about?" He traced a finger across her lips with a look that gave her a craving of a different kind.

"Like what?" she asked breathlessly.

He rolled her beneath him. "Since you seem to be recovered, maybe we can finish now?"

"Me? What about you?" She laughed. "I wasn't the only one who went into a coma."

He grinned. "I admit you drained me of everything, but I've had time to recuperate."

"Keith?" she began tentatively.

"What, *Aiwattsi*?"

"Do you intend to stay the whole night?"

He looked up in surprise. "You thought otherwise?"

"Um. I wasn't really sure." Her gaze darted away. "I just assumed that leaving was how it usually plays out."

"Sometimes it goes that way," he confessed. "But not this time." He reached out to touch her face. "Unless that's what you want?"

"No," she replied solemnly. "That's not what I want."

He pulled her into another long, lingering kiss, and then moved to the space between her breasts. He peeled the sheet back, warming her skin with his hot breath, as he slid down her belly, caressing, kissing, and swirling inside her navel with his tongue. His hands stroked up and down her thighs. Slipping a hand between them, he glanced up at her with a smug smile playing over his mouth. "You're already wet."

She blushed. "You seem to have that effect on me."

"I like it. A lot, *Aiwattsi*. It makes me want to taste you." She tensed, her heart racing as he positioned his shoulders between her legs. Her breath hitched as he nuzzled her mons. "Relax," he said. "Close your eyes. I promise you'll like it."

She gasped outright at the slow sweep of his scorching tongue.

"See? You do like that." He chuckled darkly and positioned her thighs on his shoulders. "I knew you would."

She should have been sated after what they'd already done, but apparently she, like he, only wanted more. If given the choice, she'd never leave the bed. Miranda clenched the sheets as he began pleasuring her with his magical mouth, licking, sucking, using his lips, teeth, and tongue in ways she'd never dreamed of. God, he did incredible things with his mouth. But his hands were just as talented.

Tangling her fingers in his hair, she writhed against his mouth. "Please, Keith…I want…I need."

"You want more?" he asked.

"Yes. I want more. I want you inside me."

"That makes two of us."

"Do you have—"

"Yes. I have." He sat up, retrieving a box of condoms from the bag he'd brought in with him. He offered her the packet.

She shook her head. "You do it. I haven't had much practice. At least not for a while."

After gloving himself, he knelt between her legs. Their gazes met as he teased her entrance, escalating her want, her need, her ache. She reached for him with a moan, her inner muscles clenching in rhythm with her pulsing heart. "I want to feel you inside me. Now, Keith. Please."

His penetration was agonizingly slow as he filled and stretched her. Once fully impaled, he dipped his head for a mind-melting kiss. He followed with a gasp-inducing thrust that sent a jolt of sensation careening to her core. "Oh God," she moaned. "Do that again."

He brought her legs tightly around his flanks, retreated a few inches, and thrust again. Harder. Deeper. Pure pleasure made her cry out. He stifled her sounds with another long, lush kiss. Tongues still tangling, he moved inside her again, this time in a slow, sweet, steady cadence. Thrust. Kiss. Thrust. Kiss.

With eyes squeezed shut, she clenched her inner muscles, squeezing and milking him in tempo with his advance and retreat. He grunted, jerking her hips toward him, taking her deeper. Harder.

As their mouths melded, her mind emptied to all but sensation—the sultry, breathless sounds filling the air, the scent of sex teasing her nose, their tangling tongues and the tight, wet friction of him moving deep inside her.

Thrust. Kiss. Slow and steady then hard and deep. Thrust. Kiss. Deeper, harder until her climax surged and swelled like a tsunami, cresting and crashing over her in ceaseless spasms. Pumping madly, Keith brought himself to a swift finish, emptying inside her with a feral cry then collapsing breathlessly beside her.

———∿∿∿———

The sun was only beginning to creep through the cracks between the closed drapes when Miranda opened her eyes. Carefully, she rolled onto her side to study Keith, who lay on his back, sprawled like a king. He'd flung the covers aside during the night, or maybe they'd never covered up at all. She could hardly recall anything now beyond the mind-blowing orgasms. Her insides clenched reflexively at the memory of him moving inside her.

She still didn't know what to think about this thing between them. All of it had happened so unexpectedly, from the coincidental meeting to the combustive chemistry. He was so different now from the man she'd first seen in California, and even from the one she'd met only two days ago. The brooding warrior had all but vanished. The man taking his place was warm and tender and teasing—and she was falling hard. He'd said that it was more than just a hookup, but where did they go from here? In the light of day, it seemed far too much like a fantastical journey to nowhere.

His breathing was still slow, steady, and even. She allowed herself the luxury of studying him in his full naked glory, eating him up with hungry eyes. Reaching out with an index finger, she traced the wings of the tribal eagle tattoo covering his right shoulder.

He stirred in his sleep. The sheet slid completely away. Her gaze lingered in awe on his manhood: long, thick, purple headed, and erect. *Very erect*. Unable to resist the temptation, she wrapped her hand around him, but before she could do anything more, Keith's eyes snapped open.

His hand came over hers with a mumbled curse He brought it to his mouth and kissed it. "As much as I want to, *Aiwattsi*, we can't. I still have a job to do. We should have been up and out of here an hour ago."

"I understand." Her gaze slid away. "All good things must come to an end, right?"

He reached for her, cupping her chin. "Are you okay?"

"Yeah. I'm okay. Honestly. I knew how it would be." Her heart gave a wrench as the glib words stumbled over her tongue. She'd worried that it would be awkward between them afterward, but Keith maintained his easy manner from the night before. She knew she wasn't the type for this kind of thing. The thought of parting hurt like hell, but she still couldn't regret it. If given the option of a do over, she'd do it all again. In a heartbeat.

Her fascination with him had only grown with the hours they'd spent together. The real Keith was not only naturally charismatic, but personable, knowledgeable, and confident. It was easy to see why women had flocked to him—a pang of undeniable jealousy accompanied that thought, and then a hollow ache took its place.

Stupid. Stupid. Stupid. She was half in love with a guy she'd never see again.

<center>~~~</center>

After catching a quick shower and dressing, Keith and Miranda headed out of Reno, stopping only long enough to drive through Starbucks for two Ventis before tracking back to Palomino Valley, where he loaded up the horses to be transported to the prison.

When they arrived at the prison, Miranda stayed in the background with her camera, out of sight maybe, but never out of his mind. Just being with her felt so good and right, as if she brought his world back into balance. He'd been with a lot of different women, but last night was unique in so many ways. How could he ever explain that? And even harder, how was he going to let go of it? Anything more than what they'd already shared was impossible. They were from separate worlds, and hers was everything he'd vowed to leave behind.

"You see that one over there?" An inmate named Jim Davies nudged him back to the present. Jim nodded to a flashy black-and-white pinto. With head held high, neck arched, and nostrils flared, the horse glared at several inmates sitting on the corral panel, watching him watch them. The men snickered and poked one another in the ribs, either taking bets or making dares. After a time, one of them spat a wad of chew, then climbed down from the corral panel. Eying him with suspicion, the horse blew a loud warning snort that he followed with a rebellious toss of his mane.

"Easy, ol' son." With one palm outstretched, the

inmate tentatively approached the animal. As he moved forward, the horse bared his teeth.

"Watch you don't lose an ear," one of the inmates jeered.

"What's his story?" Keith asked, nodding to the horse.

"That's one of 'em they gathered up from the Fort McDermitt Reservation last year," Jim answered.

"I heard about that one. There was a big controversy surrounding it."

"Yeah, the Paiute claimed ownership of all the horses and were going to sell them off to the kill buyer, but over a hundred of 'em were unbranded. When the activists got wind of it, it all turned into a major shit storm, with everyone suing everyone else. In the end, the mustangs were separated out and shipped over to the BLM in Fallon."

"No doubt many once *were* tribal horses," Keith said. "They bred some fantastic color in those herds. Markings like this horse has were greatly valued. He should bring a real good price at auction."

"That he would," Jim agreed, "if only we could lay our hands on him."

"What do you mean?" Keith asked.

"We've had 'im almost three months," Jim replied, "but so far none of us has been able to do a damned thing with 'im. Still can't even touch the ornery SOB."

"Three months? And you still can't touch him?" Keith remarked in surprise.

"Yup. The whole thing's an experiment gone bad."

"What do you mean *experiment*?" Keith asked, now watching the would-be horse tamer more critically. There was nothing *technically* wrong in his approach, but the animal was obviously not receptive. At all. Its entire body language declared mistrust and simmering aggression—the defensive behavior of a herd stallion. It was then Keith noticed. "He's not cut? Since when did they start sending you stud horses?"

"That's the experiment I was talking about. The activists made such a stink about the particular genetics of this herd that they got a court injunction barring the BLM from gelding the stallions. Given no other choice, they decided to try chemical castration."

The horse suddenly reared and struck out with a fore-leg, missing the man's head by mere inches. It was only the inmate's reflexive nosedive that saved him from the striking front hooves. Watching over his shoulder, he was quick to scramble back to safety.

Jim heaved a sigh of frustration. "Least no one got hurt *this* time. You might as well just load him up and take 'im back with you to PVC. He's a certified outlaw. Even if they take his balls outright, this horse is never gonna be adoptable."

Keith was struck by how similar those words matched what his family had once said of him—that he would never be good for anything. The school counselor had agreed, labeling him an intractable delinquent. When he left for the rez, his stepfather's parting remark was "good riddance to the little bastard."

"What's it gonna cost me?" Keith blurted.

Jim scratched his jaw. "Whaddya mean?"

"How much to take him off your hands? I want to adopt him."

"You're kidding, right? That horse is gonna kill somebody."

"Then I'm *dead* serious," he quipped.

"You'd be crazy to take him on," Jim insisted.

"Maybe I am." Keith shrugged. "Or maybe I just have a yen to own a sacred horse. We Injuns are kinda funny that way."

"You really want that renegade stud?"

"Said so, didn't I?" It was stupid as hell, but looking at the horse was like seeing himself, or who he would have been. He had no doubt that if he hadn't left New York, he'd have ended up in juvenile detention. Only his grandfather's patience, the freedom, and the wide-open spaces of Wyoming had saved him from that fate.

"It's your neck, I s'pose." Jim shook his head with a sigh. "Minimum adoption fee is a hundred twenty-five."

"Will you take cash?"

"Sure 'nuff. Cash is real money."

"What are you doing?" Miranda asked.

"Buying the horse," Keith replied with a shrug.

"But why? Haven't you said all along that you don't believe in mustang adoption? What are you going to do with him?"

"Dunno yet. Maybe I'll gift him to my grandfather."

"Why?" Miranda asked. "Is black and white so uncommon?"

"It's not so much the color combination as his markings. A horse like this is considered sacred in our culture. The dark place on the top of his head is called a medicine hat, and the splash of color on his chest is a war shield. These markings were highly prized by war chiefs and shaman," Keith explained. "I have a few things to take care of," he told Jim. "I'll come back and pick him up in a couple of hours."

"Suits me. I'm just happy to have him out of here.

C'mon." He clapped Keith on the shoulder. "You've still gotta do the paperwork."

Thirty minutes later, Keith and Miranda left the prison. Her boots felt more like lead the closer she got to her car. "Thank you for bringing me out here, Keith. It was very enlightening. This whole experience has been."

"Did you get everything you wanted?" he asked.

She paused. Everything she wanted? No. No, she didn't get nearly enough of what she really wanted. She wished she could voice even half of what was in her heart, but he referred only to the film. As far as that went, she'd accomplished all she'd set out to do, filming the horse gather, the processing, and had even recorded some of the inmates training the horses. She should be elated with her successes, but her heart was as heavy as her feet.

"I think so," she finally replied. "I have several weeks of editing work ahead of me to put this all together, but I'm pretty certain I know what I want to do with it. What about you?" she asked. "What will you do now?"

"I'll be here in Nevada for two or three more weeks," he replied. "After we've finished this contract, I'll be heading back to Wyoming for a couple more gathers there."

"Will you return to the reservation after that?"

"I don't know." He looked sad but resigned. "Probably not. I might look for some full-time ranch work. I haven't decided yet."

"If you want ranch work, maybe Jo-Jo would know of something?"

"Jo-Jo?"

"My grandmother. I told you she has a ranch. It's my favorite place in the world...or always was." Her smile faded.

"What do you mean?" he asked.

"It's been for sale for over a year, since my grandfather passed away. Jo-Jo really doesn't want to sell it, but she can't run it alone, not as a cattle outfit, anyway."

"What about your father? Why doesn't he help her?"

"My dad passed away when I was four. It was a stupid accident on a tractor."

"I'm sorry," he said. "I know what it's like. I lost my father too."

"I barely recall it anymore," she said "But what makes me sadder is that I hardly even remember him now, just a few fuzzy memories. He was an only son. His sister, my aunt Judith, couldn't wait to get away from the ranch. They managed to get by with part-time help until Gramps died. But now Jo-Jo can't afford to pay for more help, so she's selling out. You know, this entire experience has me wondering what it would require to take on some of these BLM horses. Do ranchers get reimbursed for keeping them?" Miranda asked.

"Yes. They get paid a per diem for each head." Keith's gaze narrowed. "Why are you asking?"

"Maybe this is another option for her to consider? It seems to me these horses wouldn't need anywhere near the time and care as cattle ranching, right? If the government offers a subsidy, maybe she could still keep the ranch?"

"C'mon, Miranda. Do you really think an old lady is capable of managing a herd of wild horses?"

"Old lady?" Miranda laughed. "You've never met Jo-Jo. She may be my grandma, but she's anything but old. She can still rope and ride with the best of them."

"She still couldn't do it alone. It's nothing like running cattle. She'd need full-time help from someone who knows these horses."

"*You* know these horses," Miranda said. "And you just told me you were going to look for ranch work."

He raised a hand. "Hold it right there. This is crazy talk. I never said anything about mustangs."

"But why not? You just adopted one, didn't you?"

"One horse isn't the same as taking on a herd of them, Miranda."

"Maybe not," she said. "But I just can't help wanting to do something."

"Isn't that the purpose of your film?"

"I thought so before I understood the complexity of the problem. Until now I even thought gathering the horses was the solution. But that's not really the case at all, is it?"

"No." He leaned back against his truck, arms crossed over his chest. "Gathering is *not* the right answer, and neither is turning your grandmother's ranch into a mustang sanctuary."

"It was only a thought," she replied, disappointed at his dismissive answer. Why had she expected more? Maybe it was all just wishful thinking that she could maintain some kind of connection with him. A long silence followed. He suddenly seemed so unreadable.

"Keith?" she began again.

"Yes?"

"Um, what if I have questions? You know,

pertaining to the film? Is there a number or email I can reach you at?"

"In case you have questions?" His mouth curved subtly at one corner, as if he saw through her subterfuge. "You have Mitch's number, right?"

She nodded. "Yeah. I programmed it."

"If you need anything more, he knows how to reach me."

He wouldn't even give her his number? Her heart sank all the way into her stomach.

"I don't have a phone or email to give you," he explained. "I don't even have a permanent address. If you need me, call Mitch."

"Oh. Okay then," she said softly. Sadly. What was left to say?

The moment she'd dreaded had come at last. She was leaving, returning to her work, to her world. Would he at least kiss her good-bye? Their gazes met and held. His eyes flickered as if he was asking himself the same question. Her pulse sped. For a moment she thought he would kiss her, but then he seemed to change his mind. She waited a few more agonizing seconds, but he made no move, just stood there watching her, his expression impassive, his hands by his sides.

Her throat tightened as she turned to her car and reached for the door.

"Good-bye, Keith," she whispered. "Thanks for... well...everything."

Did he feel nothing? Did this whole thing mean nothing? "Good-bye, *Aiwattsi*. Be well."

Be well? Was that all? The end? Their final good-bye? Her chest gave a painful squeeze. She'd never dreamed that in going out into the desert she'd end up leaving a piece of herself behind. But she had—a great big chunk of her heart.

⚊⚊

He'd almost kissed her. He still wanted to. It was all he could do to hold back, but he'd never have been able to stop kissing her once he started. So he hadn't. But he still wanted her. He hadn't stopped wanting her. The scent of her still teased him. He ached to feel himself surrounded in her warmth. There was so much he would like to have said, but what was the point? She'd come only to do a job, just as he had. Now the job was finished. She was driving back to L.A. The good-bye hurt, but a swift, clean break was for the best. This couldn't go anywhere. She had plans, a future. He had nothing. Absolutely. Nothing. A fact that gnawed at his insides when she'd asked about his plans. So instead of kissing her, he'd watched her drive away, but letting her go still left him with a huge ache in his chest.

Keith left the prison an hour later with the horse on his trailer, bound for Tuscarora, where he'd be joining Mitch's crew. He still didn't know what had prompted him to take the horse, or what the hell he was going to do with it. At first he'd thought the medicine hat stallion might make a good peace offering, but it might be interpreted as trying to buy his way back into his grandfather's good graces. He couldn't chance the risk and humiliation of a rejection. Keeping the horse for himself was impossible, even if he was inclined to train it—which he absolutely wasn't.

He was still mulling over his dilemma when he

reached the fork in the highway at Winnemucca. But instead of continuing east on Interstate 80, he turned the wheel northward onto Highway 95 with no real destination in mind. Seventy miles later, just inside the tribal lands, he spotted several bands of horses. Pulling onto the shoulder of the deserted highway, Keith cut the engine.

Nostrils flaring blood red, the horse snorted at him through the slats as he rounded the stock trailer, where he unlatched the door and flung it open. Instead of instantly springing out, as he'd expected, the stallion eyed him with suspicion.

"No tricks, ol' man." Keith turned his palms up. "Go now. You're free."

Throwing his head back and his tail in the air, the stallion lunged out of the trailer and bolted toward the same mountains that were his prior home. Watching the horse disappear in the distance, Keith whispered in warning, "You'd be wise to make yourself very scarce next time."

Chapter 15

"Good morning, bright eyes," Lexi greeted Miranda cheerily. "I didn't hear you come in last night."

"It was really late," Miranda replied. "I drove all the way from Reno."

"Reno?" Lexi looked puzzled. "I thought you went to the mountains to film wild horses? What the hell were you doing in Reno?"

"I stopped there overnight on the way back and then drove home from there." A drive that was far too long and lonely. As hard as she'd tried, she couldn't stop thinking about Keith and how it had ended. She understood his aloofness at their parting; he was trying to make it easier, but it wasn't easier. And like a fresh cut, it still hurt.

"You drove nine hours straight through? No wonder you look like death warmed over."

"Thanks a bunch, Lex."

"Here, you need this more than I do." She handed Miranda a steaming cup of coffee and then poured another, set the cup down, and plopped onto the stool beside her. "So, how was this desert adventure of yours?"

"The whole thing was so surreal. I went there think-ing I was just going to film this wild-horse roundup, but then things went awry, and I ended up trekking into the mountains with one of the wranglers."

Lexi's jaw dropped. "Oh. My. God. Please tell me he was smoking hot."

Miranda broke into a reluctant grin. "He was straight out of your wildest fantasies, Lexi."

Lexi laid a hand on her knee. "So this actually gets *good*? Or maybe you have no idea just how wild my fantasies are."

Miranda laughed. "Picture a cross between *Romancing the Stone* and *Tarzan of the Apes*, except we were in the desert instead of the jungle. For a while I even felt a bit like Jane must have, but I suppose Tarzan would have wrestled the lion."

"A *lion*? What lion?"

"We were attacked by a mountain lion. It attacked one of the horses, but all that happened after Keith killed a rattlesnake with his knife."

"All right," Lexi scoffed. "You are totally punking me. You had me going for a while, but I'm not believing a word of this anymore."

"I swear to God it's true! All of it," Miranda insisted. "Do you remember that horse-whisperer guy?"

Lexi rolled her eyes. "As if I could ever forget. Are you saying this wrangler was like him?"

"No, Lexi, it *was* him."

"You have got to be shittin' me."

"Nope. And I have film to prove it. It's mostly the horses, but there are several takes with Keith. He even put a sick foal on a helicopter. I can't wait to get into the editing lab with this."

"And get your ass canned? You'd better think again. Bad enough you were out alone in the desert with the uber-hot guy Bibi was so desperate to shag. Now you want to use her lab to edit this? Do you not see the problem here if she finds out?"

Miranda grimaced. "I guess you're right. I suppose I'll have to take it elsewhere."

"Enough about work," Lexi said. "Tell me more about your wrangler. What happened while you were alone in the desert?"

"Nothing...much."

Lexi huffed. "Don't make me pull teeth, Miranda."

"It's too personal. I really don't like to talk about sex."

A slow grin spread over Lexi's face. "So you *did* have sex?"

Miranda flushed, wanting to kick herself at the slip of the tongue. "Um, well, yeah. Sort of."

"Sweetheart. Either you did or you didn't. There is no 'sort of' when it comes to sex."

"All right," she sighed. "We were intimate, and it was amazing. Better than I ever could have imagined."

"Really? Sounds promising. When are you going to rendezvous at your oasis again?"

Miranda looked away. "We aren't."

"Why not?"

"Because he has his life, and I have mine."

"So that's it? You aren't even going to text? Call? Nothing?"

"No. I wish it could have been more, but we both knew it couldn't go anywhere."

"Now that's a surprise."

"What is?"

"That you'd give up the goods like that." Lexi grinned. "I didn't take you for a hussy like me."

"I didn't... I'm not... I mean it wasn't like that. Honestly. It was weird, Lex, how it was between us. Like it was just meant to happen. Maybe I didn't get to write my own Hollywood ending, but I'm still okay with it. I wouldn't take it back."

"I wish I could say that about even half of my past relationships," Lexi said dryly. "So what now?"

"I'll finish the film." Miranda added her secret wish with a deprecating laugh. "Who knows? Maybe one day he'll just show up, throw me on his horse, and take me off into the sunset."

———

Three weeks later, Miranda was growing frustrated with her film. "Lexi, would you take a look at this? I've already spent countless hours on postproduction, and it's just not working. I wish I could figure out why."

"Sure. I'm no film critic, but I'll take a peek." Lexi sat down in front of the laptop, where Miranda was studying the video clips.

"Keep in mind it's only the rough cut," Miranda said. "In addition to being on that helicopter, I filmed the horses as they came into the traps, so I'd have dual perspective. I also have some great stills of wild horses that I'm going to edit in."

"You've got some gorgeous video here," Lexi remarked. "Some of this desert scenery is breathtaking...but..."

"I know." Miranda grimaced. "It feels flat and passionless, doesn't it? There's nothing special here. Nothing to evoke any real emotion. Even the attempt to save the foal seems somehow lacking."

"If you wanted to tug on the heartstrings, why didn't you follow that story through?" Lexi asked.

"Because they wouldn't let me. The pilot didn't think I'd be strong enough to hold the horse. He said it was too dangerous, so I went out after the strays with Keith instead."

Lexi grinned. "Can't blame you there. As a semiemployed actress, I have to ask what you're going to do about narration?"

"I've been thinking about that. For the most part, I'd planned to use archived interviews with Wild Horse Annie. She's the one who started the whole mustang conservation movement."

Lexi gave a big theatrical yawn. "Sounds dry as the desert. What about music? Maybe you can do something cool with that?"

"I'm still looking for what I want, but haven't found it yet."

"If you really want to stir emotion, you could use 'Ride of the Valkyries.' Start it right when that chopper pops up."

Miranda snorted. "And remind people of *Apocalypse Now*? I don't think so. This whole topic is already controversial enough."

Lexi smirked. "You said you want to be evocative."

"Not in that way." Miranda sighed. "I need a unique angle, something to connect with the audience and make this feel more personal."

"Honey, what you *need* is your hot Indian wrangler."

"Keith? What do you mean?"

"I'm saying that he's your angle, and he looks incredible on camera to boot. Didn't you say he had his audience at that clinic eating out of his hand? He's the ideal connection between those horses and your viewers. You need to ask him to narrate this."

Lexi was absolutely right. Keith's passion had come through in so many ways. He'd even risked his life to go after the runaway horses. Miranda advanced to the clip to where he rode down the cliff. "Take a look at this."

Lexi gasped. "Was that for real?"

"Yes. Incredible, isn't he?"

"Oh yeah. No doubt about it. You need to change your whole angle. *He's* your real story."

Miranda shook her head. "I don't think he'd do it, Lex. I don't even dare to ask him after what happened with him and Bibi."

"Randa, honey, you asked for my opinion, and I gave you the perfect answer. Now all you need to do is find a way to *persuade* him. Seems to me you have all the right weapons in your…er…arsenal," she replied with a wink.

"But Keith was one of Bibi's clients. If I ask him and she gets wind of it, she'll toss me out like yesterday's leftovers. Or worse, she'll try to sue me."

"Can she?" Lexi asked.

"I don't know." Miranda shrugged. "Maybe. There's a noncompete clause in my contract, stating that I can't enter into any other project or endeavor that competes with the interests of Starlight Productions. Given that they produce documentaries, I have only two choices. I can trash the project and keep the job I hate…or…"

"Or?" Lexi prompted.

Miranda's stomach tightened. "Or quit the job to pursue my real dream." She'd known from the start that there was a possible conflict of interest, but she refused to give up on the film.

"It's not as simple as all that," Lexi replied. "If you cross Bibi, you might as well pack your bags. You'll never work in *this* town again."

"I know, Lex, but maybe this is exactly the wake-up I needed. Since I came back from Nevada, nothing seems to make any sense anymore. I didn't get into this field for fame and fortune. I've always wanted to use my camera to make a difference. Now I have a chance to do that. If I quit with Bibi, I'll have no reason not to see my project through."

"You'd better consider this carefully," Lexi warned. "You've worked hard. I'd hate to see it all blow up in your face. If Bibi has any sway, which we all know she does, you won't be able to do anything with that film."

"There are other opportunities besides Hollywood."

"You're thinking about leaving? Are you crazy?" Lexi asked.

"Maybe." Miranda gave a dry laugh. "You know I've never felt that I belonged here, Lex. All this time I thought Hollywood was what I wanted, but this documentary has changed everything. It's what I want to do, what I *need* to do."

"So you really are serious about quitting?"

"I think so, but I haven't made any definite decisions yet. I'm going to Montana this weekend to think things over. Where better than the ranch? Besides, I miss Jo-Jo. I haven't seen her since my grandfather's funeral."

"When are you coming back?"

"I don't know if I am or not, but if you're worried about the lease, I have enough saved to cover my half until you find a new roomie."

"Keep your money. I don't want it. You're probably

gonna need all of it to edit your film—provided you can even find a place to work on it out there in the middle of nowhere."

"I already have," Miranda said. "MSU in Bozeman has a program in Natural History Filmmaking. I'm sure I can arrange to use their equipment."

"Uh. Huh. I get it now." Lexi gave a knowing nod.

"Get what?" Miranda asked.

"The reason you're doing this. This isn't just about the documentary, is it?"

"Of course it is," Miranda replied. "Why else would I do it?"

"I don't know." Lexi pursed her lips. "Maybe to be closer to a certain cowboy? Didn't you say he was from Wyoming?"

"He is," Miranda replied. "But he could be anywhere now. This really has nothing to do with him."

"Sure it doesn't." Lexi wrapped her arms around Miranda. "You'll be just fine, sweets. Go find your horse whisperer and be happy."

Miranda replied with a teary smile. Why did Lexi always seem to see straight through her? "Thank you, Lexi. Maybe I'll do that."

Chapter 16

"RANDA JO SUTTON! YOU ARE A SIGHT FOR THESE SORE old eyes!" Miranda felt almost assaulted by the strength of her grandmother's hug. "Need some help with your bags?"

"Don't worry about it," Miranda said. "I'll ask Marvin to get them later."

"Marvin's not here anymore."

"He's not? But he's been at Circle S as long as I can remember. I thought you were keeping him on until you sold. Where did he go?"

Jo-Jo grimaced. "Don't know. Don't care."

"What do you mean?" Miranda could hardly suppress her shock. "What happened?"

"I had to let him go. Bud was the only man who could ever keep that misogynistic old bastard in his place. Once Bud passed, Marvin seemed to think he could run roughshod over me. Oh, I knew he'd always kept a flask handy, but he seemed to think he could do as he damned well pleased without Bud around. He even got a wild notion that he could take Bud's place."

Miranda frowned. "Are you saying he *came on* to you?"

"Sure did. Why so shocked? He's only five years younger than me."

"It's not that! It's just seems really weird. So what did you do?"

"I had to give him the boot, or better said, a knee to the groin. It's been just me, all by my lonesome, ever since."

Miranda laid a hand on her grandmother's arm. "Jo-Jo, why didn't you call me?"

"What for?" Jo-Jo asked.

"To come and help you. I hate that you didn't."

"Don't worry about me, sweetheart. I could handle ol' Marvin. It's the workload I just can't handle anymore."

Miranda followed her grandmother into the house.

"Are you hungry?" Jo-Jo asked.

"Not really, but I'm sure I will be by supper time."

Miranda salivated at the memory of her grandmother's cooking. No one could cook like Jo-Jo. Of course, no one probably *should*. Jo-Jo slathered real butter and cream on virtually everything. The doctor had even warned that it would worsen Gramp's heart disease, but he'd waved off the warning, saying he'd rather eat what he liked and die a happy man.

"Why has it been so long since you've come out to see me?" Jo-Jo asked. The question, posed with a mildly reproving look, made Miranda feel guilty, as was intended.

"Just really busy, Jo-Jo," she replied. "Incredibly busy with school and then work, but it looks like I may have some time on my hands now."

"Really? How's that?"

Miranda sighed. "I'm thinking about leaving my job."

"You are? Now *that* reeks of a story. C'mon to the kitchen. I'll put on a pot of coffee while you tell me all about it."

For the next two hours, Miranda sat in her favorite spot in the whole house, Jo-Jo's kitchen, sipping coffee and munching on her favorite childhood snack—Ritz crackers and Velveeta cheese.

"My entire life has revolved around certain goals, but I don't feel the same way about it as I did before. I thought I wanted to work in L.A., but it isn't at all what I thought it would be."

"If you were so unhappy, you should be glad to be free," Jo-Jo said.

"Part of me is, but change scares me," Miranda said.

"Nothing in life is ever guaranteed but change, sweetheart. Believing otherwise is only fooling yourself."

"Maybe you're right, but I still don't like uncertainty. I just don't know what I should do with my life."

Jo-Jo laid a hand on hers. "Don't fret. You'll figure it all out. Just give it some time. Why don't you tell me more about this film you're working on?"

Miranda took a savoring sip of coffee. "It started out purely by chance when my roommate Lexi told me about a wild-horse roundup. A wild-horse activist group was trying to sue over it, so the court ordered a videographer to satisfy them that the livestock company was treating the horses humanely. As soon as I took the job, I realized there was an opportunity to do so much more with it, so I decided to make a documentary."

"And now you think it's worth risking your job over? After working all this time to put yourself through film school?" Jo-Jo set her coffee cup down with a resonating click.

"Yeah. I do," Miranda said. "There is so much more to this story than meets the eye. I need to do this, Jo-Jo. I could never live with myself if I didn't see it through."

"That's my girl! I don't care what you do in this world as long as you believe in yourself and what you're doing."

"That's the only problem with this project," Miranda said. "I believe in what *I'm* doing but not in what *they* are doing."

"Why's that?" Jo-Jo frowned. "Are they mistreating the horses?"

"No. It's not that. The livestock company really seems to care about the safety and welfare of the animals. It's the program itself that's all wrong. Did you know there are over fifty thousand horses in captivity?"

"I've heard a bit about this lately but had no idea there were so many," Jo-Jo said. "Matter of fact, the BLM is looking to make deals with private ranchers. I've heard a lot of talk about that lately at the co-op and the stockyard. There's an outfit about fifty miles south of here that's preparing to take on a bunch of mustangs. Some of the neighbors are really pissed off about it."

"But why?" Miranda asked.

"A lot of ranchers fear the horses will get out and run their young calves to death. Others are worried about the impact on the elk, but I don't see the problem as long as they all maintain their fences. Horses respect them much better than cows do. Cows push through fences all the time."

Stirring her coffee, Miranda gazed out the bay window that overlooked the back pastures, which showed large patches of green even in late autumn. It was still her favorite place in the whole world. She wondered what it would be like to make a home here.

"Are you lonely out here by yourself?" Miranda asked.

"Sometimes," Jo-Jo answered. "I won't lie about that, but I still have mixed feelings about selling. Bud's granddad first homesteaded the place. It's been in the family for generations. I raised my children here. I always thought your father would run it one day, or even Judith and Robert, but they won't ever move here. Judith couldn't leave Montana fast enough. I swear she intentionally picked the nursing program that would take her the farthest from home.

"It's been a lot of work to keep the place up. I never minded when Bud and I were in it together—the ranch was our dream. But now that I'm alone, my heart just isn't in it anymore. It's all just...hard work."

For the first time, Miranda noticed the purple shadows under her grandmother's eyes. "Have you had any offers yet?"

"Not a single one, not worth considering anyway. One of the neighboring ranches inquired about leasing some of the pastureland though. I'm still thinking about it. It seems wasteful not to be putting it to any use. More coffee?" Jo-Jo filled her cup before she could reply, adding a generous amount of real cream and two heaping spoonfuls of sugar.

"Thanks." Miranda took a sip while endeavoring to corral her wild thoughts. Her grandmother had just given her the perfect opening. Maybe her involvement with the horses wasn't just about making a film. Maybe she was meant to do much more.

"Jo-Jo," she asked, "how much grazing pasture do you have here?"

"After letting all the leases go back, I still own

four whole sections—prime land with creek access on two sides."

"How many acres is that?" Miranda asked, her pulse speeding.

"A little over twenty-five hundred. That's equivalent to four square miles, with plenty of water. Water is a priceless commodity around these parts. That's why I'm not dropping my price."

"What if you could put the land to good use without it being a huge burden on you? Would you consider keeping the place?"

"I couldn't afford to keep it unless I could generate some income."

"How do you feel about mustangs?" Miranda asked. "I know it sounds crazy, but the BLM is desperate to get those horses off their hands."

Jo-Jo shook her head sadly. "I know your heart's in the right place, but I don't know the first thing about wild horses, and I couldn't do it alone even if I wanted to."

"What if you weren't alone? What if I wanted to help you?"

"Sweetheart, it would be a dream come true to have you here with me, but I don't understand why you'd want to mess with wild mustangs. Seems like nothing but a whole lot of trouble to me."

"Didn't you just say that cows are harder to manage than horses?" Miranda countered. "Maybe we could even train some of them. There are several prisons that do that and offer them up for adoption."

Jo-Jo looked doubly skeptical. "Randa, honey, you don't know the first thing about breaking a domestic horse, let alone a wild one."

"I know that, Jo-Jo. We'd have to bring someone on to do the training. I'd never be foolish enough to try something like that on my own, but I have connections now. The West family has been dealing with these horses for thirty years...and Keith has worked with them too."

"Keith?" Jo-Jo asked.

"He was a wrangler I met while working on the film. He saved me from a rattlesnake. And a mountain lion. I also nearly froze to death that night." She grinned. "But I've never had a better time in my whole life."

Jo-Jo laughed. "Sounds a little like the first date I had with your grandpa."

"Tell me about it," Miranda said.

"Bud had been coming around for a good while, helping out on the ranch. He kept eyeballing me when he thought I wasn't looking, but never could seem to find his tongue. The first time he ever spoke to me directly was the day he showed up with two saddled horses. 'Wanna ride?' he says.

"'Sure. I'll ride,' I answer. I go inside and change into my jeans and boots, and there he is, just waitin'. Doesn't say another word for two hours as we ride up into the mountains. Then he suddenly pulls up. 'You like steak?'

"'Yes. Who doesn't?' I reply. Then I noticed the little clearing with a fire pit all set up to go—neatly stacked wood, a cooler full of food, a cast-iron fry pan, coffeepot, and a box of Bisquick. I almost fell off the horse when I realized the man who'd barely spoken more than five words to me had ridden all the way up that mountain hours before just to set up for our 'date.' I suspected right then that he was the man I'd marry."

"When did you know for certain?" Miranda asked. Was it really possible to fall in love with someone so quickly?

"About two hours later, when he asked me, but it was the kiss that sealed the deal. Honey, he wasn't a talker, but that sure wasn't because he didn't know how to use his tongue."

"Jo-Jo!" Miranda cried, cheeks flaming.

"Why do you look so scandalized? I was young once too. And I never stopped liking those kisses either. The secret to a happy marriage starts with great kisses. I never had any complaints in that department...or in any other."

"Just like that? You just knew he was the one for you?"

Miranda could hardly imagine making that kind of life-changing decision after knowing someone such a short time. She and Keith had shared something special too, but how could she know if it was enough to build on? She wondered where he was at the moment, and what he was doing. It seemed the harder she tried not think about him, the more her mind seemed to go there.

"That I did," Jo-Jo continued. "You gotta understand, with men, actions speak much louder than words, especially when it comes to matters of the heart. We got married as soon as I turned eighteen. We were together fifty years, and I never regretted a day." Her eyes twinkled and then misted. "I still miss the ol' codger." She wiped a tear from the corner of her eye and sniffed. "Enough of the waterworks. Now tell me about this Keith of yours. Did you spend the night with him?"

Miranda paused, not knowing how much she should volunteer. Although her grandmother wasn't a prude by any means, she still wasn't comfortable sharing about her love life. Then again, she'd never been able to keep anything from her grandmother. Why try now?

"Yes." Miranda sighed. "We weren't *supposed* to be alone...but the others got held up. He really took care of me out in the desert. I really like him, Jo-Jo."

"*Like?*" her grandmother repeated, brows raised. Did Jo-Jo have some kind of sixth sense?

"Okay. It's more than just like," Miranda confessed, cheeks coloring. "But we're probably never going to see each other again."

"Why not? Where's he from?"

"Wyoming. His family has a ranch on the Wind River Reservation."

Jo-Jo looked surprised. "He's an Indian?"

"Yes," Miranda said. "Well, half anyway. Shoshone. I had no clue about the scope of the mustang problem until I starting looking at it through his eyes."

Jo-Jo's gaze narrowed. "So this mustang sanctuary was his idea?"

"Not at all," Miranda said. "He's totally against it. I won't deny that I'd really like for Keith to be a part of this, but I promise you I'd still want to move forward with the idea if he wasn't involved."

Jo-Jo looked unconvinced. "I'm beginning to suspect that he has far more to do with all this wild-horse business than you're ready to acknowledge, or maybe that you even realize. Before I commit to this scheme of yours, you'd better be really certain of your true motivation, Miranda Jo. This is some major responsibility we're talking about, and not the kind of thing you can change your mind about later."

"I understand that," Miranda said. "I know it would be a long-term commitment. I promise I'm not taking this lightly."

"I know your heart is in the right place, but you know even less about all this than I do. I don't understand why you'd be thinking about it at all. I thought you had your mind set on a career in movies. It's all you've ever talked about."

"It wasn't how I thought it would be, Jo-Jo," Miranda said. "I still love cinematography, but Hollywood isn't where I want to be. I don't fit in there. I wasn't happy. It hurts me almost as much as it does you to see the ranch go. Why couldn't we run it together?"

"But there's nothing for you to do here in Silver Star. It's all just ranchers. There are very few young people. You'd be bored to tears within a month."

"But I've always loved the ranch, Jo-Jo. I've never been bored here before."

"Because you were never here long enough to get bored. Besides that, we always did our best to keep you entertained. But we're not talking about a summer vacation anymore. We're talking about running a working ranch."

"Just think about it, will you? I'd honestly like to do this. If you can give me one good, solid reason *not* to do it, I promise never to bring it up again."

Jo-Jo laughed. "Don't make promises you can't keep, sweetheart. You and I both know that you're like a dog with a bone once you get an idea in your head. I know you aren't flighty, but this is a radical, life-changing decision you're talking about. You need to be damned certain it's the right one. I'm gonna sleep on this, and I'd advise you to do the same. If there's one thing I learned from Bud in all our years together, it was never to make hasty or emotional decisions. They'll always come back to bite you in the ass."

Chapter 17

Wyoming Checkerboard lands

KEITH STOOD BY WITH THE JUDAS HORSE, GAZING OUT over the sagebrush-peppered landscape of the checkerboard lands. It was a routine he could have performed blindfolded after three months of gathering hundreds of horses in as many states. This was the biggest roundup yet, but it wasn't exactly going according to plan. Over nine hundred mustangs had been served an eviction notice courtesy of Uncle Sam. Not for the first time, Keith experienced a sharp stab of conscience, as if he were a traitor, a betrayer of trust.

Ears perked, one small band warily watched the chopper's approach. A few of them snorted annoyance as the helicopter crested the horizon, then seemingly unconcerned, turned and trotted away. Another bunch appeared more cooperative at first, but suddenly spread out like fingers to gallop away into the brush.

Keith shook his head. Nope. This definitely wasn't their first rodeo. These horses had obviously been gathered before and had grown wise to the wily ways of the wranglers. Unlike the Nevada herds, they were accustomed to, even jaded by, the helicopter. They were also perfectly fat and happy in their present home and had every intention of staying.

Just like the native peoples once had, these animals

had roamed the land freely for centuries. Unfortunately, their desire to remain held no weight against the court order demanding their removal. Protecting the ecosystem was the reason behind the capture, but the truth was simple enough if one just followed the money trail. The horses were freeloaders living on the largesse of the government. Others desired use of the same lands and were willing to pay for the privilege.

He watched with a gladdened heart as the helicopter followed a band of bachelor stallions who continued their campaign of passive resistance. The pilot circled, honing in on a single horse that spun to face him with clear defiance. The chopper came closer, hovering maybe thirty feet away. The horse remained unintimidated.

The pilot rose and circled around to the other side. Two other stallions came to join the first in his stand-off. Ears pinned, they planted their hooves, stubbornly determined to hold their plot of sage-covered ground. Several minutes later, Trey backed off in pursuit of easier game.

Keith shared in their triumph as the stallions trotted off, heads high and tails in the air.

The checkerboard gather had been a long, drawn-out process. After three weeks, they still hadn't managed to get all of the horses. Given the mustangs' resistance to the helicopters, the rest would have to be caught over time by setting traps at the key watering holes. But Keith had already decided he was finished. This was his last horse roundup.

"We have a job coming up in New Mexico next month," Mitch said when Keith came by to collect his check.

Keith stuffed it in his pocket and shook his head. "I'm

done, Mitch. You already know how I feel about this whole thing. If I can't be part of a solution, I damned sure don't want to feel like I'm part of the problem."

"I don't completely agree with you on that, but I respect your position," Mitch said. "You know"—he scratched his chin—"even if you don't want to wrangle anymore, I might still have a job for you."

"I guess that depends on what you have in mind," Keith replied.

"I need someone to drive, if you're interested in just hauling the horses. I got a call yesterday about two dozen mustangs from Ft. McDermitt that they pulled from the killer auction. Matter of fact, they asked me about you."

"Why's that?" Keith asked.

"Seems they've got a freeze-branded stud in the mix that they say is registered to you. I can't quite figure that one out. You know anything about it?"

Blue Eye. Shit.

"Yup. He's an outlaw I bought from the prison. I was going to give him to my grandfather, but he musta somehow got loose."

"Somehow, huh? And then somehow found his way from Carson City all the way back to Ft. McDermitt?"

Keith had to suppress the tug of a grin. "We both know horses are real smart like that. They seem to have a sixth sense. Anytime I ever got lost as a kid, I always let the horse bring me home."

Mitch snorted. "You got a London Bridge to sell me too? I'm about as likely to buy it. Look, you're gonna have to go and pick up that horse anyway, so instead of paying your own gas, why not haul the load of 'em back for me and make a few bucks?"

"I s'pose that makes sense. How soon do I need to be there?"

"A few days. I didn't tell them for certain yet."

"Good. That gives me a little time to take care of some personal business."

"What are you planning to do with that outlaw?" Mitch asked.

"That's part of the business I've got to figure out."

Keith left Rock Springs early the next morning, heading west toward Utah. Although the section of highway between Rock Springs and Salt Lake City had always been one of his favorite drives, with his mind racing, Keith saw nothing. Miranda Sutton occupied his mind. Not that he'd ever been able to completely push her out of it. She'd lingered constantly in the periphery of his thoughts. A month had passed, but the time apart had made no difference, had done nothing to fade the memory of her face or suppress the stirrings in his groin when he thought of their last night together. So many times he'd been tempted to ask Mitch for her number, but calling would only have been futile torture. Too much distance separated them.

Until now.

His circumstances were no better than they were before, maybe even worse. Yet, coming to the junction of I-80 and I-15, he had a big decision to make — keep on heading west and forget about her, or follow his heart south to Los Angeles. There were so many reasons, good solid reasons, to stay the course, and only one reason to deviate from it, but that one reason — Miranda — outweighed all the rest.

Pulling into a truck stop, he pulled the borrowed

phone from his shirt pocket and began scrolling through the contacts. Sure enough, Mitch had her number. What would he even say to her after all this time? Would she want to see him? If he didn't ask, he'd never know. With his pulse pounding in his ears, Keith took a breath and dialed.

—⁂—

Miranda had barely opened her eyes when her phone rang. Snatching it off her bedside charger, she squinted at the display, surprised to see Mitch West's name on her caller ID.

"Hello? Mitch?" she answered.

"No. It's Keith."

Her heart skipped a beat. "Keith?"

"Yeah. I'm headed to L.A. I hoped maybe I could see you."

"L.A.?" she repeated blankly. Her heart dropped into her stomach. "I—I'd really like that, b-but I'm not in L.A. anymore."

"You aren't? Where are you?"

"Montana. I'm at my grandma's in Silver Star. I got here a few days ago."

"You're in *Montana*?" he repeated, as if he didn't believe her.

"Yes. At the ranch I told you about. I thought it would be a good place to come. You know, to figure things out."

"And have you?" he asked. "Figured things out?"

"Not completely," she replied. "But I'm working on it."

"How long are you planning to stay?" he asked.

"That's a good question," she said with a dry

laugh. "Probably until I wear out my welcome. What about you? What are you doing now? Are you still gathering mustangs?"

"No. I'm not going to do it anymore. I finished my last roundup yesterday."

"Oh. And now you're headed to L.A." Had he changed his mind about Bibi's offer? Her stomach knotted at the thought.

"I *was* headed to L.A.," he corrected, "but it seems I've just lost my whole reason for going there."

"I don't understand. Weren't you going to see Bibi?"

"Why would you think that?" he asked.

"I don't know. When you mentioned L.A., I assumed you'd had a change of heart regarding her offer."

He made a scoffing sound. "You thought wrong…at least about the job offer. As for the change of heart… maybe you got that part right."

"Wh-what do you mean?"

"My change of heart… I was going there to see you, *Aiwattsi*."

Her throat felt suddenly thick. She swallowed hard, willing herself not to attach too much meaning to his words. "You were going to drive all the way to L.A. just to see me?"

"Yeah. I was. But not now that you're in Montana."

"Oh." She tried to suppress the wave of disappointment.

"It's not that I don't want to see you," he continued. "I do, but I have to go to Fallon, Nevada, to pick up some horses. As it turns out, one of them is mine."

"Yours?" she asked. "Did you buy another one?"

"No. It's the same stallion from the prison. I released him right after I bought him, but then they caught him again. If I don't pick him up soon, I'm afraid he'll end up with the kill buyer."

"You *released* him? Why would you do that?"

"Because he'll never be adoptable and doesn't belong in a holding facility. I set him loose in the place where they caught him."

At first the news shocked her, but then it made perfect sense why he'd done it. She was glad he had. "So where are you right now?" she asked.

"Outside Park City, Utah."

"When will you be back?"

"I'll be in Rock Springs, Wyoming, tomorrow with the horses, then I'm planning to go home for a while. I need somewhere to put the horse. I'd originally thought to make a gift of him, so that's what I'm going to do."

"So you're taking him to your family's place?"

"Yeah. The ranch is on the reservation outside Riverton."

"I know how important this must be to you," she said. She hoped it would go well when he finally returned to his family. He seemed so strong and self-reliant, but at the same time lonely and drifting, as if he were lost at sea, and in desperate need of an anchor. Ironically, she was in similar straits.

"You and me both." He sounded a humorless laugh. A brief silence followed. He broke it just as she was tempted to fill it with another trite remark. "It's good to hear your voice, *Aiwattsi*."

Was that a note of wistfulness in his tone? Was he as disappointed as she was? "It's good to hear yours too," she remarked softly. "Thank you for calling me, Keith. I'm really glad you did."

"Me too," he said, adding more tersely, "we'll talk again soon."

When? She wanted to ask but bit back the question. "I'll look forward to it," she said instead.

"Good-bye, *Aiwattsi*."

"Bye, Keith." Miranda disconnected the call, hugging her phone to her chest, feeling as if she'd just ridden a roller coaster. She couldn't believe he'd called, but didn't dare think too much about what that might mean. Since her arrival in Montana, her thoughts had pinged incessantly back and forth between the ranch, the horses, and Keith. His call had both encouraged and confused her. Was he looking to pick things up? She already knew he wasn't the commitment type. His lifestyle said as much. He'd traveled from place to place for years without any lasting relationships. Why would this be any different? Still, she couldn't help hoping—for exactly what, she didn't even know.

⁓⁓⁓

"Coffee?" Jo-Jo asked as Miranda padded into the kitchen.

"Please," Miranda almost groaned. "What's that other wonderful smell?"

"Blueberry muffins. They're almost ready to come out of the oven. How did you sleep?"

"Pretty well, all things considered."

A big lie. In truth, she hadn't slept a wink. Her mind was far too unsettled. She hoped her grandmother had come to a decision about the ranch, but was almost afraid to ask.

"All things considered?" Jo-Jo prompted.

"The future, I guess," Miranda replied on a sigh. "For

years I thought I had it all mapped out, but something's changed. I don't understand how it happened, but suddenly I don't want to do what I always thought I wanted to do."

"So you're still thinking about this horse sanctuary?" Jo-Jo said.

"Yes. I am. What about you? Have you given it any more consideration?"

"Matter of fact, I did a little more than that. I made some phone calls to the regional BLM office, as well as to my neighbors."

"Why the neighbors?" Miranda asked.

"I told you there was a bunch of ranchers up in arms about the outfit down in Ennis. I don't want that same thing to happen here. Although it's my right to do as I wish with my land, it's important to keep good relations with the neighbors, especially the ones I share common fence with."

"What did they say?" Miranda asked.

"They voiced the same frets about horses getting loose, but I reminded them how many times their cows have wandered into our pastures. Dirk Knowlton over at the Flying K seemed the most concerned, since he's experimenting with a new cattle breed, but said it wasn't any business of his as long as our fences were secure. That's my other worry at this point. I think we'd have to upgrade some of the fencing, and that's a big expense."

Encouraged, Miranda asked, "I'll be happy to pay for any repairs. This whole thing was my idea, after all."

"I don't want you to drain your savings," Jo-Jo argued.

"How much do you think it would cost?"

"Probably a couple of thousand dollars, but I wouldn't know for certain without inspecting it."

The oven dinged. Jo-Jo donned a mitt and pulled out a pan of steaming blueberry delights.

"Can we?" Miranda asked. "Inspect it?"

"Sweetheart. It would be a waste of time. I don't have any money to put into fencing."

"But maybe I do," Miranda said. "Depending on how much we're talking about. I have a little bit saved up. If that's the main thing that's stopping us from doing this, I'd really like to know what it'll cost." With a pleading look, Miranda laid a hand on her grandmother's shoulder. "Please, Jo-Jo. Let's at least find out before you decide anything."

"All right." Jo-Jo sighed. "We'll investigate, but don't get your hopes up."

"Thank you, Jo-Jo." Miranda smiled. Although Jo-Jo tried not to show it, she was definitely softening to the notion.

Jo-Jo placed a basket of muffins on the table beside the large crock of salted butter. "Eat up, now, cowgirl. We've got us some fence to ride."

—◦◦◦—

Tails wagging madly, Jo-Jo's three old herd dogs trailed hot on their heels as they left the house for the main barn. As she slid back the metal door, the mixed smells of alfalfa hay, fresh manure, and oiled leather greeted her, filling Miranda with remembrances of the happy summers she'd spent on the ranch. It was here she'd learned to ride a horse, and even drive. Gramps had taught her how to shift and clutch at the age of twelve, when he'd put her behind the wheel of the old farm truck in the back pasture.

She'd always loved the visits, but she had never considered making a life out here until now. Silver Star was a tiny community with only a post office to even mark its existence, and the nearest town, Twin Bridges, wasn't exactly a metropolis. If she sought entertainment of any kind, Butte was an hour away and Bozeman a good eighty miles. Would she grow bored with it as Jo-Jo feared?

She recalled Keith's words about yearning for a simpler, quieter life. Would that kind of life suit her? She was beginning to believe it would. She'd always been a homebody anyway. During four years in L.A., she'd been out only a handful of times. The only things she'd ever really needed to be content were her camera, an Internet connection, and Netflix.

Jesse and Doc pulled away from the hayrack to greet them with quiet nickers. "Hello, boys," Miranda said, stroking one head and then the other. "I hate to interrupt their breakfast."

"They have nothing to fear," Jo-Jo said. "We'll be taking the ATV."

"Why not ride the horses?" Miranda asked.

"Because I haven't put a saddle on either of those ol' timers in almost two years."

"Oh," Miranda remarked in surprise. Most of her childhood memories were of her grandmother on a horse. Jo-Jo had always loved riding. She never thought Jo-Jo would give it up as long as she was still able to sit a horse. "You don't ride at all anymore?"

"Nope. I quit after Bud passed," Jo-Jo said sadly. "Haven't been able to bring myself to get on a horse since. I sold all but these two retirees. Bud built these stalls to shelter them from the harsher weather, and I soak their feed every night. We never pampered our ranch horses, but these two old boys have earned a comfortable retirement." She patted Doc's neck. "I hope someone does the same for me one day."

Miranda had never imagined her fiery grandmother needing that kind of care, but it seemed the years were finally beginning to catch up with her. "I'll take care of you, Jo-Jo. I promise."

"Are you really planning to hang around here that long?" Jo-Jo asked.

"Yes," Miranda replied. "If you'll let me. I really do want to make this my home."

"Then you better know up front that I refuse to live on Jell-O, applesauce, and instant potatoes in my old age."

"I promise to make you pureed roast beef and gravy at least twice a week," Miranda teased.

Jo-Jo grinned back. "Then I'd best teach you how to cook!"

Chapter 18

KEITH WAS GROWING EDGIER BY THE MILE. AFTER TRANS-porting the horses he'd picked up in Nevada, he was finally headed home. As he pulled through the gate leading to Two Rivers Ranch, Keith's mind exploded with memories. Suddenly he was thirteen again, fighting the urge to squirm under his grandfather's penetrating, hawk-like eyes.

They'd picked him up in Cheyenne, his grandmother standing silently in the background while his grandfather silently scrutinized him. "You have the look of your father." The terse statement, accompanied by a curt nod, was Keith's only sign of acceptance.

"Where is my father?" Keith asked. "Why isn't he here?" His grandparents exchanged a look he couldn't decipher. His grandmother's lips quivered. For a moment, she appeared as if she might cry.

"He could not come," his grandfather had said with-out any elaboration. Days later, Keith learned from his cousins that his father had been accused of murder and taken back to prison. The news had shocked him. Was he predestined for the same fate? His family in New York had believed so.

He recalled climbing into the beat-up ranch truck, the silent four-hour drive leading to the ranch. Now, his palms were sweating as he drove slowly up the long gravel drive. He parked his truck, wondering if he should knock or just walk into the house as he always had. He'd never given it a thought until now, but he'd also never been so uncertain of his welcome.

It was afternoon. Chances were good that his grandmother would be in the kitchen. Figuring his best strategy was to go around to the back, he knocked at the kitchen door. Huttsi was his best way back. If he caught her alone, she wouldn't turn him away.

Tonya answered, "Hey, Cuz."

"Hey, Ton. How are you?"

"Busy as usual, but staying out of trouble." She flashed a toothy grin. "Mostly, anyway. C'mon in."

Wiping his boots on the mat, Keith stepped into the kitchen, instantly inhaling the wonderful, memory-inducing smell of fry bread. His grandmother stood in her usual place, with flour up to her elbows. Some things never changed.

"Huttsi, look who's back," Tonya prompted.

He waited with bated breath for her to acknowledge him.

"Two Wolves? You've returned?"

His grandmother's tone was neutral, but her gaze was reassuringly soft. He slowly exhaled in relief. "Yes," he replied. "Just got back from Nevada. I was gathering mustangs for the BLM."

"How did it go?" Tonya asked.

"Well enough." He gave a dismissive shrug.

Huttsi snorted. "We know all too well how the government 'manages' these things. Have you seen your grandfather yet?"

"No. I just arrived. But I brought a gift for him. A horse."

"A horse?" Her smile began in her black eyes and moved slowly to twitch the corners of her mouth. "That was a wise decision." They both knew that horses were his grandfather's weakness. "If you wish to find him, he's in the sweat lodge. He spends much time there, I think in prayer for you, Two Wolves. You see? All is not lost."

"Thank you, Huttsi." He stooped to plant a kiss on the tiny woman's weathered cheek.

She winked. "Come back in an hour if you want some fry bread."

He grinned. "I'd love some."

Tonya accompanied him outside. "That didn't go badly. Then again, she's always had a soft spot for you."

"What of Kenu?" Keith asked, still apprehensive of his reception from his grandfather. Would he welcome Keith back or send him packing?

"He hasn't spoken of you. But that doesn't mean anything when she said he prays for you. That *does* mean something," Tonya reassured him. "Now what's this about a horse?"

"Come," Keith said. "I'll show him to you."

He led her to his parked trailer. She peered inside through the aluminum slats where the horse was pacing and snorting. She gave a low whistle. "He's a looker all right."

"Is there a vacant corral where I can put him? I'll need six-foot-high panels." He answered her questioning look. "He's an outlaw."

Tonya regarded him with open skepticism. "And you're giving him as a *gift*? What's grandfather going to do with a horse like that? He doesn't break them anymore."

"I thought maybe you—"

Tonya stopped him with a glare. "Don't even go there, Cuz! I'm not about to get on some crazy mustang when we have a couple dozen nice, docile, hand-raised two-and three-year-olds in our own pastures."

"Maybe he could keep him for breeding. You don't find color like his very often."

"But people 'round here don't want mustangs. It's hard enough to sell registered horses these days. You know that better than I do. Why not break him yourself and ship him overseas? You were in the money when you were doing that."

"Isn't that exactly what everyone had such a problem with? That I was exploiting my heritage for money?"

Although they also raised cattle, their primary business was horse leasing. Running a business that depended heavily on the tourist trade, the ranch had always experienced the constant ebb and flow of a fluctuating economy, until Keith's popularity had opened new opportunities abroad. But no one besides Tonya wanted to acknowledge that his prosperity had helped to keep them afloat while others floundered. He still deeply resented the judgment he'd suffered over it.

"What else can you do with him?" she asked. "I'm wondering why you picked him up in the first place. I thought you didn't want anything more to do with horses."

"It was a moment of weakness," he said.

"More like madness."

"Maybe." Keith sighed. "If Kenu doesn't want him, I'll figure something out. In the meantime, I've got to unload him from this trailer."

"C'mon," Tanya said. "There's an empty corral you can just back up to."

———

Keith waited on a stump outside the sweat lodge for almost two hours before his grandfather emerged, wearing only his breechcloth. Steam rose from his body into the frosty air like a mist over a winter lake, but he seemed completely unaware of the cold.

Keith offered him a blanket and a pouch of loose tobacco. His grandfather accepted both with a nod, betraying no emotion. Although clouded by cataracts, his gaze seemed just as sharp and penetrating as when they'd first met.

"I knew you would come," he said after a time. "I saw it in a vision."

"I brought you another gift," Keith said. "A spirit horse from the Paiute lands."

"A spirit horse?" Keith instantly perceived that he'd breached a wall. Horses were the common love that had brought them together so many years ago. The old man nodded his gray head. "I will see this gift."

"A beautiful animal," Kenu remarked as they approached the corral where the horse paced, "but his spirit is much agitated." The animal greeted them with flattened ears and a broad backside. Kenu eyed the horse again with a slow shake of his head. "I cannot accept your gift, Two Wolves."

"Why not?" Keith asked, his chest tightening. He'd hoped to put an end to his rootless existence, only to be turned away again, his gift rejected.

"Because this gift is as incomplete as the giver."

Keith wanted to gnash his teeth in anger and frustration. As he'd feared, his peace offering had been appraised and found lacking. Just as he had been.

"Why did you take me in when I first came here?" he demanded, prepared at last to hear the brutal truth. "Was it only because you lost your son?"

His grandfather met his gaze, but this time there was a difference. Pain flickered in Kenu's black eyes. "I never could have survived losing my son had you not come, Two Wolves. You were a gift I did not seek, but I knew you were never meant to remain."

"But I want to stay," Keith insisted. "Why won't you let me?"

"Because your place is not here, Two Wolves."

Keith gave a deprecating laugh. "It's not out there either." He'd thought coming home to Wyoming would be the easiest path. He didn't want to forge a new one on his own. Not again.

"Then you have not looked hard enough," Kenu replied. "The easiest path is not always the answer."

"I *do* belong here," Keith insisted. "I know I screwed up. Why won't you let me make amends? Give me a chance to prove myself."

The old man shook his head sadly. "It is not for you to prove anything to me, Two Wolves. It is for you to find your purpose. A man with no purpose is a man with no soul."

Did Kenu really believe he lacked a soul?

"I don't know what I'm supposed to do with my life. In all this time the answer has never been revealed to me, so how am I ever to know it?"

Kenu once more regarded the horse. "Did you ever consider that this animal might be the answer? Perhaps it is *he* that is meant to show you."

In that moment Keith understood. The truth was indeed brutal, piercing like an arrow to the heart, but not in the way he'd expected. He wasn't being sent away for lack of love, but because of it.

Keith was loaded up and headed for Rock Springs to return Mitch's trailer when his phone rang. "Keith, it's Mitch. I know you just got back a couple of days ago, but I'm in a bit of a tight spot."

"How's that?"

"I just got a call asking if I can haul a load of horses from Gunnison."

"The prison?" Keith asked.

"Yup," Mitch said. "They're shutting down their mustang program due to an alleged mishandling of funds. It's a huge blow to the entire inmate training program."

"Don't they house several hundred horses at that facility?" Keith asked.

"Over eleven hundred, and the BLM's scrambling to find places for the horses. They've got less than thirty days to remove all of them. We all knew it wouldn't be a pretty sight when the shit finally hit the fan. But we also knew it was inevitable. Rock Springs is almost at capacity, but they're still going to take fifty horses. I've got three trailers available to haul them, but I need another driver. Would you be willing to make the trip?"

"When?" Keith asked.

"We need to get them as soon as possible," Mitch replied. "I predict that we'll be spending the next couple of months doing nothing but hauling horses 'cross country."

Mitch voiced Keith's fears, but his first loyalty had to be to Mitch, at least until the current crisis was over. "Yes. I can go. I'll head out first thing in the morning."

He cursed his luck. For days he'd been looking forward to seeing Miranda, but now it looked like that was no longer in the cards, not if he wanted to keep his job, anyway.

"Great," Mitch said, sounding relieved.

Keith went to pocket the phone but then dialed it again. Although he couldn't see Miranda as he'd planned, that didn't mean he couldn't at least call her again.

"Hello?" Miranda answered on the third ring.

"Hey. It's Keith."

"You called back. I was hoping you would."

"I'm sorry it took me so long."

"Did you go home?" she asked.

"Yes," he replied.

"How did it go?"

"Not how I'd hoped."

"What does that mean?"

"It means I'm going to be living on the road again, working for Mitch." His feelings about his return were still confused. He hoped she wouldn't press. He wasn't ready to say more.

"I thought you'd decided not to gather horses anymore," she said.

"I'm not wrangling. I'm driving," he explained. "I have to make a trip to Gunnison, Utah. It's kind of an emergency. We have to move over a thousand horses."

"Wow! That many? Where are they all going?" she asked.

"Pretty much to whoever will take them. The BLM is dispersing them all over the western states."

"So you're going to be on the road for a while?"

"Yeah. I'm going to be gone for several weeks. Maybe longer."

"Oh. I'd hoped…"

He grimaced at the note of disappointment in her voice. "Me too." He raked a hand through his hair with a sigh. "I'm really sorry I won't be able to see you. This isn't what I wanted, but I owe Mitch. He's always treated me well and pays decently. I have no reason to complain—other than the schedule."

"When do you leave?" she asked.

"I'm headed to Utah right now. I wanted to call you and explain while I still could. I'll probably lose cell service any minute."

"Keith? Is there any chance I could go with you?"

"To pick up the horses?"

"Yes. I'd really like to. Do you think I could meet up with you in Idaho?"

He considered the request, and then dismissed it as impractical. Although he really wanted to see her, it made no sense to take her to the prison. "I don't think it's such a good idea," he said. "It's a bigger and tighter-security facility than the one in Nevada. I doubt they'd let you in, even with me."

"Oh," she replied softly, sounding as deflated as he felt. "Then I guess we'll just have to wait for a better time."

"Yes, *Aiwattsi*," he replied, his disappointment matching hers. "I still want to see you, but I'm afraid we'll have to wait. I'll call you as soon as I get back."

Her reply was garbled and then, just as he'd feared, the phone went dead.

Damn it all. He hadn't even said good-bye. He was so damned tired of waiting, of putting his wants and desires on hold for others. A few miles later he realized he couldn't wait any longer.

Still unable to make a call, he pulled off the road to

text Mitch. Going to be late to Gunnison. Had something come up that can't wait. Will be there first thing in the a.m. He hit Send, pocketed the phone, and then reprogrammed the GPS.

Six hours later, he pulled his truck and trailer through the gates leading to the Circle S Ranch in Silver Star, Montana. Pulling up in front of a large outbuilding, he parked and cut the engine. The place was large and neat but seemed completely deserted—except for a trio of barking canines: a blue heeler and two Australian sheepdogs.

A middle-aged woman, presumably Miranda's grandmother, emerged from the house, wearing an inquisitive look. Miranda followed, her mouth falling instantly open. "Keith!" she exclaimed. "What are you doing here? How did you find me?"

He grinned. "Wasn't too hard. Silver Star isn't a very big place. I only had to ask for the Sutton ranch."

"B-but I thought you were en route to Utah."

"I was," he confessed, "but I decided to take a little detour."

"Hundreds of miles is hardly little." She laughed.

He'd almost forgotten her contagious laugh and dimpled smile. It was only her grandmother's presence that kept him from pulling Miranda into his arms and greeting her the way he wanted to. Once more, his wants and needs were on hold, but at least it was only hours now instead of weeks.

"Keith, this is my grandmother," Miranda said. "Jo-Jo, this is Keith Russo. He's…he's…the wrangler…I told you about."

He tipped his hat. "Good to meet you, Miz Sutton."

The awkward introduction stung a little, but how else was she supposed to introduce him?

"Jo-Jo, please," the older woman replied. "Or Jo, if you like. It's what all my friends and family call me."

"Am I a friend if I tell you I've come to take your granddaughter away?" Keith asked.

"Depends." Jo-Jo eyed him appraisingly. "Do you intend to bring her back again?"

"Yeah. I promise to bring her back. I was on my way to Gunnison to pick up a load of mustangs when Miranda said she'd like to go with me."

"Do you mind if I go?" Miranda said to her grandmother.

"When will you return?" Jo-Jo asked.

"Coupla days," Keith answered. "It's seven hours from here to Gunnison, then I have to haul the horses to Rock Springs, which is another four or five. Back here from there is another seven on top of that. We'll have to break up the drive, especially since I'm hauling livestock. If that makes you uncomfortable, we can get separate rooms." Not that he'd sleep in his.

Jo-Jo gave a resigned sigh. "I appreciate the gesture, but Miranda Jo's well past the age of consent."

"Yes, Jo-Jo, I am," Miranda said. "Just give me a minute to run upstairs and throw a bag together. I won't be long." She dashed into the house, leaving Keith alone with her grandmother.

"You came a long way to see her," Jo-Jo remarked, her faded gray eyes holding his.

"Yes, I did." He wasn't ready to volunteer anything more, not when he didn't even understand what had compelled him to go six hours out of his way. "Miranda speaks very fondly of you," Keith said.

"She and I have always had a special bond," Jo-Jo said. "I'm glad she's come, but I'm a little concerned about this sudden interest of hers in wild horses." She eyed him speculatively. "She's always been a grounded and sensible girl, which makes me wonder why she's so determined to take on a herd of mustangs."

"She's spoken to you about that?" Keith remarked in surprise.

"Yes. I hate to be blunt, but I'd like to know if you had anything to do with this. Did you put the idea into her head?"

"Absolutely not," Keith scoffed. "She hasn't talked you into it, has she?"

"Not yet, but I admit I've been chewing on this whole thing. I had an hour-long discussion with the regional BLM wild-horse administrator yesterday. It seems they're pretty desperate to find a place to pasture several hundred horses they just gathered in Wyoming."

"The checkerboard herds," he said.

"You know something about it?" she asked.

"Yes. I was there. They were all taken to Rock Springs, the same facility that's now been forced to take three loads of horses from Gunnison, Utah."

"That explains a lot," Jo-Jo said. "No wonder the BLM agent called me back so quickly."

"What did he say?" Keith asked.

"That they have a greater than anticipated surplus of wild horses and are actively seeking pasturing agreements with private ranches."

Keith laughed outright. "That's an understatement if I ever heard one. I'm sure they're chasing their tails, looking at any possible prospect to unload horses. What do you plan to do, Miz Sutton?"

"I'm still undecided. I really don't want to sell my ranch. On the other hand, I don't want Miranda to make any commitments she'll later regret. She has a compassionate nature, but this would be a life-changing decision. I'm not sure she understands that."

"I agree," Keith replied. "Are you going to try to dissuade her?"

"I've tried, without much success."

"It's a long drive to Utah. Maybe I can talk some sense into her."

"Good luck with that." The corners of Jo-Jo's lips twitched in a hint of a smile. "I'm afraid Miranda takes after me. She's like a dog with a bone when she sets her mind on something."

Miranda appeared in that moment with purse in hand, backpack slung over her shoulder. "Talking about me?" She flashed a mischievous grin. "You don't really have to answer that. My ears were burning the whole time I was gone. Ready, Keith?" she asked.

"Yeah, I'm ready."

"Bye, Jo-Jo." She planted a quick, parting peck on her grandmother's cheek. "Thanks for understanding. Keith and I really do have a lot to talk about."

Jo-Jo's gaze darted from one to the other. "I know you do, sweetheart, but it's not the *talking* that I worry about. You'll take good care of her?" Jo-Jo asked Keith, worry etching lines around her mouth.

"I promise she's in safe hands with me, Miz Sutton," he reassured her.

"We'll call you as soon as we get to Gunnison," Miranda said.

Keith tossed Miranda's bag into the back seat and

then handed her up into the cab of his truck. She gave him a look of apology when he joined her inside. "I'm sorry if my grandmother gave you the third degree."

"Doesn't bother me." He shrugged, started the engine, and began backing out of the drive. "She doesn't know me from Adam. It's only natural she'd worry about you. I'm glad she cares. Everyone needs someone who cares."

"You speak as if you don't…have anyone that does."

He kept his hands on the wheel and his tone light. "Maybe I don't. At least not anymore. I have a habit of alienating anyone who cares about me."

"So I guess it didn't go so well with your grandparents?" she said softly.

"No, it didn't. I've tried to make amends for my mistakes. I cut all ties to my old life. I even cut my hair as an open act of contrition, but my sacrifices have all been in vain."

"What do you mean you cut your hair? I don't understand the connection."

"In my culture, a man's hair is a source of personal pride. Cutting it is often an act of penance or an expression of profound grief. For me, it was both, but the elders don't easily forgive or forget."

"What about the horse?" she asked.

"Let's just say my grandfather found my gift as lacking as he still finds me."

"I'm so sorry, Keith. I know that must really hurt."

He looked away with a shrug. "I screwed up. I have to accept the consequences."

"Maybe in time…"

His grip tightened on the wheel. "I don't want to talk about it anymore."

Taking his cue, she quickly changed the subject. "You really surprised me, showing up like you did. I still can't believe you came all the way up here. I thought I'd never see you again."

"I didn't think so either," he replied. "But I've thought about you, *Aiwattsi*. Every day. I missed you, but there just didn't seem any point in pursuing it, given the distance."

"Then what changed your mind?"

"You came out here and changed everything. The distance has lessened."

"Yes." She leaned toward him. "Less distance is always good."

He glanced in the rearview mirror to ensure they were out of view from the house, and then put the truck in park. He reached for her hand, twining his fingers with hers. "I have responsibilities I can't shirk, but I couldn't wait to see you…to be with you."

"Me too," she whispered back.

He didn't need any further invitation. He cupped her face, kissing her slowly, lips gently brushing, then hungrily melding. Their tongues tangled. His heart hammered and pulse roared. One kiss had his body almost trembling with want. Until this moment, he hadn't realized just how much he needed this. Needed her. Soon, he reminded himself.

"Keith?" Desire had darkened her eyes to the color of slate. "Did you really mean what you said about getting separate rooms?"

He ran a thumb over her kiss-swollen lips. "I said we *could* get separate rooms. I never promised we would."

Chapter 19

MIRANDA FELT LIKE SHE'D CRAWL OUT OF HER SKIN WITH anticipation as the truck slowly ate up the miles of highway between Montana and Utah. For the past two hours they'd stolen sidelong glances, both outwardly ignoring the sexual tension that electrified the air. They'd carried on sporadic spurts of small talk, while under it all every muscle felt tight and every nerve ending twitchy.

Casting another covert glance, she studied his profile, the high cheekbones, deep-set eyes, strong, masculine nose, and full, sensuous mouth, fixing on the last. Her insides quivering at the thought of those soft and knowing lips, on how he'd used his mouth on her body, on her sex. From the roots of her hair to the tips of her toes, she was hyperaware of him.

"Don't you get lonely, driving as much as you do?" she asked, breaking another long silence.

"Sometimes," he said. "But I've gotten used to it. I've been traveling for a long time. Off and on for eight years."

"I wouldn't think the time would make it any easier. Does it?"

"No. Not really," he confessed.

"Then why did you do it for so long?" she asked. "Did you really like it so much? Traveling all the time?"

"I did in the beginning. I was restless. I loved the freedom of a life on the road. I could do whatever I pleased, and I did. I got to see new places and meet lots of different people, but I soon got caught up in chasing things I thought I wanted—selfish things, material things—everything I was raised to despise. It was a real ego trip in the beginning, especially after my YouTube videos went viral, but I later came to see that I'd created an empty illusion. It was all about my persona, it wasn't really me. They didn't even know *me*."

"But was it really their fault?" she asked. "I mean, how could it be? When you aren't yourself, how can people ever get to know the real you? We see only what others allow us to see. We touch only the parts they allow us to touch." And she ached to touch him now.

He caught her gaze and held it, his mouth curving smugly at the corners, as if reading her lust-filled thoughts. "Soon." He tore his eyes away, murmuring the single syllable almost to himself.

"Soon?" she inquired softly.

"When we arrive," he answered. "I thought we'd overnight in Provo. It's only an hour from Gunnison. We can stay there tonight and pick up the horses in the morning."

She shivered at the thought of another entire night alone with him.

"Do you always stay in motels when you're on the road?" she asked.

"Not always," he replied. "It all depends on where I am and the weather conditions. Sometimes I camp out in the truck bed. I keep an air mattress under the seat, just in case the mood strikes me. I prefer sleeping under the stars."

"I enjoyed it too," she said, then added with a grimace, "except for the mountain lions."

"That was unusual," he replied. "I've never had such a close encounter with one before."

"Just my luck then." She gave a dry laugh. "But it didn't scare me off for good."

"You'd do it again?" he asked, as if surprised.

"Yes. I would. As crazy as it sounds, I'd do it all over again. Maybe I'd even try your roasted rattlesnake."

"Would you now?" His lips curved at the corners.

"Yes. I think I would. I can't explain it very well, but that short trip into the desert was life-changing for me. I found the whole experience liberating. Then again, I suppose that might have a lot to do with my two near-death experiences," she added with a laugh. "I liked the solitude and being away from it all. Even with the discomforts, I think I'd enjoy doing it again."

"If that's the case, there are a number of places I'd like to show you," he said, "beautiful places—awe-inspiring canyons and breathtaking waterfalls—that few people even know about. But these sights are off the beaten track and not easy to get to."

"I'm not daunted. Not with you as my guide."

Their gazes met and held. "I'd gladly be your guide anywhere you choose to go, *Aiwattsi*."

The look in his eyes made his double meaning clear. Her nipples tightened and mouth grew dry. "How much farther?" she asked.

"Three hours, but if nature's calling, we can stop in Pocatello," he said, apparently misreading her impatience. "It's the halfway point. We need gas soon anyway."

A few miles later they pulled off the highway.

While Keith filled the tank, Miranda climbed out of the truck, glad for the chance to stretch her cramped legs and relieve her bladder.

"Hungry?" he asked after paying for the gas.

"Ravenous," she replied, but food wasn't going to satisfy her real hunger. Did he feel it too? She'd thought so earlier, but he seemed so restrained now.

"There's a good diner nearby called Elmer's," he said. "I'll take you there."

As Keith promised, the food was both good and plentiful, but by the time they walked back to the truck, Miranda didn't even remember what she'd eaten. Her mind was too full of Keith, of the night to come. She didn't understand her physical reaction to him. She'd never felt like this with anyone. He reached behind her to open her door, enveloping her in his musky, masculine scent, a scent that had teased her the entire drive. "Three more hours?" she whispered.

Her remark snagged his full attention. "So impatient, *Aiwattsi*?" His expression confirmed that he really could read her mind. "Don't think I haven't also been counting down the hours. My thoughts have been filled with what I want to do with you…to you…from the moment you climbed into this truck."

Her pulse fluttered. "Then why haven't you?"

"Because I have responsibilities. I'm already a day late due to my detour to Montana. I'd planned for us to drive through to Provo and then spend the night together. It was a sensible plan."

"Yes," she agreed, "very sensible."

"It was," he said, stepping into her space. "But I'm liking it less every passing minute." The look in his eyes made her breath hitch. If she'd wondered about his interest, there was no doubt now.

"Is there any alternative to that plan?" she asked.

"There is if you don't mind getting up before the crack of dawn to drive to Gunnison."

"I don't mind," she said. "What do you want to do?" she countered, her eyes searching his.

"What do I want?" His arms caged her on either side, his body pressing hot and hard against hers. "You, *Aiwattsi*. Only you."

They barely made it into their room before his mouth claimed hers, hot, aggressive, and devouring. Mindlessly she flung herself into it. Mouths melding, tongues thrusting and retreating, moans mixing and mingling. Dizzying, devastating, drugging kisses. Searching hands peeled away clothes. Touching, teasing. Sucking and stroking. Agonizing emptiness. Merciless need. Their limbs tangled and entwined.

Restless and writhing, he reached out. Gazes locking. He probed, then pierced hard and deep, shock and pleasure surging, senses swimming. Primal, pulsating pleasure.

Blissful friction. Rasping, ragged breaths. Erotic echoes of slapping flesh.

He plunged and pummeled in a ruthless, relentless rhythm.

Frantic and feverish. Edging them toward ecstasy.

Aching, quaking, quivering. Surging swells and sinuous spasms. Clutching, clawing, clenching, convulsing. Two voices cried out in ravaging release.

Sweating and spent, Keith lay watching Miranda. She opened her eyes to his. Her sleepy gray pools stared back at him and a sated smile gave a soft lift to her mouth. "I don't understand what you do to me," she said. "I've never felt this way with anyone."

Neither had he. He was more comfortable with Miranda than he'd been with anyone in a very long time—maybe ever. He'd hidden himself from others, but he hadn't hidden from her. He didn't want to hold anything back. He wanted her to see him clearly, not as a romantic hero, but exactly as he was, with all his flaws and foibles, to know and accept and trust him as a friend as well as a lover. He reached out to trace her lips with a finger. "Are you content?"

She arched against him with a feline stretch. "Right now I am."

He rolled her on top of him. "Tell me what else makes you happy, *Aiwattsi*."

Her lips twitched. "Besides orgasms?"

"Besides the orgasms *I* give you?" he teasingly corrected.

"I've never known any other kind." She looked down at his chest, tracing a circle around his nipple, her golden brows furrowing. "I've never really thought much about it. I guess my best times have always been spent with the people I love. I was happy when my father was alive. I hardly remember him, but I always feel warm and fuzzy inside when I think of my early childhood. I get the same feeling when I think about the times I spent at my grandparents' ranch. So I guess that's happiness."

"What about your work?" he asked. "Does it make you happy?"

She hesitated. "That's a completely different feeling. It's like magic happens when I capture something special on film, but working for Bibi was all about the money not the magic."

"Are you going back to California?"

"No. I'm not going back," she said resolutely. "I know my options in Montana are extremely limited, but I've thought about this long and hard. I'm going to look for freelance opportunities. Worst-case scenario, I can always fall back on commercials and television work."

"But not filmmaking," he said.

"Probably not, aside from my documentary," she replied sadly. "I thought I wanted to make movies, but that life is all about money, beauty, power, and influence. Who you really are as a person means almost nothing out there. That's not what I want." She looked up, seeking his gaze. "What about you? What makes you happy?"

"This," he said simply. "I like being with you." He wanted to say so much more, but fear kept him in check.

"But what do you want from life?" she asked.

"I don't know," he said. "I'm still trying to figure it out. I've done a lot of soul-searching in the past year, but I still don't have any answers. I don't know what I want or where I'm going beyond here and now."

"Do you intend to keep working for Mitch?"

"I haven't decided," he said. "It's what I'm doing now, but I've quit thinking beyond the present. There's little point when all my needs are met."

"Are they all? Truly?" she asked.

"Yes," he replied. "My needs are very simple—air, food, water, clothing, and shelter. I have all of these."

"But those are just physical needs," she argued. "Life is more than just feeding and clothing the body, isn't it?" Her voice was soft, but her words hit hard.

"The body feeds the soul. Haven't I shown you this? That's all I have to offer you, Miranda. Do you understand that? Only the here and now. If you expect more from me, you'll only be disappointed." He knew it was more than just lust between them, but how long would it last? He didn't know. The last thing he wanted was to hurt her with promises he wasn't sure he could keep.

Her gray eyes grew cloudy, changing the mood as abruptly as a brewing storm changed a sultry summer day. "Why do you say that? How can you know what I expect? Or what I desire?"

"I think I know your desires better than you do," he replied.

She pursed her lips. Her color rose, flushing her pale cheeks to a deep shade of pink. "That isn't what I meant. This is new territory for me too. Please don't make light of it."

"All right then." He crossed his arms over his chest. "Tell me. What would you expect?"

She licked her lips. "My desires in a relationship aren't anything extraordinary. I think I want what everyone wants—companionship, trust, mutual respect, friendship"—her gaze darted to his—"fidelity."

His shrug was purposely careless. "Maybe that's why I've avoided it. I won't live for others, Miranda, and I don't expect anyone else to live to please me."

"But isn't that part of any kind of relationship? A desire to make someone else happy?"

"I've never been able to live up to anyone's expectations," Keith bit back. "I'm done failing. I'm done trying." It was better to be alone than to get hurt.

He knew he'd only sabotaged himself. Was he about to do it again with her? He was beginning to think he already had, but trust came hard. Too hard. With trust there was always a risk of rejection. So he simply didn't take those chances.

"But we all need someone." Eyes locked with his, she whispered, "Please, Keith, tell me what you need and how can I give it to you. Let me touch you. Let me feed your soul."

He froze, heart hammering against his chest, while for long, labored seconds, his mind raced. It was as if she'd reached deep inside him to a place so heavily guarded he'd thought it untouchable. Others had taken from him, but no one had ever really cared what he wanted or needed. But he wasn't ready to let his guard down. Not yet. He couldn't afford to make himself any more vulnerable than he already was.

There was one sure way to end this discussion, and he wasn't beyond using it. He rolled her beneath him. "I told you what I need. Maybe it's time I show you again?"

He kissed her before she could reply. The moment their tongues tangled, his lust roared back to life. He wanted her with an ache that reached deep into his bones, but the ache was more than sex alone could relieve. She'd asked him before if his life was lonely. It was. Lonely, empty, unfulfilled. He hadn't even realized how empty he was until now. Was he damaged beyond repair? Beyond any hope of redemption? He didn't know. It was damned hard to fix what you didn't even know was broken.

He suddenly thought of his cousin's words. *You don't even know who you are anymore, and you won't belong anywhere until you do*. Maybe he had lost his way for a while, but he was trying real hard to find his way back, and Miranda suddenly seemed like a homing beacon.

Let me touch you. Let me feed your soul. How could he tell her she already had?

Chapter 20

MIRANDA SENSED THERE WAS SOMETHING SPECIAL GROWING between them, but how much more of himself was Keith willing to share beyond sex? He'd succeeded in turning her desire against her to stem the flow of questions. Was he already looking for an escape from any emotional entanglements? Would he try to find an excuse to break it off because she was getting too close? Her head roiled with unanswered questions, but the moment their mouths met, her mind blurred to all but the need to feel him inside her again.

Breaking away from her mouth, Keith worked his way down her body. Miranda shut her eyes to scorching sensation lapping at the place between her thighs. Hot. Wet. Slick. His tongue sliding and swirling, every flick and dart eliciting an answering flutter deep inside her. Her arousal shortened her breath, hardened her nipples. Her lungs burned for air. She ached to be filled, the emptiness like a piercing pain. She reached out for him with a needy sound.

Pressure, sweet and steady, answered her prayer.

Probing fingers teased and tormented, wreaking havoc on her senses. Long, lush lashes of his tongue. His lips pressing against her clit, gently squeezing, insistently sucking. Alternating anguish with bliss. Her pulse thudded a pounding drumbeat in her ears as he coaxed her to climax. Her orgasm came slowly, swelling and spreading in low ripples of sensation that left her panting.

He came over her, eyes dilated with desire. She parted her lips in expectation of his kiss and got his fingers instead. Wet. Slick. Scented, like his breath, with the remnants of her climax. He stroked them over her mouth and then reclaimed what he'd given her with lush licks of his hot tongue. Adding tiny flicks and teasing nips, he sucked her lower lip into his mouth and then breached her in a long, slow penetration, stretching, joining her body with his. Eyes locked on hers, he moved inside her, slow and deliberate, every thrust claiming another little piece of her soul. Whether he knew it or not, wanted her or not, she was his. It could never be like this with anyone else.

———～ッ～———

With almost four hours of driving ahead of them, they had to rise well before the sun to make up for the hours they'd spent making love. Although bleary-eyed and sleep-deprived, Miranda didn't regret a minute they'd passed exploring each other, but this morning she once again sensed Keith's withdrawal, could almost see him recoiling into himself.

The silence as they drove was now charged with another kind of tension—uncertainty and unease. It had all happened so fast. They both needed time and space to figure it out. So she gave him space—or as much as the truck cab would allow.

She was glad she'd brought her iPad. At least she could pretend to read. She kept her eyes glued to the screen even as she felt his gaze seeking hers. She wondered what he was thinking but didn't dare ask, knowing any perceived pressure on her part would lead only to further retreat on his.

She wondered why Keith had chosen such a solitary path. Did he keep himself apart purely out of fear of rejection? Freedom and independence were long cowboy traditions. But with freedom and independence often came isolation and loneliness.

She stole another glance at him. Tension sharpened his features, and his hands were tight on the wheel. She was suddenly reminded of the mustang stallion that had leapt out of the holding pen, leaving the others behind, because his freedom was more important than even the familial bonds with his herd mates.

Although he'd tried not to show it, she'd felt his pain when he'd spoken of his family, and partially understood his wariness after the hurt and rejection he'd suffered. There were only three people she'd ever trusted implicitly, and two of them, her father and her grandfather, were both gone. Only Jo-Jo remained.

After a time, the quiet became stifling. "Do you mind if I play some music?" she asked.

"Go ahead," he replied. "The truck doesn't have an MP3 jack, and the radio reception out here is piss poor, so I always carry CDs in the glove box."

Curious to know what kind of music he listened to, she opened it to take a look. She found Iron Maiden, Manowar, and Anthrax on top of the stack. "Wow. I never would have figured you for a metalhead." There was so much she still didn't know about him. They'd jumped into bed so quickly that they hadn't had a chance to truly get to know each other.

He shrugged. "A lot of the metal bands honor Indian culture. Just listen to 'Run to the Hills,' 'Spirit Horse of the Cherokee,' or 'Indians.' Or if you want to hear some hardcore NA death metal, listen to 'Warpath' by Dark Kloud."

"No thanks," she replied. "I prefer to keep my rage bottled. Do you have any music that isn't dark or depressing?" She flipped through a few others in the stack. Staind. Breaking Benjamin, Linkin Park, Seether. "Ah, here's one." She popped Nickelback into the player, skipping to her favorite power ballad. Shutting her eyes, she immersed herself in the music. They arrived in Gunnison without speaking another word.

Although Keith was able to get clearance for her to go inside, the invasive and humiliating body search was unavoidable. Miranda endured it with stoicism. For the next hour she remained inside the truck, while Keith oversaw the loading of twenty-some horses onto the trailer, a process that moved quickly and without incident.

"I'm sorry, *Aiwattsi*," Keith apologized when he climbed back into the cab.

"It's all right. You warned me how it would be."

"Do you regret that you came?" he asked, glancing her way. He posed the question casually, but his shoulders were square and rigid.

"No," she replied. She knew he referred to more than the prison experience. "I don't. Are you sorry you brought me?"

"No, I'm not." His shoulders eased, and his lips curved slightly at the corners, the first hint of a smile she'd seen all day. It was enough to break the remaining tension. "But I am sorry I've been bad company. I've got a lot on my mind."

"It's okay. I understand. Don't feel you have to entertain me. How far is it to Rock Springs?" she asked.

"Less than five hours," he replied, dropping his hat behind the seat.

"What happens after we drop them off?" Keith had told her the horses that had been handled by the inmates had already been shipped to adoption centers. She wondered about the fate of the mares they now transported.

"I'll drive you back to Montana and then return here for another load."

"*Another* one?"

He shook his head with a sigh. "I wish it was only one more."

"What do you mean?"

"Mitch texted me early this morning, asking if I can trailer a load to Colorado and then another one to Arizona. I expected as much when I heard about this situation, but it's still put me in a pissy mood."

"Is *that* why you've been so aloof?"

"Yes. I really don't like this situation."

"Are you going to do it?" she asked.

"I have to," he replied. "It sucks, but it's my job."

"How long do you think it will take to find places to put them all?"

"Weeks? Months?" He shrugged. "Who knows?"

"What about your horse?" she asked. "You never said what you're going to do with the one you adopted. Where is he?"

"My cousin Tonya is looking after him, but it's only temporary. As soon as we've settled the Gunnison horses, I'll probably take him back to the BLM. He'll never be adoptable, so I'm hoping he'll find a permanent home on one of the long-term pastures."

"And then what?" she asked.

"And then nothing. He'll live out his life."

"That sounds so…empty. Aren't you even going to *try* to gentle him?"

"No. His needs will be met."

"His *physical* needs," she stated, once more vividly reminded of Keith.

"What else is there? He's only a horse."

"You don't believe that any more than I do. Wasn't it you who told me they have emotions? Doesn't he deserve more from life?" She couldn't believe he'd just give up on the creature like that. Once more his negative outlook had let her down.

"Maybe we all do, but that doesn't mean we'll get it."

"Why are you so cynical?" she asked.

"I have good reason to be. Why does that horse matter so much to you?" he snapped.

"I don't know. He just does. Why do *I* need a reason?"

He didn't answer. Just stared at the road. She knew he was growing annoyed, but she pressed on. "What are your plans after all this?"

"I know nothing more about my future today than I did yesterday, Miranda. Nothing has changed."

"But it doesn't have to be that way," she insisted. "You *could* change things if you really wanted to."

"How?" he demanded. "I see no path forward, and I can't go back. I'm stuck in this situation whether I like it or not."

"No you aren't. You just refuse to open your mind to new opportunities."

"What do you mean?" he asked.

She'd been chewing on the idea for hours and now saw her chance. "I've been talking to my grandmother about turning the ranch into a mustang sanctuary. She's giving it serious thought and has already made inquiries with the BLM."

"She told me. It's a crazy notion, Miranda."

"Why?"

"Because you know next to nothing about handling those horses."

"Then we'll have to hire someone who does. You said you were interested in ranch work—"

"I'm *not* going to work for you, Miranda."

"Why not? It would be full time, and you wouldn't have to travel anymore."

"Because we're lovers, that's why not. Business and pleasure mix about as well as oil and water. It could only lead to trouble."

"You're being completely unreasonable," she said. "The horses need a home, and Jo-Jo has twenty-six hundred acres of pasture that's going to waste. She'd like to keep the ranch, and I'm willing to do whatever I can to make that happen, but I need help. You know these horses better than anyone except maybe the West family. Please tell me what I'm missing here."

"I already did. I can't work for someone I'm involved with."

"Technically speaking, you'd be working for Jo-Jo, not me," she argued.

"Doesn't matter. Our relationship still makes this whole proposition impossible."

"But you're wrong," Miranda insisted. "This could

be the ideal solution for all of us." The more she considered it, the more convinced she was. "Is our personal relationship your only objection?"

His brows contracted into a deep frown. "I don't need any other reasons. I could probably come up with plenty more if I thought about it long enough, but I'm not about to waste brain cells on the activity."

His body language said it was time to back off, but she'd already committed herself. "Would you consider taking the job if we weren't intimate?"

"This entire discussion is pointless, Miranda. I don't do hypotheticals."

"It's not strictly hypothetical," she said.

His gaze snagged hers. "What are you saying?"

Miranda knew what she was risking. She wondered if taking a step backward was the right answer. Maybe that's what they really needed in order to move forward. Although her body still hungered for Keith, her heart hung in the balance. Until he found what he needed, he'd always hold back. She fingered the bear tooth around her neck and then took a deep breath. "I'm saying that if we didn't sleep together anymore, your entire argument would be moot."

He pulled off the road, put the truck in park, and faced her with gaze narrowed. "Do I understand you right? Are you breaking it off with me?"

"It's not what I want, but maybe it's for the best. You've made it clear you aren't looking for a relationship."

"That doesn't mean I want to end this," he said.

"You can't always have it both ways, Keith. I'm trying to get my life back on track too. I think the mustang sanctuary is the answer for all of us. I'm willing to make a personal sacrifice for the greater good if you won't consider it any other way."

—∞—

Keith cursed under his breath. "I can't fucking believe this." She was mistaken to think he'd take the job if they ended their involvement. Sure it was a valid reason for his refusal, but it wasn't the only one. He resented her attempt to manipulate him into accepting her offer. Rather than persuading him, it only made him balk harder. "I've already told you what I think of all that greater good bullshit."

She stared back at him, looking almost incredulous that he'd refused. "Why? I don't understand why you're so set against the idea. It makes no sense to me."

"I can't be part of this, Miranda. If you're determined to go ahead with this, you'll have to do it without me." He didn't want to be on the road anymore, and he didn't want to be alone, but he'd already compromised his principles too many times. He refused to commit to something he didn't believe in—even for her.

A vision suddenly appeared of the black wolf baring his teeth at the white wolf.

He let out a bitter laugh as his grandfather's words sounded in his brain. *It is not for you to prove anything to me, Two Wolves. It is for you to find your purpose. A man with no purpose is a man with no soul.*

Chapter 21

IT WAS BARELY SIX O'CLOCK WHEN MIRANDA STEPPED ONTO the front porch, she shivered in the chill morning air and then sucked in a cleansing lungful, feeling like she could never get enough of it after her years in the smog-filled San Fernando Valley.

Winter would come soon. The few leaf-bearing trees surrounding the house were nearly barren, and the ground glistened white with frost. Gazing beyond the fenced pastures at the Tobacco Root Mountains, gray and purple shadows capped with white, she was still unable to believe that this was really her new home, her new life.

For weeks, she'd kept herself almost manically busy, preparing the ranch for the horses and making weekly trips to the university film lab to edit. The film had begun to come together in a way she hadn't expected, but Lexi was right that Keith's narration would be the key to its success. Unfortunately, the time had never been right even to ask him. Now she feared she'd never have another chance.

Although he'd been on the road constantly since the trip to Gunnison, her decision about the horses had driven a deep wedge between them. She'd finally accepted his reasons, but still couldn't overcome her profound sense of disappointment. They'd exchanged a few brief phone calls but hadn't seen each other. She realized too late that she'd pushed him too hard. Perhaps if she hadn't, he would have eventually come around. She recalled how the prison inmate had tried to gentle the stallion. He'd slowly closed the distance, hand tentatively outstretched, only to be violently rejected. Keith had explained that a horse with no trust would have to be enticed to make the first move. That was exactly the mistake she'd made with Keith. She wondered wistfully if she'd ever see him again, but knew he had to make the next move.

When she returned to the house after her barn chores, she found Jo-Jo sipping coffee. Miranda shut her eyes to sniff the air and smiled. Cinnamon. Her next favorite after blueberry. She reached under the napkin for a muffin.

"I guess today's a big decision day," Jo-Jo said, handing Miranda the contract she'd received from the BLM the day before. The approval had taken almost a month. Although it felt like eternity, it was lightning fast by government bureaucracy standards. "The agreement looks pretty straightforward," Jo-Jo said, "But Bud never signed anything without due diligence."

"Due diligence?" Miranda asked, perusing the document while slathering a warm, moist peace of heaven with soft, creamery butter.

Jo-Jo snorted. "Just a fancy term for legal fees, but I'd rather pay a lawyer to take a look at this than make a big mistake over something I didn't fully understand."

"I agree," Miranda said between eye-rollingly delicious bites. "How soon do you think you can get someone to review it?"

"I already have an appointment I made weeks ago with Wade Knowlton to talk about some estate-planning concerns. I asked him to take a look at this as well. Would you like to drive into Virginia City with me?"

"Sure, Jo-Jo," Miranda said. "Is the Star Bakery still open? I used to love that place, though their muffins can't compare to yours."

"We can stop there for lunch." Jo-Jo looked at her watch. "My appointment's at nine, so you'd best put a wiggle on it."

Miranda scarfed down the rest of her muffin, and then downed her coffee in three long, scalding swigs. Twenty minutes later she was showered and dressed with purse in hand. Jo-Jo joined her a moment later, contract in one hand and truck keys in the other.

"You want to drive?" Jo-Jo asked.

"We could always take my car," Miranda suggested.

"Sweetheart, that vehicle may be purdy to look at, but it's going to be mighty impractical around these parts."

"I know." Miranda sighed. "I've been thinking the same thing. Once we get everything settled, I'll probably trade it in for something with four-wheel drive."

"Won't you miss it?" Jo-Jo asked.

"I'll get over it. I'll have more than enough mustangs on my hands soon enough."

~~~

"Hello, Jo-Jo. It's been a dog's age. What have you been up to?" A plump woman rose from her desk to greet them with a bright smile.

"Nothing special," Jo-Jo replied. "I think I'd have died of boredom long ago if Miranda hadn't come to save me. Iris, have you met my granddaughter, Miranda?"

Miranda stepped forward, offering her hand. "Nice to meet you, Iris."

"A pleasure," Iris said. "Are you visiting for long?"

"Actually, I'm thinking about settling here and helping Jo-Jo run the ranch."

"You're taking it off the market?" Iris asked Jo-Jo.

"I guess it all depends on the answers Wade gives me to my questions."

"He just ran over to the courthouse and should be back shortly." She looked to the door with a laugh. "Well, speak of the devil!"

Miranda's gaze riveted to the man who'd just entered. Was this the lawyer? Her gaze traveled appreciatively over his tall, lean frame. In boots, jeans, and cowboy hat, Jo-Jo's attorney was hardly the stuffed shirt she'd expected. He was also much younger and far better-looking.

He doffed his hat. "Miz Sutton! I'm so sorry to keep you waiting."

"Hello, Wade. I don't think you've met my granddaughter," Jo-Jo supplied. "She's going to be a famous filmmaker one day. Mark my words on it."

He directed an intense blue gaze at Miranda. Her cheeks heated with embarrassment as his big, warm, and surprisingly callused hand swallowed hers. "It's a pleasure to meet you. Can I offer you ladies some coffee before we get started?"

"No, thank you," Jo-Jo replied. "We're going to have lunch at the Star when we leave."

He flashed a dimpled grin. "Best place in town. Why don't you step on into my office and tell me what I can do for you."

Miranda's gaze wandered over the office as the lawyer reviewed the contract. Jo-Jo had told her that the building had been a bordello in the gold rush days, but little evidence remained. The oak plank flooring was polished to a gleam. The furniture was burgundy studded leather, masculine, soft, and comfortable. One wall was lined with the requisite bookcases, teeming with intimidating legal tomes and a few hunting trophies. A framed watercolor Western landscape hung next to it.

"It all looks clean to me," Wade remarked, handing the contract back to Jo-Jo.

"What do you think of the idea?" she asked.

"It could turn out to be a fairly lucrative arrangement in the end, but ten years is a big commitment. Are you sure you don't want to try to negotiate a shorter term?" he asked.

"I thought about that, but we're taking on only two hundred to start with," Jo-Jo said. "I insisted on that provision to test the waters before I get in over my head."

"That was a smart move," he agreed.

"My real concern is Miranda here," Jo-Jo continued. "Ten years might not seem like a lifetime to someone her age, or yours, but I'm seventy-two. I might not even make it to eighty-two. That's what worries me most about this. I don't want to see her saddled alone with all this responsibility."

"I understand that, Jo-Jo," Miranda said. "But I still want to do it."

"If we go ahead," Jo-Jo argued, "it's gonna tie you to the ranch until you're thirty-six. I have some big concerns about that."

Wade sat back in his chair, fingers steepled. "What are you thinking you'd like to do, Miz Sutton?"

Jo-Jo's faded gray eyes narrowed. "I want to ensure

that Miranda has a way out of this in the event something were to happen to me. Can you do that, Wade?"

"If anything were to happen to you, Miz Sutton, all of
those decisions would automatically fall on your executor. Upon your passing, this agreement could either be
nullified or renewed according to their wishes."

"But what if Aunt Judith wants to sell the place?"
Miranda asked. "You know she would, Jo-Jo."

"Yes. She would," Jo-Jo agreed. "And that's part of the
reason I brought you here. A few weeks ago I instructed
Wade to designate you as the executor of my estate."

Miranda's hand flew to her mouth. "You did?"

"Yes. I rewrote my will," Jo-Jo said matter-of-factly.
"Judith and Robert have no children and no desire to be
saddled with the ranch. Of course, you'll have to work
out some kind of deal with them in the event of my passing. You might have to sell a section of the land, but all
decisions regarding the ranch proper will yours."

"You're willing the ranch to me?" Miranda repeated
incredulously. "Jo-Jo. I don't know what to say."

"Can I take off my lawyer hat and voice a personal
concern?" Wade asked.

"Sure," Jo-Jo replied.

"I'm just wondering how you two ladies are going
to manage this all by yourselves. I think you'll need
some help."

"Hiring someone will be my next move after we sign
the contract," Jo-Jo said. "The revenue generated from
the horses should be enough to pay someone."

"It should be more than sufficient," he agreed. "Do
you have anyone in mind?"

"I know someone who has experience with

mustangs," Miranda said, "but I haven't yet been able to talk him into it." Although Keith was the best candidate, they'd hardly spoken in weeks, not that she put much faith in changing his mind. She hated how they'd parted, but she'd promised herself not to repeat her mistake. She was waiting for him to reach out to her. Problem was, he still hadn't.

"Ranching is a very small world," Wade said. "Mind if I ask who it is?"

"His name is Keith Russo, but he also goes by Two Wolves," Miranda replied. "His family has a horse-leasing outfit outside Riverton, Wyoming."

Wade's gaze narrowed. "How do you know Keith?"

"I met him first in California where he was doing a horse clinic, and then again in Nevada when I was filming a wild-horse roundup. Do you know him?" she asked Wade.

"Not personally," he replied. "But I saw him years ago when he used to do his wild-horse routine at the rodeos. He did some pretty amazing things with that horse, but I don't know if he was really the one who trained it or not."

"He was," Miranda said. "I heard the whole story. Plus I saw him with those mustangs. He was amazing."

"I'm not saying anything against the man," Wade said carefully. "I just don't know if you could count on him."

"The question is moot at this point," Miranda said. "He isn't interested in the job."

"Then I'd be glad to put the word out for you, maybe even help screen some ranch hands. My brother Dirk and I know a lot of cowboys around these parts."

"That's very kind of you," Jo-Jo said. "We just may take you up on that."

"Are you ready to move forward on this, or do you need some time to think about it?" Wade asked.

Miranda eyed her grandmother.

"I don't guess there's anything more to discuss," Jo-Jo said.

Wade leaned forward, handing her a ballpoint pen. "If there are no questions, all I need is your signature on that line right there."

"No. No questions." Jo-Jo's voice was resolute. Miranda's pulse raced as her grandmother plied pen to paper and scratched her signature.

⁓⁓⁓

"My lawyer's quite a hottie, isn't he?" Jo-Jo remarked with a coy look. "They say he's the most eligible bachelor in the whole Ruby Valley."

"I admit he wasn't at all what I expected," Miranda confessed. "But you're wasting your time if you're trying to play matchmaker, Jo-Jo. I'm not looking for a relationship."

Jo-Jo pursed her lips. "Still hung up on that Keith?"

Miranda sighed. "There's just something about him, Jo-Jo. When I first met him, I thought he was a phony and a womanizer, but that's not who he is at all. It was just this persona he'd created. I really care about him, but I'm also very confused."

"I thought his interest in you was pretty obvious," Jo-Jo said, "but his actions prove he's not someone you can rely on." She hesitated, brows furrowed. "I don't know if a man like that is any good for you."

"Why do you say that?" Miranda asked, suddenly defensive.

"You hear nothing from him for weeks, and then he shows up out of the blue. Next, he disappears again. A woman needs a man who's going to be there for her through thick and thin."

"That's not his fault, Jo-Jo. It's his job that's taken him away."

"A job he doesn't believe in?" Jo-Jo said. "Makes me wonder about his character."

"He doesn't have a defective character, Jo-Jo. He's just trying to figure out what he wants from life. A lot of people feel lost at different times in their lives. Just like me, he's been struggling, but unlike me, he's estranged from those he cares most about."

Jo-Jo's gaze narrowed. "Why is he estranged?"

"His grandparents think he exploited his heritage. He wants to reconcile with them, but it's a really complicated situation. They're still angry about some things they didn't approve of and won't let him come back home."

"It's called tough love, Miranda. Sometimes we have to make things unpleasant for those we love in order for them to see the light."

"I know, but I really hurt for him. I think part of his refusal to work here is that deep down he wants to be a part of something and not just hired help. That's what he really needs, Jo-Jo. To belong."

"Don't we all?" Jo-Jo said.

Their conversation paused as the waitress appeared with two huge slices of chocolate cream pie. Miranda rolled her eyes in bliss with the first bite. "It's not *quite* as good as yours, but pretty darned close."

"Not even close," Jo-Jo said. "I'll prove it to you this Thanksgiving. I'm glad you'll be here this year. I spent all three holidays last year with Robert and Judy in Phoenix, but I'd much rather have been at home. I enjoyed seeing them, but six weeks was far too long, especially since we spent so much of it looking at condos in retirement communities."

"Is that what you want?" Miranda asked in surprise. "To move to Phoenix with them?"

"It's what *they* want, but not exactly *with* them. All the places they took me to were at least twenty minutes away from their house."

"I'm speechless, Jo-Jo."

"You don't have to say a word, sweetheart. It's true that actions speak louder, and that trip told me everything I needed to know. They don't want me in their lives, they just want control. Judith invited me down again this year, but I'm not going. If they want to celebrate Thanksgiving as a family, they'll have to come up here. If they don't come, that's just fine with me. The two of us will spend it together."

"I haven't had a real Thanksgiving in ages," Miranda said. "I spent it alone for three out of the four years I was in California. Last year was the only exception. I was invited to dinner with some of Lexi's friends, but it didn't feel much like Thanksgiving."

"Why's that?"

"They were Buddhist vegetarians, so there wasn't even a turkey. We ordered takeout Thai food instead."

Jo-Jo's eyes widened. "*Thai food* for Thanksgiving?"

Miranda laughed. "Yup. Pretty much anything goes in L.A. They aren't so big on tradition there, but I'm a

SADDLE UP   215

traditional girl. That's another reason I didn't fit. I'm glad to be here with you this year."

"So you still don't have any regrets about leaving?"

"No, Jo-Jo. I don't. I thought I might when I told Bibi I wasn't coming back, but I have perfect peace about it. Helping those horses makes me feel like I'm finally doing something right with my life. I feel like it's what I was meant to do."

"You once felt that way about your filmmaking," Jo-Jo reminded her.

"Filmmaking was all about me and my desires. This is so much bigger than just me. I haven't given up on films completely, but right now I feel like I can make a difference, and I *want* to make a difference, Jo-Jo."

"I think you know by now that I'll always support whatever you do, as long as your heart is invested," Jo-Jo said.

"It is." Miranda added wistfully, "I just wish Keith's was as well."

"I guess we'll have to take Wade up on his offer to help us find someone," Jo-Jo said.

"Yeah. I guess so," Miranda reluctantly agreed. It was so frustrating to think how Keith chose to waste his talents.

"When we're finished here, we should also go and take a look at some used equipment. With winter coming on, we're going to have to feed a lot of hay to those mustangs. I think we might need a bale splitter. I wish I hadn't already sold ours, but I didn't think I'd ever need one again. I'm hoping we might be able to rent one."

"Shouldn't we wait until we hire someone to help us?" Miranda asked.

"I suppose we could," Jo-Jo agreed. "I've just become used to doing everything myself. To be honest, now that you're doing my morning chores, I'm not even sure how to occupy my time."

"That's probably a good thing. You've worked hard for a lot of years. You should do something for yourself now, Jo-Jo. Something you enjoy."

"You mean like reading, knitting, or needlework?" Jo-Jo rolled her eyes. "I've tried all of those things over the years, but never could sit still long enough to do any of them."

"Then maybe you need to find something more active? How about a yoga class?"

"Yoga? Sweetheart, I've had no reason to put my legs around my neck since Bud passed on."

"Jo-Jo!" Miranda squealed.

"Don't look so scandalized." Jo-Jo laughed. "I'll have you know I've read the *Kama Sutra* cover to cover." She added with a wink, "You gotta spice things up from time to time when you're with the same man for fifty-some years."

Miranda wondered what it would be like to grow old with someone. She immediately thought of Keith. But what future could there be for two people who wanted completely different things?

Chapter 22

"IT'S BEEN BRUTAL THESE PAST WEEKS," MITCH SAID, "BUT I don't see it getting better any time soon. We're taking off the next few months, but come spring, we'll almost certainly be going back to Nevada."

"You'll be doing it without me this time," Keith said, closing the steel door behind the last horse and then proceeding to unhook the trailer. After six weeks and eighteen trips, carrying over three hundred horses as far west as California and as far south as Oklahoma, he was weary and more than ready to retire from driving. "I'm done traveling. All I want now is to lay my head down at night and remember where I am the next morning."

Mitch clapped him on the shoulder. "Can't blame you for that, but it's even better when you have someone keeping the sheets warm for you." He winked. "So what's your plan?"

"Don't know yet. I'm hoping I'll figure it out soon."

"I hear Miranda Sutton's convinced her grandmother to take on some mustangs," Mitch said. "The BLM just approved it."

"How many?"

"They're starting with two hundred, but plan to take more next year if it all works out."

Keith shrugged. "Miranda Sutton's gonna do whatever she wants, no matter how ill-advised it might be."

"Why do you say that? It could turn out to be a good deal all around," Mitch said.

Keith shook his head. "It's more than two women can handle, especially with one in her seventies and the other who knows almost nothing about ranching and even less about mustangs. Hopefully, they'll have the good sense to hire someone who does."

"It ain't rocket science, Keith. Miranda's a smart girl. She'll figure it out, but I do know they've been looking for some help. She called me a couple of days ago to check references on a wrangler that used to work for me."

"What'd you tell her?"

"I said he had too much cowboy attitude and was rough with the stock. I also told her I knew someone else who'd be perfect for the job." He gave Keith a pointed look. Mitch obviously wasn't aware that he and Miranda had called it quits.

"She already asked, and I refused," Keith said. Not that he hadn't had second thoughts about it afterward. He had. Several times during the countless hours of staring down a never-ending highway he'd almost called her back about the offer, but he just couldn't bring himself to pick up the phone and dial her.

"They need your help," Mitch said.

"She ignored all my advice," Keith groused. That was one more thing that stuck in his craw—that she'd moved forward without even talking to him about it. They'd spoken only a couple of times in the past month. Miranda was determined to go her way, so he had no choice but to go his. "Their timing sucks to be doing this. I don't know why she couldn't have at least waited until spring. They're going to need to truck in a shit-ton of hay to get the horses through winter, a huge up-front expense they wouldn't have had if Miranda wasn't so damned hardheaded."

"Given the dire situation, I'm sure the BLM can be persuaded to bring in the first load of hay," Mitch said. "After that, I can help them find a good price. I buy all mine from a big alfalfa grower down in New Mexico. I can maybe hook them up."

"I'm sure they'd appreciate it."

"Maybe you should reconsider that job, Keith. Although I'd hate to see you go, I can't think of anyone better suited to help them get this thing off the ground. God knows we need to find more homes for these horses."

And Keith really wanted to get back to ranch work. It was true that they needed experienced help, and he needed a break. Even the chores he used to despise most—posthole digging and pulling wire—suddenly seemed more appealing than his current situation.

"All right, Mitch. I'll make the damned call." Snatching out his phone, Keith punched the number. Four rings later, her voice mail picked up. "Miranda? It's Keith. If you're still looking for help, I'm available to get everything set up to bring the horses in. You can reach me at this number until tomorrow."

He didn't know if she'd even call him back after the way things had ended. It wasn't an ugly breakup; they just hadn't seen eye to eye. Was it really over between them? He'd soon find out.

~~~

Miranda awoke with a strange feeling of anticipation. She threw back the handmade quilt and snatched her robe from the bedpost, shivering as her feet hit the icy floorboards. She then peered out the frost-etched window. As forecasted, a light dusting of snow had fallen during the night, just enough to give everything a magical glow in the early morning light. It was a breathtaking scene that filled her with dismay. Winter was right around the corner, and they were miles of fence from ready.

After dressing and swigging down her coffee, Miranda snatched a second muffin from the basket and stomped into the pair of rubber muck boots sitting beside the kitchen door. Mug in hand, she nearly skipped toward the workshop-cum-stable. She'd finally begun to adapt to her new schedule since she'd insisted on taking over the morning ranch chores. Although she hated rising with the sun, she loved the warm nickers from Jesse and Doc when she appeared every morning with their feed buckets.

After the horses finished their breakfast, she led them out to pasture, and then turned her hand to mucking out the manure from their stalls. It was messy, smelly work, but she loved the earthiness of it. In truth, there was nothing on the ranch that she'd ever really minded doing. She wondered if that would change in time.

Returning after her morning chores, she found a missed call from Keith. She'd almost given up on ever hearing from him again. Although they'd spoken on the phone a couple of times, they hadn't seen each other since their fateful trip to Gunnison. Her pulse raced as she played his terse voice mail. She didn't know what had brought about his change of heart, but it didn't matter. Even with their differences, there was still no one else she'd rather hire. Her heart clogged her throat as she hit redial. Three rings, and he answered. "Hello? Keith? It's Miranda."

"I know your voice, *Ai*—Miranda."

The sound of *his* sent a warm ripple down her spine until she realized he'd reverted back to her real name. Had he done it intentionally to create more distance? The idea stung.

"I just got your message," she said. "You've changed your mind?"

"If the offer is still open," he said.

"It is. We've been approved to take two hundred horses and have been looking for someone to help us. I'm certain Jo-Jo will agree that you're the best person. We can pay you a salary based on a percentage of the per diem we receive, plus room and board. There's a cabin you can have all to yourself. And you can even bring your horse with you. It's not a lot, but at least you won't have to live on the road anymore."

"The offer is more than generous," he said, "But I won't accept your money."

"What do you mean you won't accept it?"

"I don't need your money. I'll come because you need the help."

"I don't understand you at all, Keith, but I'm not about to refuse. There's a lot to be done before winter sets in. Thankfully, we don't need to do all the fencing right away, just enough to accommodate the first two hundred horses. How soon can you come?"

"I'll drive up tomorrow." A long silence followed. "I need to make something clear up front, Miranda. My feelings about all of this haven't changed. I'll help you with your fences and getting everything ready, but I won't be staying on once the horses are settled."

Her stomach dropped with disappointment. "Oh. I see."

"Knowing I'll stay only a few weeks, do you still want me to come?" he asked.

"Yes," she replied softly. "I still want you to come."

"All right then. I'll be there by noon."

When Keith hung up, Miranda felt more confused than ever. She was disappointed at his lack of enthusiasm, but refused to allow it to mar her happiness. Although his feelings about her pet project hadn't changed, his actions told her that he still cared for her. There was no other explanation for his call, and that alone gave her reason to hope it wasn't over between them.

After showering and changing, she went back downstairs to find Jo-Jo sitting in her grandfather's old La-Z-Boy with a big tangle of yarn in her lap. "What are you doing?" Miranda asked.

Jo-Jo scowled over the reading glasses perched on her nose. "Taking your advice and trying to knit, but making a huge muddle of it. To hell with this! You can't teach an old dog new tricks." She tossed the tangle to Miranda. "Maybe you can figure it out and show me."

Miranda caught the yarn with a laugh. "I'll have to check and see if there's an app for knitting."

"You think a computer is going to teach you to knit?" Jo-Jo asked.

"Why not?" Miranda replied. "There's an app for almost everything these days. I came down to tell you there's no need to make that phone call to Wade."

"Why's that?" Jo-Jo asked.

"Because I just heard from Keith. He's coming to help." She couldn't hide her giddy grin. "He said he'll be here around noon tomorrow."

"Well, that's quite a turnaround," Jo-Jo remarked dryly.

"Maybe not," Miranda said, her smile fading. "He's not planning to stay after we bring the horses in."

"How do you feel about that? Do you still think he's the right one?"

"Yes. There's no one better to help us, Jo-Jo."

"I just hope you and he can manage to work together," Jo-Jo said skeptically.

"I'm sure we can, Jo-Jo. Keith's extremely competent. You won't be disappointed with him."

"It's not my disappointment I worry about, Miranda Josephine. It's yours."

―∿∿―

"Here's your phone back, Mitch," Keith said. "Looks like I won't be needing it anymore."

"So you're going to take the job after all?" Mitch asked.

Keith shrugged. "I'll help them get started, but I don't plan to stay."

"That so?" Mitch cocked a brow. "I've got a notion you might feel differently after you get there."

"I won't be changing my mind. I'm only helping them out to prevent a disaster. I'll be back in Wyoming in a couple of weeks."

"If that's the case, you might as well hold onto the phone. You can give it back when you return."

Keith pocketed the phone. "Thanks, Mitch."

"When do you leave?"

"I'm heading out tomorrow."

"Then I'll text you that contact for the hay. Do they need anything else besides forage?"

"Not that I'm aware of. She said everything seems to be in good shape, other than needing to upgrade the fence."

"What about saddle horses?" Mitch asked. "Need any of those?"

The suggestion gave Keith pause. He recalled how much Miranda enjoyed riding. She'd told him that her grandmother had sold all the riding horses and kept only a couple of old retirees. Although most outfits had long ago switched to ATVs for most of the real work, it seemed a shame for her to be living on a ranch with no horse to ride. "What do you have?" Keith asked.

"How about a coupla mares?" Mitch suggested. "Sadie's fully recovered from her leg injury, and I've got a filly of hers that might suit you well enough."

"You looking to sell or lease them?" Keith asked.

"Neither. You can take them as a gift," Mitch offered. "I've got too many that aren't earning their keep. Might as well reduce the herd before winter."

Why not take the two mares? Keith had already decided to bring the mustang he'd intended for his grandfather— the one he hadn't been able to bring himself to return to BLM even after it had failed to win Kenu's favor. Since he'd now resigned himself to keeping the renegade, it was past time to teach him some manners. Working with the horse would also be the best way to keep himself occupied and his hands off Miranda—if he didn't get himself killed first. Then again, in that event, he wouldn't have to worry about keeping his hands off Miranda anymore. Just being near her again would be a huge temptation, one he wasn't sure he'd be able to resist.

Chapter 23

MIRANDA WAS SITTING ON THE FRONT-PORCH SWING WHEN Keith pulled into the yard. She tossed her iPad down and descended the steps, her pulse skittering as she walked toward his truck. By the time he'd parked, her heart was racing like she'd run a marathon. What would she say? Would it be awkward now? She hoped not. She really wanted it to work out between them. She needed this to succeed for all of their sakes.

He climbed out of the cab, greeting her with a tip of his hat and a tentative smile. Clearly, he felt as uncomfortable as she did.

"Hi, Keith." She stopped abruptly, an arm's length away. "Did you have a good trip?" she greeted him lamely, feeling twice as uneasy as she'd imagined.

"It was long," he replied. "I'm happy not to do it again for a while…I'm even happier to see you."

"I…um…*we're both* really glad you came," Miranda said. "I was half-afraid you'd change your mind."

His black eyes captured and held hers. "I don't make many promises, Miranda, but I always keep the ones I make."

She could see he was trying, but it still seemed impossible to just pick up where they'd left off. It would take some time to find their footing with each other again.

"Jo-Jo asked me to apologize for not being here to welcome you. She had to run into town for some groceries. I'll warn you ahead of time that she's a fantastic cook, as long as you don't follow a low-fat diet."

"Are you kidding?" His chuckle sliced the tension. "I grew up on fry bread. It's cooked in Crisco."

"Then you should love Jo-Jo's cooking. I've gained five pounds already. If I'm not more careful, I'm going to have to buy some bigger clothes."

"You look good to me," he said, his eyes raking appreciatively over her. "I think ranch life must suit you."

"Thanks. You look good to me too." He was dressed in his customary faded jeans and a worn denim jacket, but Keith would look good in a burlap sack. "Um, how do you want to do this?" she asked.

He nodded to the trailer behind his truck. "How about we start by unloading the horses?"

"Horses?"

"Yes. I brought three. The two mares are a gift for you...from Mitch," he quickly clarified. "You may have to check fences and might need to ride out among the herd from time to time, so we hoped they'd be useful to you. One of them is Sadie, the horse you rode in Nevada."

"I remember her. She was a great little horse." Miranda gave a gleeful squeal. "Wow. I can't believe this. I don't even know what to say."

"Say you'll accept them."

"Of course I will! That's so generous of you... of Mitch. I can't even tell you how badly I've missed riding since I've been here."

"I also brought Blue Eye."

"Blue Eye? The mustang you adopted? You didn't take him back?" she asked in surprise.

"No, I didn't," he replied. "We'll need to keep him separated from the mares and any other horses you have, at least until I've decided what to do with him."

"What do you mean by that?" she asked. "Aren't you going to train him?"

He shrugged. "If he'll be trained. Some refuse."

"Horses are a lot like people, aren't they?" Her gaze sought his. "You have to earn their trust."

"Yes," he agreed. "But trust comes much easier to some than to others."

She knew he wasn't just speaking of the horse.

"There shouldn't be any problem keeping them apart," she said. "We have a large, round pen we can put him in. It's where I learned to ride."

"Is there room to back the trailer up to it?" he asked. "The trailer is partitioned, with the mares together in the front and him in the back, so I have to get him off first."

"Yes. There's plenty of room."

Miranda showed him to the small corral. A few minutes later he backed up flush against the gate. "You'll need to stand on the other side of the panel and out of his way," he instructed. "I still don't trust this horse any farther than I can throw him."

"Even now?" she asked.

"Yes. Even now. The chemical castration was ineffective. I have a good hunch they tried the drugs on him because no vet cared to risk his life cutting him. He's aggressive as hell. I've been on the road so much that I haven't had time yet to teach him any manners, but at least he's accustomed to fencing. I doubt he'll try to go through it, and hope he can't get over it."

He opened the gate to the pen and then moved to

release the trailer door. In a few swift and efficient movements, he released the latch and stepped behind the door. The horse stuck his head out, made some low grunting sounds, craned his neck, and raised his upper lip, but made no move to get off the trailer.

"Why isn't he getting out?" Miranda asked.

"I'm guessing he doesn't want to leave the mares."

"What's that funny thing he's doing with his lip?"

"It's called flehmen. Horses have a special olfactory organ located above the roof of the mouth. Raising the lip helps a stallion to determine if a mare's in season for breeding. It's the wrong time of year, as mares only cycle from spring to early fall, but that won't stop him from hoping he has a chance. Gelding him is the only sensible thing to do. Keeping him intact is only going to frustrate the hell out of him."

As if on cue, the horse looked Keith's way with a glare and a snort.

"Horses get sexually frustrated? Like we do?"

"They do," he replied slowly, maybe even cautiously. "A stallion's sex drive is a powerful force."

"He's so proud and full of himself," Miranda said. "I love watching him."

"He's full of himself all right," Keith remarked dryly.

"How are you going to geld him if nobody can go near him?"

"It'll probably take a tranquilizer gun to get the job done."

"Will it really help his behavior?"

"It should, but who knows. He's already had large doses of medication to lower his testosterone, but he still thinks he's a stud. Sometimes it takes a while for the testosterone levels to drop, but he should have already settled down."

She nodded to the stallion. "He's still not getting off the trailer. What are you going to do?"

He leaned back against the corral panels, propping a boot heel on the steel rail. "I'll give him a few more minutes to figure things out before I interfere. Would you do me a favor and grab the bungee cord out of my truck?"

"Sure? Where exactly is it?"

"Under the passenger seat."

When Miranda returned, Keith used the bungee to secure the trailer door to the corral panel. He then climbed over the corral, dropping to the ground beside her. They stood watching the wary stallion, who still evinced no desire to leave the trailer.

It was the closest they'd been to each other in a long time, and his proximity hit her hard. Any resolution she had to keep things on a professional level melted that moment. Fifteen minutes in his company already had her aching for his touch. How could she ever last a whole week? A day? Even another hour? Miranda suddenly felt a lot like that horse. Now that Keith was here, it was impossible *not* to think about being with him again. Did he feel it too? Did he still want to be with her?

"This is a real nice place." He nodded to the house and surroundings, still revealing nothing of his thoughts. "I didn't really get to see it last time I was here."

"It's been my grandmother's home for over fifty years," Miranda replied. Now that he'd set the tone, she had no choice but to follow suit with inane small talk. "It's also where my grandfather grew up. His parents

homesteaded the place during the depression. They
came out West and never looked back."

"You sound like you're happy here," he remarked.

"I am. I never could have imagined doing anything
like this, but everything just seems to have led to it."

"There isn't any chance I can still talk you out of it,
is there?" he asked.

"No, Keith. The deal is signed. I couldn't back out
even if I wanted to, but I don't want to. I'm even hoping
you'll come to see this as a good thing."

"That's doubtful," he said.

The two old geldings grazing in the pasture suddenly
caught the stallion's attention. He blew out a loud snort
and leapt off the trailer to charge down the fence line,
neck arched and ears flat. Keith sprang into action, closing the trailer door and then the corral gate to lock him in.

"We need to be very careful to keep him away from
them." He nodded to Jesse and Doc. "Blue Eye is going
to see any other male as a threat to his harem. There
wouldn't be an issue if there weren't any mares around,
but once mares are in the mix, a stud horse can be a real
pain in the ass to keep. It probably would have been
better if I'd brought geldings instead of mares. It also
wouldn't be a bad idea to keep the mares separate from
your geldings, just in case this guy should get out."

"It shouldn't be any problem. There's plenty of room
here. The ranch has two corrals and over two thousand
acres of pastures."

~~~

After they unloaded and fed all the horses, Miranda
showed Keith around the ranch. Even though he'd come

with the best of intentions, his resistance was slipping fast. It had taken him less than five minutes to realize he'd only been fooling himself to think he could ever maintain a platonic relationship with Miranda. He'd been fighting the urge to touch her from the moment he climbed down from his truck.

"Do you want to see the bunkhouse now?" she asked.

"Sure. Let me just grab my stuff."

Walking side by side, he noticed her long strides perfectly matched his. He didn't stifle the impulse to rest his hand on her lower back. She glanced up at him, her gray eyes flickering. He broke the contact only to grab his two bags. His hungry eyes were glued to her shapely little denim-clad ass as he followed her to the bunkhouse. His thoughts and emotions were jumbled as she fumbled with the lock. His resolution was already weakening.

She opened the door to the single-story split-log cabin and beckoned him inside. "It's not much, but I hope you'll feel at home here. This is the living area. We cleaned the place and aired it out last week, and replaced all the linens. There's a fridge, microwave, and coffee pot in the kitchenette, but we're happy to feed you over at the house."

He gave the room a cursory inspection. It was sparsely furnished, just an overstuffed sofa, end table, a television, and a recliner. There was a multipurpose wood-burning stove between the living room and kitchenette. It was more than adequate for his needs.

She turned to face him, her expression soft and inviting. "I really mean that, Keith. I want you to feel welcome here. Your coming means more than I can say."

"I already told you not to read too much into it," he

replied brusquely. "I'm not a convert to your 'save the mustangs' campaign, Miranda."

"But you *are* here," she countered. "I think I'm reading that part right enough."

"I'm here for *you*," he said.

"Is that so?" she whispered. "Then what are you waiting for?"

The look in her eyes was a blatant invitation, but Keith still resisted. "I told you before that it's a bad idea to mix business with pleasure."

"But you didn't want the paycheck, did you?" she countered softly.

"No. I don't need your money," he said.

"Since you refused my offer of payment, technically this isn't a business arrangement, is it?" She toyed with a golden curl. "The way I see it, it's more like a friend doing a favor for a friend."

"Even so, if this is going to work out, we need to set some ground rules and abide by them."

"Should I show you the rest?" she asked, ignoring his remark. "The bedroom used to have two sets of over-sized bunks," she said. "We've replaced those with a full-size bed. I think you'll find it quite comfortable." She licked her lips. "Do you want to see it?"

He hesitated. The last thing he needed was to be alone with her in a bedroom. It wasn't that he didn't want her. He did, maybe too much, and that was the root of the problem.

"I'm not so sure we should go in there. If we do, there's no turning back again." If they continued down this path, all his good intentions would soon be nothing more than the paving stones to hell.

She tipped her chin to meet his eyes. "But I don't want to turn back. We've had too much of that already. I want us to move forward again. The real question is, do you?"

"I've already told you I can't make any promises. I don't know what my future holds."

"I don't care about the future," she said. "Why not concentrate on the present and hold *me*?"

He dropped his bags with a thump, freeing his hands to clasp her waist. Hers crept up his chest to loop around his neck. They stood like that, body to body, heartbeat to heartbeat for long, silent seconds.

"Keith? When the time is right, how do they go about it?"

He shook his head with a look of confusion. "How does who go about what?"

"The stallion and mare," she said. "How does she let him know that she's receptive?"

"If she's not in season, she'll either show no interest in him at all or try to kick his teeth out. If he knows what's good for him, he behaves like a gentleman until he's clearly invited."

She took his hand, leading him toward the next room. "What happens once he knows she's interested?" she asked. "Does he just climb on top of her and go at it, or is there some kind of mating ritual?"

Her question took him off balance, but the glimmer in her eye brought instant understanding. *Hell yeah*. He could certainly get into this game. "A good stallion woos his mare."

"He woos her?" Her brows rose. "How?"

"It's really not so different from our foreplay." He

dipped his head close to her ear. "He begins by seducing her with sounds."

"He whispers sweet nothings?"

"More like murmurs nasty somethings," he replied darkly. "Mares like trashy talk. It excites them."

Her pupils flared. "What kinds of things does he say?"

"I suppose he tells her how excited he is, how much she turns him on. He probably doesn't have to say much more than that. Being well hung and turned on probably works in his favor," he added with a teasing smile.

He slid his hands from her waist and over her hips to cup her ass. He was already hard as a post. He rocked his pelvis into hers. The surprise in her eyes said she knew it.

"Does she get more turned on knowing he's big enough to satisfy her, or just knowing how much he wants her?" she asked, her breaths coming shorter.

"Both."

"Wh-what about him? What gets him excited?"

"Mainly her scent. When he senses her receptiveness, the courtship moves on to smelling." He dipped his head to hers, breathing in a teasing hint of her. "The most powerful aphrodisiac to a stallion is the smell of an aroused mare. It's almost a drug."

He then nuzzled her throat and hair, filling his lungs with her. Miranda arched her neck with a little sigh, giving him better access. She shivered lightly as he moved up her neck to her ear.

"What's next?" she asked. Her pale face was tinted a rosy shade, and her eyes had darkened to slate.

"The stallion and mare begin touching noses and sniffing each other. They then progress to nibbling and licking," he murmured into her honeysuckle-scented hair.

"Are you saying that horses *kiss* each another?"

"Yes." He skimmed his mouth over her face and hovered inches from her lips. "I guess you could call it that, although he does most of it."

"Are there certain places the mare likes him to kiss her?"

"Yes, *Aiwattsi*," he replied. "He begins with her face." He cupped hers, brushing his lips softly from cheekbone to cheekbone, across her nose, and then back to her lips. "He licks and nibbles until he senses that she wants more."

She raised her hands to his head, guiding him toward her softly parted lips. He accepted her offering with a long and leisurely kiss. Lips melding, teeth nipping, tongues tangling, he took his time, exploring every sweet inch of her mouth. She arched into him with little moans and sighs. He deepened the kiss, skirting his hands downward to grip her hips, molding them tightly to his.

He released her to unbutton her blouse. "He works his way down her body, nuzzling, nipping, and licking her. All of this excites both the stallion and the mare." Kissing, licking, and softly biting her soft, sweet flesh, he worked down her body, taking his time to slowly peel away the rest of her clothes, down to her lacy white underthings. He slowly removed her panties and knelt to pay proper homage, delving into her with his tongue, teasing and tasting until his mind blurred with blinding lust. She tried to squirm away, but he held her hips firm, fingering and licking until she was shaking and panting.

He pulled away with a smirk. "By the time he's done licking her, she's ready for him to mount."

"How?" she asked breathlessly.

"From behind. It's the only way with horses."

"Don't some people like it that way as well?" she asked.

"Yes," he replied, wondering what she was getting at. "It's particularly pleasurable for men."

"Why?" she asked, reaching for his belt.

"Because men are visually stimulated. We like to watch. And some men are especially aroused by a woman's ass."

She arched a brow. "What about you, Keith? Do *you* like to watch?"

"I do. And I've always loved your ass. You have no idea what you do to me, *Aiwattsi*. I hope you know what you're doing now. You've led my mind down a path that my body wants to follow."

"I want whatever you want." Her expression was an irresistible combination of innocence and seduction as she backed toward the bed. "I want you to show me what you want."

He followed her with his eyes as he undressed, his gaze slowly devouring her—from the red-gold curls cascading down her shoulders and over her erect pink nipples, to her smooth pale belly, her golden nest, and then down her long, slender legs to her pale pink toenails and back up again. "Are you sure? I won't be gentle," he warned.

She eyed his erection and then replied, "I don't want or need gentle. I want you, Keith."

It was all he needed to hear. He shoved a hand into his pocket to retrieve his wallet and the lone condom he hoped was still there. His hands shook as he gloved himself.

"Turn around," he commanded. "Spread your legs."

Hardly giving her a chance to comply before grabbing her hips, he spun her around. Holding her hip with one hand, he glided the other between her legs. She clamped her thighs together on a hiss, trapping his hand in her sex. He shut his eyes on a groan as her hot, wet heat greeted his fingers.

"You're very wet," he murmured, his mouth playing on her shoulder.

"And you're very hard," she rasped, letting out a little moan as he pressed his erection against her ass while simultaneously stroking and caressing her clitoris.

"I've had a raging hard-on since you started this whole damned breeding discussion."

"That *was* the idea," she confessed with a giggle.

"I should punish you for that. Maybe I will. Maybe I'll make you beg for it."

"Maybe you'll beg first," she rejoined, arching her back and teasing him with her ass.

He squeezed his lids shut on a groan. *Holy shit.* Maybe she was right.

"Keith? What happens once the stallion knows the mare is ready for him?"

"She spreads her legs and lifts her tail. Bed. Now," he growled, throbbing with the need to penetrate. "I want you on your elbows and knees."

She climbed up onto the mattress, presenting herself, ass raised. The vision of her pale round globes and glistening pink sex were almost more than he could take.

"Now what?" she asked, looking over her shoulder.

"He mounts her by taking hold of the back of her neck with his teeth, and penetrates." Sliding between her legs into liquid silk, he began rhythmically rocking his hips, coating himself in her sweet, wet heat. She let out a gasp as he simultaneously sank his teeth into her shoulder and pierced her. "Is this what you wanted?" he ground out, sweat beading his brow in his effort to hold back.

"Don't stop," she hissed, arching her back and taking him deeper.

Stifling a groan, he slowly withdrew and thrust again, hard and deep, Pleasure jolted through him like an arrow piercing his body. Setting a ruthless rhythm, he drove in and out, stretching and filling her while the echoes of softly slapping flesh melded with guttural grunts and reciprocal moans. Pouring everything into her, he slammed into her harder, faster as his balls tightened with explosive need.

"Now, *Aiwattsi*," he growled.

She cried out as her body seized beneath his, her sheath clenching and quaking in spasms that stunned him with sensation. He threw his head back on a feral cry as she milked him to his release. Sweating and panting, Keith collapsed over her, his mind numb and his body spent.

Chapter 24

MIRANDA STIRRED AGAINST HIM WITH A CONTENTED PURR and then suddenly froze. "Did you hear something?" A soft knock followed her question.

"Hello? Is anyone here?"

"Damn! It's Jo-Jo!" Roused instantly to wakefulness, she leaped from the bed. "What are we going to do?"

"Not much we can do." Keith shrugged, tossing her a boot as she snatched up her clothes. "Either we ignore her and hope she gives up looking for you, or we go out there and admit we're caught."

"I can't let her see us like this!" she hissed, frantically wriggling into her jeans.

"Coward." He jerked his on as well and stomped into his boots. "Do you really think we can hide this from her?" His gaze narrowed. "Or is that what you really want, Miranda? To keep our relationship a secret?"

"Of course not!" she protested. "But how is it going to look to her? You just got here, and we're already…"

"We're what?" He cocked a brow.

"We're…we're…" She flushed deep pink.

"Can't say it, Miranda?" he taunted.

"I could if I knew what *it* was!" She threw her arms into her blouse. "What *are* we doing anyway, Keith?"

"Your shirt's inside out," he remarked calmly.

"Crap!" she cried.

"Miranda? Keith? Are you here?" Jo-Jo pushed the bedroom door open.

Miranda gasped. Keith was still shirtless, and Miranda's was inside out. She also wore only one boot. Jo-Jo regarded them, her forehead puckered and lips pursed, as her gaze raked over their half-dressed state. "I...um...we were just...er...ah..." Miranda stammered.

Keith stepped forward. "Miranda was just helping me to get settled."

Jo-Jo's frown deepened as she took in the disheveled bed. "I can see that," she replied.

"I know how this looks," Keith said, "but I swear I meant no disrespect to you, Miz Sutton. Maybe I should go."

"Please, no," Miranda whispered, almost a prayer. She held her breath for several agonizing seconds. She feared she'd pass out from lack of oxygen before Jo-Jo finally exhaled an exasperated sigh.

"I don't think it needs to come to that."

Miranda blew out an echoing breath.

"I just came by to see if you needed anything." Jo-Jo averted her eyes as Miranda handed Keith his shirt and adjusted her own clothes.

"I don't think so," Keith replied evenly. "But thank you for asking."

"We need to go to the co-op tomorrow for fencing supplies," Miranda said. "After that, I figured we'd drive up to the Wal-Mart in Butte. If he needs anything, I'll take care of it."

"Absolutely not. You'll take my credit card and charge whatever you need to my account," Jo-Jo said.

"Don't trouble yourselves on my behalf," Keith interjected. "If I need anything, I'll get it myself."

"Don't be silly," Jo-Jo said. "You came here to help us."

"I didn't come as a hired hand, Miz Sutton. I'll pay my own way."

"Please call me Jo-Jo," she insisted. "I don't think we need to stand on ceremony, especially now," she added dryly. She then turned toward the door. "Supper'll be ready in an hour. I'll expect you both."

Miranda stared after her grandmother for a long, speechless moment.

"Is she always so open-minded?" Keith asked.

"In some things I suppose, but this is all new territory," Miranda replied. "I'll talk to her as soon as I go inside. I don't want this to get any more awkward than it already is."

"I should talk to her. I'm the one who committed the trespass."

"You certainly weren't alone, Keith. And if anyone is really guilty, it's me. I knew you wanted to keep things platonic."

"Maybe that was my initial intent," he said, "but that plan went out the window the minute I saw you."

"Really? I never would have guessed it by the way you acted."

"Because I'm better at hiding my feelings than you are. You wear everything on your face, *Aiwattsi*."

"Then you have me at a strong disadvantage. I don't know how to read you at all."

"Am I really so hard?" he asked.

"Yes. You are." She frowned. "I can't seem to figure you out, no matter how hard I try."

He smiled. "Then I'll try and make it easier for you."

"I wish you would," she replied with a slow grin. "I feel like I've been riding a roller coaster since I met you."

One corner of his mouth curved upward. "That makes two of us."

"What are we doing, Keith?" she asked. "I'm not trying to pressure you. I just need to know. Is this just fucking?"

"I thought you hated dirty words."

"I do," she said. "But if that's all this is, there's no point in sugarcoating it."

"Is that what *you* think this is?" he asked.

"No," she replied. "It's never felt like that with you. What we just did and how we did it was really naughty"—she blushed—"but in a fun way. It didn't feel cheap or dirty."

He grinned. "Maybe in time you'll grow to like cheap and dirty."

"Maybe," she said. "But one step at a time, right?"

"Yes, *Aiwattsi*." He stroked the backs of his fingers over her cheek. "One baby step at a time."

She caught his hand and held it there, searching his eyes. "You never answered my question."

"I didn't think it deserved an answer. Do you think I would have come all the way here if all I wanted was a fuck?"

"No," she confessed, her heart racing. "You'd never have to drive six hours for that. You could have any woman you wanted." She knew it was true. His sex appeal was undeniable.

He slid his hand down her cheek to cup her chin. "Is that what you think?"

"Yeah, I do," she replied softly.

He dipped his head and murmured against her mouth,

"Would it surprise you to know the only one I've ever really wanted was you?"

Jo-Jo was peeling apples for a pie when Miranda entered the kitchen, feeling much like a dog with its tail between its legs. "I'm sorry, Jo-Jo."

"For what you did or for getting caught doing it?" Jo-Jo asked.

"For disappointing you. I was so very happy to see him again. One thing just led to another."

Her grandmother replied with a sympathetic smile. "You don't have to apologize to me. I was once young and horny too. Hell, I was once old and horny. Now I'm just plain old. At least I'm not dead. I admit I was a bit shocked, but I should have seen this coming."

"What do you mean?"

"You're in love with him. It's plain as the nose on your face. I just hope you're not making a mistake. It's never a good idea to get involved with people who work for you."

"But it's not like that, Jo-Jo. He came here because he wanted to help. He won't take our money."

"That does put things in a slightly different light." She handed Miranda the peeler. "Would you finish these for me? I need to sit down for just a spell."

"Sure," Miranda replied, taking up an apple. "Are you feeling okay, Jo-Jo?" Miranda asked, noting her grandmother's pale color.

"Just a tad under the weather," she replied. "I've been a bit light-headed off and on for the past few days. It'll pass if I just sit down for a bit."

"Do you want a drink of water?"

Jo-Jo waved away the offer. "I'll be fine in a minute. It's nothing to be concerned about."

"Have you seen a doctor?"

"Sweetheart. I'm just old," Jo-Jo insisted. "There's no pills to cure that." Jo-Jo turned the conversation back on topic. "I'll admit Keith wouldn't have been my first choice for you."

"Why not?" Miranda asked.

"I had hoped you'd hit it off with my handsome young attorney, Wade Knowlton, but I'm not going to judge a man I don't even know. I'll give Keith the benefit of doubt, because I know you're not a fool."

"I'm not sure how to take that, Jo-Jo."

"I mean, I trust your good sense. I don't believe you'd take up with someone who wasn't worthy. I can see for myself that's he's a straight shooter. I respect that at least. He fessed up right away and shouldered the blame. That shows a protective streak. Coming here also proves he's loyal. There's another point in his favor." She rose to pull the rib roast out of the oven. "How long does he intend to stay with us?"

"I'm not sure. He's said he plans to leave right after we bring the horses in."

"If all goes according to schedule, that'll be right before Thanksgiving," Jo-Jo remarked. "Do you think he'll want to stay here with us for the holiday or spend it with his family?"

"I don't know," Miranda said. "Come to think of it, I don't even know if they observe Thanksgiving on the reservation, do you? The Pilgrims' arrival and establishment in the New World hardly seem a reason for them to celebrate."

"I guess you're right," Jo-Jo said dryly. "I never thought of it that way."

"I never did either, but I look at a lot of things differently since I met him."

"Whether he celebrates it or not, I'm sure he won't want to be by himself," Jo-Jo said. "Judith and Robert are coming up. Judith almost had a heifer when I told her I wasn't moving to Phoenix. I think she'll try to bully me into changing my mind."

"Have you told her about the mustangs yet?" Miranda asked.

"I mentioned it only in passing, but haven't told her the rest yet. I'd rather wait and do it in person. Speaking of that, I could use some reinforcements. You can tell Keith if he wants to stay, I'll make him the best damned stuffed turkey and pumpkin pie he ever ate."

Miranda bit her lip. "So you're really okay with him and me?"

"Sweetheart, I don't have to love it to accept it. You're a grown woman. I only ask for a little discretion. Silver Star is a very small town, and people love to gossip."

Miranda kissed her grandmother's cheek. "You have my promise."

Keith took a quick shower and changed into his best shirt and a fresh pair of jeans. Hat in hand, he knocked on the front door, ready to do whatever he could to mend fences with Jo-Jo Sutton.

"C'mon in, Keith." She beckoned him inside. "Miranda went upstairs to change. She should be down in a minute or two."

He wiped his boots on the mat and followed her inside. "Miz Sutton—Jo-Jo," he amended, "I really did mean what I said about leaving if I've offended you." He hesitated. "Just say the word, and I'll grab my things and go."

"It's all right, Keith." She gave him a reassuring smile. "I was just taken off guard, but not really offended."

"I wish I could promise you it won't happen again, but..." He gave a fatalistic shrug. "I really can't make that promise."

"Miranda and I have already talked about it. What happens between the two of you is your business, as long as you're discreet about it, and it doesn't interfere with the running of this ranch."

"It won't. You have my word on that."

"Your word is good enough for me."

"Thank you, ma'am."

"I hope you don't mind eating in the kitchen," she said. "I rarely use the dining room since my husband passed. When Miranda came to stay, I tried to switch back to using it, but she said she prefers the kitchen. It's her favorite room in the house."

"Me too," he said. "I love the smells. I've always felt the kitchen was the heart of the home. I was raised by my grandparents and always used to sit with my grandmother while she made bread."

"Does she like to bake?" Jo-Jo asked.

"Yes, but our bread is deep-fried rather than baked. Fry bread is a staple on the rez."

"Then I'll have to see if I can make you some. Do you have the recipe?"

"Actually, I do. Right here." He tapped his head with

a grin. "But don't tell anyone. Where I grew up, men aren't supposed to know anything about cooking."

"Do you like to cook?" she asked.

"Sometimes. But I only know how to make a few of my favorite things."

"Like what?"

"Mostly game dishes—venison, rabbit, elk, black bear. Bear is my specialty."

"So you do a lot of hunting?"

"Yes. We stock the freezer with fish and game. We buy little meat."

"Bud loved to hunt bighorn sheep," she said. "Used to go every year with some buddies of his. We've got a whole trophy room, if you'd like to see it later."

"I'd like that, Jo-Jo."

"I didn't get a chance to say so earlier, but I'm glad you've come, Keith."

"I'm happy to help you out," he said.

"But then you plan to leave again."

"Yes."

"Back to Wyoming? That's a lot of distance to try to make a relationship work," Jo-Jo remarked.

"It is," he agreed. "I'm thinking about looking for some ranch work that's closer."

"Why not just stay on here?"

"I have some very good reasons for not accepting the job, Miz Sutton. Personal reasons."

"If you're serious about ranching, there's an outfit about twenty miles down the way that's probably looking. The Knowltons are raising some new hybrid cattle and might be needing some help come calving season. There are a few other places that always hire extra hands for branding. 'Course, that kinda work doesn't pay a whole lot. If you wanted to reconsider staying on with us, I could try to make it worth your while."

"I don't need your money," he said. "I have no debts and lead a very simple, uncomplicated life. I mostly work because I want to, not so much because I have to."

"Oh?" Her brows rose inquisitively. Her gray eyes, so much like Miranda's, pierced him with her next question. "Do you eventually plan to settle down somewhere?"

"Yes... Eventually. I've drifted mainly because I haven't had a good reason to put roots down."

"I saw your horse out in the small corral. He's quite a looker."

Keith breathed easier at the change of topic. "Looks are about all that horse has going for him at the moment," he replied.

"What do you mean?" Jo-Jo asked.

"He's been in captivity for over six months, and no one's been able to do anything with him yet. I was planning to work with him in my spare time."

"Are you talking about Blue Eye?" Miranda asked, entering the kitchen.

"Yes," he replied, relieved that the grilling was over.

"I'd love to film you working with him. Would you mind?"

"No, I don't mind."

"Thank you," she said. "Supper smells great, Jo-Jo. I'm starving."

"I'm not surprised." Jo-Jo flashed them both a mildly chastising look. "I'm sure you've both worked up *quite* an appetite."

Chapter 25

MIRANDA EXITED THE HOUSE THE NEXT MORNING WITH A thermos in one hand and a basket in the other. She was surprised to find Keith waiting on the front porch. "Keith! You missed breakfast. I've got some coffee and biscuits if you want them. I was just heading over to the bunkhouse to bring them to you. I thought maybe you'd overslept."

"I've been up for about two hours," he said.

"I don't understand. Why didn't you come inside?"

He shrugged. "Wasn't real hungry, and once a day is enough to impose."

"It's not like that!" she protested. "Jo-Jo likes feeding people. In fact, I think she lives for it. But if it really makes you uncomfortable to come over in the morning, we can always go into town later and pick up a few groceries after I take care of the horses."

"Already done," he said. "I fed them all and turned the geldings out so we can get started on the fence. Have you ridden out and checked for weak places?"

"Yes. Jo-Jo and I already did that. We know exactly where the bad spots are. We'll need to replace a few rotted posts and raise the perimeter fence height."

"Do you want to ride out now to show me where those bad posts are?"

"Sure," she replied. "That's probably the best place for us to start."

"How many need to be replaced?" he asked.

"About a dozen," she replied.

"The ground's probably too frozen to dig holes for wood posts, but I'm hoping I can still drive in some metal ones. Got any T-posts and a driver?"

"Yeah, in the workshop," she said. "There's a big stack of them."

After loading up the utility cart with T-posts and tools, they rode out together on the ATV, her arms wrapped around his waist. It was bitter with the wind, but she hardly noticed in her excitement to show him the ranch.

"Our summer grazing's on the eastern slopes." She gestured to the nearby mountains as they pulled up to the first post that she and Jo-Jo had flagged with survey tape on their prior inspection. "We have river access on both the north and south boundaries, so we've never had to worry about water. You see how ideal this is for the horses?" Miranda gushed as she pointed out the boundaries of the place that had become her pride and joy.

"I can't argue that," Keith said. "It's a shame she ever thought of selling it."

"The very idea nearly broke my heart, but there's no way she could have kept running it on her own."

"She could have leased it out for the income," he suggested.

"She had an offer to do that but refused. She said she couldn't stand by and watch someone else run the place that had been hers for so long. She said she'd rather sell it outright, but she really didn't want to do that either. It's her home. And now it's mine too. I love it here, Keith. I feel like I was always meant to be in this place."

"That's how I felt when I first arrived in Wyoming. Everything about it spoke to my heart."

"But you don't feel that way now?"

He sighed. "I don't know anymore. I thought I did because I missed it so much, but when I went back, it all felt so different to me. Like I didn't belong anymore. So many things have changed… I've changed."

"Change isn't always a bad thing," she said. "Sometimes it hurts, but it's also what helps us to grow. I've changed a lot too, and I'm much happier for it. I've always believed that everything occurs for a reason. Just look at how we met in Nevada. All of this was meant to happen… You and I were meant to happen." She bit her lip, realizing she'd said too much, implied too much. "I didn't mean to suggest…"

"I know what you meant," he said. "I've had the same thoughts."

"You have?" she said softly, watching him unload the posts.

"Yes," he replied. "I don't believe in coincidence either. Why do think I came?"

"I don't know," she replied, afraid to ascribe too much meaning to his words. She wondered if he'd pull back again. In the past, he'd let her get only so close before shutting her out.

He stood and pulled off a leather glove to touch her face. "Because I want to be with you, Miranda. I was about to drive all the way to California when I first called you. I've never felt this way about anyone before."

Their eyes met. Her heart raced. She swallowed hard and whispered, "Me too. Not even close." She laid a hand on his arm. "Please, Keith, why don't you stay?"

He shook his head with a look of regret. "I just can't. I've told you why." He laid his bare hand on hers. It was still warm from the gloves. "Just give me some time, okay? This is new ground for me. I need to work all this out in my head."

She returned a wistful smile. "Okay."

For the next several hours they worked to reinforce the posts. Although it was cold enough to see their breath, Keith quickly worked up a sweat in his attempt to pound the posts into the frost-hardened ground. Panting from his exertions, he threw down the post driver with a muffled curse. "It's no good. I can't get deep enough. I'm just wasting energy and bending the posts."

"Is there something else we could try?" Miranda asked.

"Yes. A hydraulic post driver," he suggested. "It's the only option." He snatched up his discarded jacket, mouth compressed. "I don't know why you couldn't have waited until spring to do this."

"Because the situation is urgent now," she replied. "You know that as well as I do."

"Urgent?" He tossed the bent posts back into the trailer with a mumbled curse. "I don't think so. Look, you're not saving the world here, Miranda. Hell, you're not even really saving the mustangs. You're only sticking your finger in the dike. I would have thought you'd understood that by now."

"Maybe I can't save the world, but at least I'm doing *something* instead of living in my own little bubble."

His head snapped around. A scowl darkened his brow. "Is that what you think? That I live in a bubble?"

She jutted her chin. "I think you purposely hold yourself apart, just like that horse of yours, intentionally keeping everyone at a distance, when what you really need is right in front of you."

"What makes you such an expert on what I need?"

"I can see that you aren't happy. I know what I'm saying, because I was that way too until now—unhappy, restless, unfulfilled. Maybe you don't want to admit it, but I think that's the real reason you're here. You want to feel a sense of purpose."

"You sound just like my grandfather," he scoffed. "He's always preaching how every living thing has a reason for being."

"You don't agree with him?"

He shook his head with a snort. "If I did, then I'd have to accept that I'm the sole exception to the rule."

"Just because you haven't discovered your purpose yet doesn't mean you don't have one," she argued.

Her words seemed to strike a raw nerve. His gaze hardened. He picked up the post driver and threw it into the cart. "We're done here. Let's go."

His tense silence all the way back to the house told her he'd withdrawn, just as she'd feared he might, but if they were going to pursue a relationship, she needed to be free to speak her mind. She hoped he'd come to realize the truth of what she'd said. Either that or he'd pack up and leave. The thought filled her with dismay. She wanted him to stay, but not if she had to walk on eggshells just to keep him happy.

‸

Things were strained between them for the rest of the day. Keith drove alone to Butte to rent the post driver and then begged off for supper. The next morning when she rose, he was already gone with the ATV. Although disappointed and hurt, she knew he needed space. He'd implied as much the day before. She was surprised by a knock on the door later in the afternoon. Her heart hammered as she rose to answer.

"Hi," she greeted him tentatively. Had he come to say good-bye?

He returned the greeting with a terse nod. "I reinforced half of the posts and got about a mile of wire strung."

"Why didn't you wait for me this morning? You knew I wanted to help."

"I didn't see much point in both of us freezing our asses off."

"But we would have made more progress with two of us working," she countered.

"That's doubtful," he replied with a hint of a smile. "I know you have good intentions, but you don't have the body strength or the know-how for this kind of thing. I've been pulling fence wire since I was thirteen. I can do it faster alone."

"What about just keeping you company?" she asked softly.

He sighed and tipped his hat back. "I needed time alone to think."

"Oh... Did you? Think?" she prompted.

"Yes. I did. I'm not here just to give you a progress report. I came to apologize."

"You did?" She stepped out onto the porch, shutting the door behind her. It was too cold to be without a jacket, but she wasn't about to let him off the hook now.

"I didn't mean to be so abrupt or so hard on you yesterday. You touched a nerve, or maybe a bunch of them.

You have to understand that I want to make it work with you, but I don't know how. I'm not even sure that it can."

"Why not? What makes us different from any other two people who want to be together?"

He scrubbed his face. "The short answer is that I still don't have my shit together. I've been trying really hard for months, and you've only given me reason to work at it even harder, but I'm just not there yet. I need you to be patient with me, *Aiwattsi*." His black eyes met hers. "I don't want to let you down."

"I don't know how you could," she replied, hugging herself. "You came here, didn't you?"

"Yeah. I came. I swore I wouldn't have anything to do with this, but I'm beginning to think even wild horses couldn't have kept me away from you."

He cupped her face and kissed her, softly, sweetly, with toe-curling tenderness. The kind of kiss that hinted at secrets hidden in the heart. He released her slowly. She shivered and chaffed her arms. "It's getting really cold out here. I need to go back in. Will you join us for supper tonight? Jo-Jo said she was making something especially for you."

"She is? What is it?" he asked.

She grinned. "The Food Network did a segment on fry bread yesterday. They had several different recipes, so she decided to give Indian Tacos a try."

He laughed. "Sounds great, but could you ask her to hold off for a bit? There's still about an hour of daylight left. I was hoping to work with the horse. Did you still want to watch?"

"Yes, I do! Just give me a minute to grab my camera and a jacket."

A few minutes later, Miranda stood outside the corral with her video camera poised as Keith climbed over the panels and into the pen, a coiled rope in hand. He dropped softly to the ground. Fear gripped her as the horse spun to face him, neck arched, teeth bared, and ears pinned.

"Be careful, Keith!"

"I'm always careful," he said.

"What are you going to do?" she asked.

"I'm just going to stand here quietly, looking down at the ground. I won't make a single move as long as he doesn't. If he's feeling purely defensive, he should just stand there, watching and waiting on me, but if he makes an aggressive move, I'll have to counter in the same way. As a stallion, his sole purpose in life was to procreate and to protect. His instincts taught him to fight anyone who threatened his position. It's not going to be easy to change lifelong behaviors."

"How do you go about it?" Miranda asked.

"With time and patience." He kept his eyes glued to the horse as he spoke. "He basically has to be reprogrammed, but I can't even begin the process until he accepts that I'm not a threat to him." Even while he was speaking, the horse lowered his head, stretched his neck, and charged.

Miranda cried out, but Keith darted out of its path and threw the looped end of his lasso at the horse, startling him into turning away. Blue Eye circled him several times, plunging and kicking, but Keith stood his ground, using the rope to keep the animal at a safe distance.

"If I back down or retreat, he wins," he explained. "And that's what he'll remember the next time." After a minute or two, the horse snorted and withdrew to the far end of the pen, still watching Keith with a wary glare until Keith lowered the rope and climbed back over the panel.

"That's it? That's all you're going to do?" Miranda asked, befuddled.

"Yup. My only goal was to show him he can't intimidate me, so I'd call that one a win."

"It looked a lot more like a draw to me," Miranda said dryly.

"In reality, there was no winner or loser, but I achieved what I wanted. I didn't let him exert dominance. Once he backed off, I rewarded him by removing the pressure. This isn't going to be about coaxing, cooing, and trying to woo him. That kind of courtship approach already failed with this horse. The next time I go in there, we'll see who can move whom. Herding is how horses exert dominance over one another. If I win, we can move forward."

"And if you don't?" she asked. "What if he runs through that rope of yours? What if he hurts you?"

"Then I'd have a real tough decision to make. An aggressive horse is as dangerous as a rabid dog. I won't keep an animal that I can't turn my back on."

"Are you saying you'd euthanize him?"

He nodded. "But only as the last resort. It's still way too early to judge."

Watching Keith with a horse was an almost magical experience. It was uncanny how well he read and understood them. "I just don't understand why you aren't doing this full-time," she said. "You have such a talent. It seems such a waste not to use it."

"I've already told you why I can't."

"But your reasons are nonsensical," she protested. "Why can't you at least give it a chance? I really think this could be a good thing for all of us. I don't understand why you don't see it, too. Whether you want me to be part of it or not, you still need to move forward with your life, Keith. You can't let the past keep clouding your future."

"My future?" He shook his head. "This is not *my* future, Miranda, or my dream. It's yours."

Her lips quivered. "I thought… I hoped…that maybe it could become ours together."

He tossed his rope down with a shake of his head. "I'm sorry to disappoint you, but you thought wrong. I'm not one of your mustangs. I don't *need* saving."

"Don't you?" she asked softly. "It's not a weakness or a character flaw. It's human nature to need someone. We all do. You need this, Keith. These horses need you. And *I* need you."

—⁓—

I need you. His chest tightened. When had anyone ever said that to him before? He gazed sightlessly out at the mountains, digesting her words. For the second time, it was as if she'd reached out and touched that aching place in his soul.

"You're asking too much," he said with a jerk of his head. "I told you I'm not here for the horses. I'm here for you. I came here to help *you*. Damn it, Miranda! Why can't that be enough?"

She stood with hands on hips, her gaze meeting his squarely. "Because you're too obstinate to recognize what would truly fulfill you."

"Look, Miranda, there are two kinds of people in

this world, sequoias and tumbleweeds. You're the sequoia. Your convictions are strong, and your roots run deep. I'm the tumbleweed. All my life, I've taken a day at a time. I've never had a serious relationship or any real responsibilities. I've never even stayed in one place for more than a few months at a time. And that kind of life suited me just fine."

"Does it still?" she asked. "Is that the kind of life you want?"

"No," he said. "It's not what I want anymore, but staying here with you is asking for commitments I'm not sure I can make. I don't know if I even have it in me." He gripped her shoulders. "Can you understand that? I don't know if I can change. And I don't want to hurt you if I can't."

She tore her gaze away and looked into the distance. "Are you saying you think you'd just pick up and disappear one day?"

"Maybe." He released her to answer with a single shoulder shrug. "I've done it before. If the mood struck me. I might do it again. It's how I've always been."

"Maybe that's how you *were*, but I don't believe for a minute that you would. You're one of the most responsible people I know. You've worked for Mitch for months, under really tough conditions, and you never let him down, even when you hated it. You don't hate it here, do you?" she asked.

"No, I don't hate it."

"Do you think maybe you could grow to like it?"

"Maybe I could," he said, adding pointedly, "I have good reason to. That's the only part of all this that I'm certain about."

"What part is that?" she asked.

"You, *Aiwattsi*. I meant it when I said I've never wanted anyone like I want you."

She broke eye contact again. "Didn't I already prove you can have me just about any way you like?"

Her flippant answer told him she was afraid to take his remark to heart.

"That's not what I meant," he said. "I need you to understand that it's never been anything more than sex for me before you. This is different between you and me. It's more."

"What do you mean more?" she asked, warily. "How much *more*?"

"I don't know the answer."

"Then I have to ask if you *want* to know."

"I do."

"Then stay with me, Keith. Let's just give us some time to figure it all out. It's the only way we'll ever know. You don't have to work for Jo-Jo and me, if that's what bothers you. Maybe you could just lease the facilities from us and train some of the horses. Give the throwaways another chance. I'm certain the BLM would support you. Maybe they'd even give you a contract, like they've done with the prisons. At least think about it, will you?" Her eyes pleaded.

She'd waged a hard campaign, chipping away at him piece by piece with her determined persistence. He'd balked and bucked from the very start, but she was wearing him down. He had little fight left in him when she looked at him like that.

He doffed his hat and raked his hair with a sigh of defeat. "All right. You win. I'll stay on until spring. If I think by then that I can do anything with these horses, I'll talk to the BLM."

The words were barely out of his mouth before she flung her arms around him with a squeal. "You will? I'm so happy, Keith! I can't even tell you how happy I am."

He flashed a lecherous grin. "Then maybe you can show me instead?"

Chapter 26

THE NEXT TWO WEEKS PASSED QUICKLY AS MIRANDA AND Keith fell into an easy routine of rising early to care for the horses, then riding out to work on the fence. Although she hardly knew the front end of a hammer from the back, she loved helping him, even if she wasn't actually a whole lot of help. Keith was patient and took the time to show her how to pull wire. Working together, they managed to complete the work on the south pasture just barely ahead of the first big snowfall.

On the days they finished before dark, Keith made slow but steady progress with Blue Eye. They were still more or less at a standoff, as the horse still hadn't approached or let Keith near him, but at least the stallion's aggression had diminished. Keith marked it as a baby step, but progress nonetheless.

With the long hours they'd put in, they hadn't had any trouble keeping their promise to be discreet. In truth, they hadn't had any energy to do anything besides work, eat, and sleep. But now homebound by the snowfall, Miranda was secretly thrilled for the chance to spend some time relaxing together. When he didn't come to the house for breakfast, she decided to bring it to him… in bed.

She opened the door when he didn't answer her knock and caught him just stepping out of the shower, wrapped in only a towel. "You didn't show up for breakfast."

"Wasn't real hungry."

"I brought you some anyway." She set it down on the counter. Her gaze roved appreciatively over his flexing muscles as he toweled his head dry. "I'm really disappointed that I'm too late to scrub your back."

"I'm all clean, but I sure wouldn't mind getting really messy," he replied with a grin that heated her insides.

"Are you letting your hair grow back?" she asked. She hadn't noticed before how long it was getting, since he always wore a hat. It had grown a couple of inches in the months since she'd they met in Nevada, and now almost touched his shoulders.

"Yeah." He smiled self-consciously. "I've felt really naked without it."

"Your nakedness is perfectly fine with me," she replied, stripping off her coat and toeing off her boots. When she looked up again, he'd dropped his towel. She inhaled a sharp breath to see him in his full natural glory. Her insides clenched with desire as he approached. Her gaze dipped and lingered in awe on his manhood: long, thick, purple-headed, and erect. *Very erect.*

"Ready so quickly?" she asked.

"Yes. I've been fighting this particular state of 'readiness' since the moment I opened my eyes. I was half inclined to take care of it myself."

"But that would have been such a waste." She reached out and wrapped her hand around him. He shut his eyes on a guttural sound as she stroked his hard, hot length. "I'm more than happy to take care of it for you."

"I was hoping you'd say that. Two weeks is too damned long just to think about it. My body might be exhausted, but my mind's been working overtime."

"Oh yeah?" She cocked her head. "So what has you so preoccupied?"

"Do you remember the first time we were together, when you were afraid to let me kiss you 'down there'?"

She laughed softly. "Why does that seem like a life-time ago?"

"Because you're no longer the shy girl, *Aiwattsi*. I'm glad you enjoy what happens between us. I enjoy it all the more because you do. I was wondering if you'd come to me. I was hoping you would. I woke up with my head filled with all the things I still want to do to you."

"Really? Do tell."

"Tell?" He cupped her face and kissed her deeply, passionately. "How about if I show you instead?"

∼◆∼

Miranda opened her eyes, spooned against him in a warm postcoital cocoon. "Jo-Jo asked if you have plans for Thanksgiving. I told her I wasn't even sure if you celebrated it or not."

"It's not our custom," he said, "but some of us do. Did you know that Thanksgiving was really an Indian harvest celebration way before the Pilgrims ever landed? There are those who feel the white people hijacked our holiday. A few bands in New England have even gone so far as to designate it as a great day of mourning."

She rolled over to face him. "How do you feel about that?"

"I think the past is the past. We need to let the bit-terness go. As far as the holiday is concerned, it's just another day to me, but I do like turkey."

"Were you planning to go and see your grandparents?"

She added hopefully, "Or would you like to spend it here with us?"

"I wasn't planning to leave, not with the horses arriving so soon."

The frown etching his brow told her it was more than just the horses arriving that kept him from going home. His pain was deep, and a wound she ached to soothe. She hoped that time would bring about a reconciliation with his family.

"I'm glad you're staying," she said. "I just hope you don't mind my aunt Judith and uncle Robert. They're coming up from Phoenix tomorrow. When Jo-Jo told them about the mustangs, they booked the first flight to Montana. Jo-Jo said Judith is having a real cow over it."

"Why should they care?" Keith asked.

"Because Judith is a real control freak. She had it all planned out for Jo-Jo to move to Phoenix with them, whether it was what Jo-Jo wanted or not. I just hope they don't cause any trouble."

Keith shrugged. "They might not like it, but there's not much they can do, given it's all a done deal." He fingered one of her curls. "It doesn't sound like you're too fond of your aunt."

"No, I'm not. She's a real be-atch. She and Jo-Jo don't get along very well either. Judith hated the ranch and couldn't leave soon enough. She went away to nursing school, married an oral surgeon, and never came back. He's a real asshat too. The man extracts wisdom teeth for a living but acts like it's neurosurgery."

"Have you heard yet when they'll be bringing the horses?"

"The guy from the BLM is supposed to come out

tomorrow to look things over. If he gives us the final stamp of approval, we can expect them the day after."

"Are you nervous about it?" he asked.

"I guess I am a little nervous. This is a really big commitment. I just hope Jo-Jo never regrets that I talked her into it."

"You understand that there's no turning back once they unload those trailers."

"I know. I'm ready. I'm just really glad you're here with me. I don't know how I could have done it without you."

His brows pulled together. "But you were determined to do it anyway, weren't you?"

"Yes," she admitted. "I was. And I still would have, but part of me could never quite believe that you'd let me down. I think I always knew you'd come through in the end."

"So much faith in me, *Aiwattsi*?" he asked softly, his mouth forming a hint of a smile.

"Yes," she said, rolling on top of him. She loved feeling him beneath her almost as much as on top. "Supreme faith. You're not at all the person I once thought you were. You came even though it wasn't what you wanted. And the fact that you are still here with me makes everything feel complete."

"How does your grandmother feel about me being here?" he asked warily.

"She likes you, Keith. A lot. She's just been worried all along that you might not stick around. She's afraid you'll break my heart. You won't, will you?" she asked softly, her eyes searching his. "You'll keep it safe, right?"

He wrapped his arms around her, pulling her close

enough that she could hear his heart beating. "I would never intentionally hurt you, *Aiwattsi*. If I ever did break your heart, it would break mine too."

———

"You're up early. Where's Keith?" Jo-Jo asked.

Miranda bit her lip with a guilty look. "Um. He said he wanted to sleep in today."

"I suppose it was all that fence work that wore him out." Jo-Jo's knowing wink said she knew exactly what had tired Keith out and where Miranda had spent most of yesterday and all of last night. "Maybe you and he ought to cool it down just a bit while Judith and Robert are here."

"We will," Miranda promised. "When are they arriving?"

"At three. Should we flip a coin?" Jo-Jo asked. "Heads picks up Judith and Robert, tails gets to stay here?"

Miranda set her cup down with a laugh. "I don't mind picking them up, but that would mean you'd have to ride the property with the BLM agent. I was thinking that Keith and I should do that in case he has any questions about the work we did."

"I suppose you're right." Jo-Jo sighed. "I'm just glad they're staying only a few days. The thought alone is enough to bring on a migraine."

"I knew you and Aunt Judith weren't close, but I didn't know it was *that* bad," Miranda remarked.

"To be honest, I'm mostly worried about how she's going to treat you and Keith. She made several derogatory remarks when I told her you'd come here to stay, and that was even before I mentioned Keith or the horses. *That* business about sent her into orbit. I don't even dare tell her about the changes I made to my will."

"I'm so sorry, Jo-Jo. I never meant to come between you."

"You haven't. She's always been a hard pill to swallow, but she's only gotten worse with age. It's too bad they couldn't have kids. I think motherhood might have softened her. It does with a lot of women, but Judith could never carry to term, and Robert refused to adopt, so they just gave up. She's been miserable ever since."

"I didn't know about her miscarriages," Miranda said. "That's so sad."

"It is sad, but she's too mean to feel sorry for. Oh, well," Jo-Jo groaned. "I guess I'll be the one driving to Butte to pick them up. At least I already made all the pies. I've got an apple, two pumpkins, and a banana cream. That's still your favorite, isn't it?"

"Yes," Miranda said, "but you didn't have to go to all that trouble."

She smiled. "It was no trouble, and it just happens to be my favorite too."

"Is there anything I can do to help you get ready?" Miranda asked.

"Not today, but I'll happily put you back in charge of the vegetable peeler tomorrow."

"Gladly." Miranda kissed her cheek. "Please drive carefully, Jo-Jo."

⁓⁓⁓

Keith spent the afternoon driving the property with the BLM agent, Bill Watson. After riding the fence he'd repaired, they returned to find Miranda waiting.

"So, what's the verdict?" she asked.

"There's plenty of fresh water, the fence is high enough, and all the wire appears tight," Bill said.

"My grandparents ran four hundred head of cattle at one time, so we're pretty well equipped," Miranda replied. "We were also careful to check all the posts. Keith did a lot of work on them for us."

"Well, everything looks good from our end," Bill said.

The look of worry eased from Miranda's face. "So we can take the horses?"

"Sure enough. Can you take them this week?" Bill asked. "I know it's a holiday and all, but we're in pretty desperate straits."

Miranda looked to Keith. "What do you think? Are we ready?"

Keith replied, "I think the sooner the better. Let them get the lay of the land while they can still see it. Most of the snow from the prior storm is already melted, but there's more forecasted."

"I admit it surprised the heck out of me that you were willing to take them on this close to winter," Bill said, "but we sure do appreciate it."

"We don't usually get a real heavy snow load here in the valley," Miranda said. "And, fortunately, what we get doesn't stay long. Can you get a driver to bring them this close to the holiday?" she asked.

"We'll get a driver, no worries there," Bill reassured her.

"Would you like to come in and warm up?" she asked. "I already put a pot of coffee on."

Bill hesitated. "Thanks, but no. Got a lot of paperwork to do before I can get those horses transferred. I'll call as soon as we have it all lined up." He offered his hand. "Look forward to working with you."

"Me too." Miranda shook his hand heartily. "I'll be waiting for that call."

Bill tipped his hat in a parting gesture. As soon as he got in his truck, Miranda turned to Keith. "Thank you so much, Keith. We never could have done it without you."

He flashed a wolfish grin. "You can thank me properly later."

She frowned and shifted her weight. "About that... Jo-Jo thinks we should cool things down while my aunt and uncle are here." She added with an apologetic look, "I won't be bringing you breakfast in bed for a while."

"That's mighty disappointing. It's become my favorite meal...or, better said, you have."

She swatted his shoulder. "None of that kind of talk either. You'll get us both in really hot water. We already have a couple of strikes against us."

"What do you mean?"

"They don't like that I've come to live here."

"That so? Then they're sure to be real happy about me."

"I don't think Jo-Jo said too much about you."

His brows met in a frown. "So I'm to be presented as just a hired hand, as far as they're concerned?"

"That's probably what they'll think you are, especially since she fired Marvin, the guy who used to work here. Do you mind just leaving it at that?" she asked. "It would be a whole lot easier all around. And it's only for a few days."

"I don't like it, but I suppose I could be bribed." He cupped her head, tilting it back to kiss her. One kiss stretched into two, and then three, until their mouths just merged for long, breathless, thoughtless minutes. Lost to time and place, they were still standing on the front porch locked in that embrace when Jo-Jo's Expedition pulled into the drive.

"Crap! They're here." Miranda jerked back with a curse. "Do you think they saw us?"

"I think they'd be blind if they didn't. Busted twice?" He chuckled. "We're not very good at covert ops."

She scowled back at him. "This isn't anything to make light of, Keith. Things are about to get damned awkward."

When the vehicle came to a stop, Miranda marshaled a smile and sallied forward. Keith followed, hanging back a few steps as Miranda greeted the new arrivals. "Aunt Judith! Uncle Robert! How great to see you."

The couple who climbed out of the truck greeted her with less enthusiasm. Her aunt was a fairly attractive woman in her forties, with the same red-gold hair as Miranda's, but cropped short to her chin. Her uncle was a trim middle-aged man with a bored air. Miranda's aunt Judith stepped forward with an air kiss to her niece's cheek. "Miranda. What a surprise to find you here."

"What brought you out to the ranch?" her uncle inquired. "Last we knew you were studying cinematography out in California."

"I was," Miranda replied, "but I graduated almost two years ago."

"No job prospects out in Hollyweird?" he asked with a hint of a smirk.

Keith could almost see Miranda bristle. "I had a job with a well-known production company, but I left it to work on an independent film project."

"Oh?" His brows arched. "What kind of project would bring you all the way to Montana?"

"It's a documentary about mustangs," she said. "I filmed the first part of it in Nevada and plan to finish it out here."

"You'll have to tell us all about it later," Judith said. "Right now I need to get out of the cold. My thin Arizona blood can't take these temperatures anymore. We'll need help with the bags. Where's Marvin?"

"I sacked Marvin months ago. I thought I told you that," Jo-Jo said.

"Maybe you did." Judith gave an impatient wave. "You know I don't keep track of those kinds of things." For the first time she looked to Keith. "Could you please get our bags?"

"Keith isn't an employee," Jo-Jo quickly interjected.

"Oh?" Judith arched a brow and gave him a critical once-over.

Jo-Jo turned to him with an apologetic smile. "Keith, this is my daughter, Judith, and—"

"*Dr*. Pearson," Miranda's uncle interjected before Jo-Jo could complete the introduction.

The guy really was a self-important ass. It seemed that Judith and Robert were a matched pair. Keith tipped his hat and stepped forward, hand extended to make his own introduction. "Good to meet you both. I'm Keith Russo." Darting a look at Miranda, he added, "Your niece's fiancé."

Miranda's eyes widened and jaw went slack. He didn't know what devil had suddenly taken charge of his tongue, but it was done now and not to be taken back.

"*Fiancé?*" Judith repeated. "No one said *anything* about an engagement." She turned to Jo-Jo. "Mama, why didn't you tell me? I would have at least brought a gift."

Jo-Jo looked baffled. "I didn't know myself." Her

gaze flickered from Keith to Miranda and back again. "When did you two decide this?"

"Only yesterday," Keith answered smoothly. "We'd planned to keep it a secret until after I picked up the ring."

"Yes. It had to be sized," Miranda blurted. She held up her left hand, following his lead. "See, I have really skinny little fingers."

"This is rather abrupt, isn't it?" Judith remarked, eyeing Miranda up and down. "Or perhaps you have a pressing reason?"

"What do you mean?" Miranda asked.

"With the way this came out of the blue, I thought maybe…" Judith gave a blithe shrug. "It's nothing to be ashamed of… It happens all the time these days."

"What happens all the time?" Miranda asked.

Keith stifled a chuckle. "I think she's wondering when we expect little Keith to arrive."

Miranda's face suffused with color. "I'm *not* pregnant, Aunt Judith," she replied through her teeth.

"How terribly awkward," Judith remarked.

"I suppose congratulations are in order," Robert said, offering Keith his hand with a supercilious smile. "When is the big day?"

Miranda flashed Keith a warning look.

"We haven't discussed a date yet," he answered.

"We'll look forward to hearing the whole story once we get settled." Judith looked to her husband. "Won't we, Rob?"

"Absolutely," Robert agreed, wooden faced.

Judith frowned. "Now then, what are we going to do about the luggage? Rob can't lift anything since he threw his back out playing golf."

"I'll get it," Keith volunteered.

"*We* will," Miranda corrected. "Got the remote thingy for the back, Jo-Jo?"

"Sure thing." One click opened the tailgate. Judith and Robert each grabbed a small bag and then headed for the house, leaving four more for Keith and Miranda to haul.

"Thank you for the help," Jo-Jo murmured to Keith, "and for putting up with their crap. As for the bomb you just dropped…" She gave Keith a pointed look. "We'll talk later."

Miranda stood gaping while Keith finished pulling the bags out of the back. She drew in an audible breath and confronted him, hands on hips. "Um…what the *hell* did you just do?"

He grinned. "Just saved our asses. I thought I was pretty smooth about it too."

Her brows knitted over stormy eyes. "By faking an engagement? How does that help?"

"It sure makes things more pleasant for me," he said.

Her lips compressed. "How do you figure that?"

"As your fiancé, I now have every right to some PDA. What's wrong?" he asked, noting her scowl. "You don't like being engaged to me?"

"I don't like lies and deceit, even in exchange for PDA."

"It's only for a few days," he said. "What else could we do after they caught us lip-locked?"

She exhaled a defeatist sigh. "I suppose you're right. You just shocked me with that. By the look on her face, you shocked Jo-Jo too. For the record, I don't think she pegged you as marriage material."

"Do you?" he asked, turning suddenly serious.

"I never thought about it," she said. "But I guess I have a hard time imagining you as a husband or father."

"Why not?" It wasn't as if he'd ever fantasized about that role either, but it irked him that she hadn't. Isn't that what all women did once they entered a relationship? "In what way am I deficient?" he asked.

"I didn't say you were deficient…exactly. I guess it's just that you've never talked about those things. Maybe I thought you didn't want them." Her gaze searched his. "Am I wrong?"

"I don't know," he replied. "I never gave it much thought before."

But he *was* thinking now. Suddenly it wasn't hard at all to imagine waking up every morning, cocooned with her after a night of lovemaking. He wondered what it would be like to put down roots and build a life with her. The engagement announcement that had sprung thoughtlessly from his mouth a short while ago no longer felt like a joke, and her rejection hurt more than he'd have thought possible. He told himself she was right. They weren't nearly ready for that kind of step, but his pride was bruised to think she'd take him as a lover but didn't consider him worthy of anything more.

"I don't understand you," she said. "You've insisted all along that you don't want commitments or ties; that you don't like to think about the future; that you prefer to live in the present. You've made it clear I shouldn't expect anything from you beyond staying a few weeks and helping us with the horses. Isn't that what you want?"

"Maybe it was," he said slowly. "But my wants seem to be changing."

He'd recognized long ago that he had feelings for her, but hadn't dared to put a name to those feelings. Until now. He was suddenly aware of a terrifying truth—he was falling in love with Miranda. Although he hadn't gone crashing instantly to the ground, he'd begun a free fall their first night together. He hadn't noticed because it had been such a slow and easy descent, every smile, laugh, and kiss pushing him a little further, but in the end, he'd landed at her feet.

———

Miranda's heart drummed loudly in her ears for one, two, three beats. "What are you saying? Don't play games with me, Keith."

"I'm not playing games," he said. "Maybe your aunt's assumption got me thinking. What if we weren't playacting? What if we wanted this to be real?"

Was he serious? Did he just propose in a vague and oblique way? The thought of it thrilled and terrified her. She had no doubt of her feelings for Keith, but they were still so early in their relationship that an engagement would be like trying to build a house on quicksand.

She licked her lips and slowly answered, "Then I'd have to say we aren't ready."

He blinked, and then his expression went blank. "You said 'we' but you really mean *me*, don't you?"

Miranda's throat tightened. "Keith, it's just…I didn't mean—"

"You don't have to explain anything. If you want a great fuck, I'm your man, but I'm not the one you're dreaming about making babies with one day. I'm not the one you think you'll ever be able to count on, the one who will be there for you in the long run. Do I have that straight?"

Keith's anger took her completely aback. Had he really been thinking about marriage? Family? His reaction told her he had. "You're putting words in my mouth," she said. "I only meant that we aren't ready for the next step."

Keith grabbed a suitcase with each hand. "Then it's a damned good thing we are *just* playacting."

Arriving upstairs, hand poised to knock, Keith halted at the sound of Judith's raised voice.

"I can't believe this situation!" Judith hissed. "We turn our backs for one minute, and that little bitch sneaks in to turn Mama against me. I'm not going to stand for it, Rob. If she doesn't want to sell, fine, but this ranch is rightfully *mine* when Mama passes. And what the hell is the deal with that Keith anyway? Who does he think he is, moving in lock, stock, and barrel?"

"He's a drifter and an opportunist if ever I saw one," Robert said. "A damned wolf in sheep's clothing! That's what I see."

"Well, I'm not going to stand by and watch Mama get fleeced. Dear God!" Judith said tearfully. "The two of them are plotting to take over the ranch. We can't let this happen, Robert."

"You shouldn't have to."

"But what are we going to do?" she asked.

"We'll start by calling Marvin," Robert said. "He should be able to fill us in on what's happening here. I certainly don't trust this Keith guy."

"And then what? How are we going to convince Mama to come to Phoenix?" Judith asked.

"She needs to be made to see that she's bitten off way more than she can chew."

"But I've already tried that, and she won't listen. I haven't been able to talk any sense into her."

"If we can't convince her, I have something in mind that should put an end to all this horseshit," Robert answered. "Just trust me. I'll handle it."

I'll handle it? What the hell did *that* mean? Keith waited, but the voices faded away. When it appeared they weren't going to say any more, he rapped on the door. "It's Keith. I've got your luggage."

"Just a minute," Judith answered seconds later, swinging the door open and inclining her head as if he were her porter. "Just put it right there on the bed."

"Sure. No problem." After dropping off the four large bags, he headed back downstairs.

What were they up to? No good, for certain. And what did this guy Marvin have to do with it? Maybe it was none of his business, but then again, if anything threatened Miranda, he'd damned sure make it his business.

Chapter 27

"MORE POTATOES, KEITH?" JO-JO ASKED, EXTENDING THE bowl before he could reply.

"Thank you." Keith took up the serving spoon and dug in for his third helping. "These are really great, Miz Sutton. The whole meal is." He'd forgotten how good a real holiday meal could be. He couldn't even remember the last one he'd eaten at home in Wyoming. The only thing missing was fry bread.

"I bought the biggest fresh bird I could find," Jo-Jo said. "I never buy frozen turkey."

"We always got ours fresh too, straight from the fields," Keith said.

"You're a hunter?" Robert asked.

"Yes," Keith replied. "Almost everyone hunts on the rez. Our family rarely buys meat. We fish and bow hunt for it. My grandfather taught me when I was young. He prefers the old ways."

"You should see him throw a knife," Miranda gushed. "He's incredible."

"Knife throwing?" Judith laughed. "Doesn't seem like a very practical skill."

Miranda looked up from her plate where she'd been pushing her food around. "It is when you're faced with a Mojave rattler," she remarked with a shudder.

"When did you encounter one of those?" Robert asked.

"When I was in the Calico Mountains, filming a

wild-horse roundup," Miranda explained. "Keith was working as the head wrangler for the livestock company when I went out there to film. I was gathering firewood when I came across the snake. It was poised to strike when Keith impaled it with his hunting knife."

"Is that really true?" Robert asked skeptically.

"Yes," she said. "That's how Keith and I got together. But it wasn't just killing the snake that did it for me. It wasn't even after our encounter with a hungry mountain lion. It was before all that, when he called in a helicopter to save a dying foal." Miranda's gaze skittered across the table to snag Keith's. "I think I knew even then that I was falling in love. Saving my life only clinched it."

Although voiced playfully, her confession made his heart slam against his chest. Her gaze held his steadily, and for a suspended heartbeat they were the only two people in the room. Hell, maybe the only two in the world.

"So that's how you met?" Judith asked.

"Not quite," Miranda said. "We were first introduced when Keith was conducting one of his clinics in California."

"Clinic?" Robert's brows rose. "Are you a physician, Keith?"

Keith shook his head with a laugh. "Not that kind of clinic. I'm an equine behaviorist…" He looked to Miranda. "Or I was."

"A *horse shrink*?" Robert released a snort. "Is that even a real job?"

Ignoring the heat creeping up his neck, Keith responded levelly, "Yes. I traveled the country conducting clinics on how to manage problem animals, although in reality, the horses weren't usually the problem. Most behavioral issues are caused by owners who don't understand them."

Judith chortled. "And they actually *paid* you for this?"

"Quite well. I spent the better part of three years touring in Europe."

"Oh." Judith's mouth snapped audibly shut.

"Is that still your primary occupation?" Robert asked.

"No," Keith replied, slanting a look at Miranda. "I gave it up almost two years ago. Since then, I've been wrangling mustangs."

"So what brought you out to my mother's ranch?" Judith asked.

"Miranda," Keith replied.

"I asked him to come and help with the horses," Miranda said.

"Horses? What horses?" Judith asked.

"The mustangs," Miranda replied. "Jo-Jo and I are turning the ranch into a mustang sanctuary. The first of two hundred horses are supposed to arrive tomorrow."

"*Two hundred mustangs?*" Judith dropped her fork with a clatter.

"Yes." Miranda looked to her grandmother in question. "I thought Jo-Jo told you about it."

"She told me you were preparing to adopt some horses, which is ridiculous enough," Judith retorted, "but she said nothing about turning the entire ranch into some kind of petting zoo! What is this about, Mother? Have you lost your mind?"

"It's not a zoo, Judith," Jo-Jo said. "It's a federally subsidized wild-horse sanctuary."

"Zoo? Sanctuary? You're just splitting hairs. Messing with wild horses is pure insanity!"

"No, it isn't," Jo-Jo insisted tersely. "It's a means of keeping my home. The horses will generate enough income for me to do that."

"But you're selling the ranch and moving to Phoenix," Judith said.

Jo-Jo shook her head. "No, Judith. I already told you that I've changed my mind about Phoenix. I took the ranch off the market weeks ago. This is my home. It will always be my home. I expect you to bury my bones here, or at least cast my ashes."

"But I don't understand," Judith persisted. "We spent months talking and planning your retirement."

"*You* spent months talking and planning, Judith. You never asked what I wanted. I considered it only as briefly as I did because I didn't want to be alone, but Miranda's arrival has changed all that. Now we're contracted with the BLM to provide a permanent home to several hundred wild horses. Gravy anyone?" Jo-Jo asked, practically shoving the boat across the table.

"No, thank you." Judith waved it away.

"What about you, Keith?"

"Sure," he replied, flooding his potatoes while intently watching the exchange. The mustang announcement had exponentially escalated the tension at the table.

Nearly hissing with rage, Judith spun on Miranda. "This is all your doing, isn't it? She's an old woman! She doesn't need this kind of stress! Do you want to put her into an early grave?"

"That's enough, Judith!" Jo-Jo stood, hands braced on the table. "I've done less real work around this place since Miranda's arrival than I've done in the past two years. She's been a godsend to me."

"If you were struggling here, why did you let Marvin go?" Judith asked.

"I told you why," Jo-Jo replied. "And I didn't replace him because I couldn't afford to."

"Well," Judith huffed. "I guess there's nothing more to say about it."

"Good," Jo-Jo replied with a brittle smile. "Does anyone want pie?"

———⚬———

After doing the dinner dishes, Miranda and Keith escaped to the front-porch swing, where they snuggled up together in a blanket. She drew a breath of air into her lungs and exhaled a wispy cloud of vapor, silently watching it dissipate into the night as she composed her thoughts.

"Dinner tonight went about as horribly as I could possibly have imagined. I'm really sorry about the third degree you got from Robert and Judith and how rude they've both been to you, Keith."

"It means nothing to me, *Aiwattsi*. They mean nothing to me. I only care about the opinions of people who matter."

"I know you're right." She sighed. "But Jo-Jo matters to me, so I hate to have come between them."

"It's not you. It's your aunt. She is a very unhappy woman." His arms tightened, pulling her closer. In his arms, all of the unease that had preoccupied her since their tiff the day before melted almost instantly away. "It'll be all right, *Aiwattsi*," he reassured her. "They're only here for a few days. Then all will go back to normal."

She wondered what normal was. Nothing about her life was normal anymore. "I hope so," she said. "The time can't pass quickly enough for me."

A coyote howled in the distance. Another one echoed the call, vividly reminding her of another cold night she'd spent wrapped in Keith's arms. So much had changed since then. It now seemed like eons ago.

"It's so clear out here," she murmured, gazing up at the heavens. "So peaceful and beautiful. There's nothing like the Montana sky at night."

"I'd argue the same about the Wyoming sky," he said. "I'd love to show it to you one day."

She turned to face him. "Do you still miss home so much, Keith?"

"Yes." He stroked her hair. "I miss how it was, but things have changed. It feels less like my home now. They say home is where the heart is… My heart is with you, *Aiwattsi*."

Hers gave a lurch into her throat. "What about the sequoia and the tumbleweed?" she asked.

"Did you know tumbleweeds are actually dead?" he said. "The only living parts of them are the seeds they carry and spread around. You see what a great metaphor that was for me? Rolling from place to place just spreading my seeds?" He gave a derisive laugh. "But I don't want to be a tumbleweed anymore. You've changed that. How can I convince you that I can be what you need?"

"You don't have to do anything," she whispered. "I already know I can count on you. I've just been waiting for you to convince yourself."

He cupped her head and kissed her deeply. "Come to bed with me, *Aiwattsi*, let me show you in truth that I'm convinced, converted, and persuaded…that I'm a man reborn."

Chapter 28

MIRANDA AWOKE, STRETCHED, AND THEN GRABBED HER ROBE and padded straight to the window overlooking the south pasture. Just gazing out on the horses was a simple pleasure she'd come to look forward to every morning.

The hay truck had come first, an entire semitrailer they'd parked behind the main barn. After that, the horses began to arrive, trailer by trailer, over the next three days. Two hundred twelve mares in all. Through it all, Blue Eye had paced his paddock, out of his mind with excitement over his would-be harem in their thousand-acre pasture. She felt bad for the stallion to have them within sight and smell but ever out of reach.

She squinted but was still unable to see through the fog that enshrouded the ground. Even the mountains were obscured, appearing as a barely discernible shadow. Although mildly disappointed, she knew the fog would soon fade away with the rising sun. The forecast had promised mild temps and plenty of sunshine.

Keith had suggested taking a ride together if the weather cleared. Between all the fencing, filming Keith and Blue Eye, and editing her documentary, she hadn't yet had a chance to ride Sadie. She was elated at the prospect of getting on a horse again and spending time alone with Keith, doing something they both enjoyed. Although they were back on even footing again, Keith had seemed strangely preoccupied and a little aloof since

Judith and Robert had left. She couldn't understand why she and Keith seemed destined always to take two steps back for every step forward. She hoped today would be another forward step.

He was in the kitchen, sipping coffee with Jo-Jo, when she came downstairs. "Good morning, Jo-Jo, Keith." Miranda reached for the coffee pot, noting that they both looked strangely out of sorts. "Is something wrong?" Miranda asked.

"Let's just say something's not right," Keith replied with a frown.

Miranda grabbed her cup and sat. "What do you mean?"

"Blue Eye's gone."

"*Gone?*" she gasped. "What do you mean gone?"

"As in he's not in his corral."

"Do you think he jumped out?" Miranda asked.

"It's not impossible," he said slowly, his expression dubious. "But I'm confounded that he hadn't done it sooner, if he had the ability to clear that height."

"Maybe all those mares finally got to him?" Miranda suggested.

"If that's the case, we'll know right where to find him."

"Are you going to look now?" she asked.

"Can't. It's like pea soup out there."

"You're right about that. I couldn't spot any of the horses from my bedroom window and could barely even make out the barn."

"We'll have to wait for it to clear up a little bit," he said. "Riding into a herd in the fog would only spook them."

It was almost noon before the haze burned off. Walking out into the pasture, Miranda and Keith scouted for Blue Eye. Although hundreds of hoofprints pockmarked the frosty ground, there were no horses in sight. "Where are they all?" Miranda asked, baffled.

Keith shook his head with knitted brows. "I've got a weird feeling in my gut about all this."

"It's almost a thousand acres," Miranda said. "They could be anywhere."

"True, but they usually splinter off into small groups. Mustangs don't tend to all stay congregated. In any case, there's no point in speculation. Let's just saddle up and go take a look."

Miranda rode by Keith's side as they set out at a ground-covering trot. Scouting the periphery and creek banks, where the animals would go for water, they still came up clueless, until reaching the northernmost periphery and base of the mountains that her grandparents used to lease for summer grazing.

"I'll be damned! Look at that!" Keith exclaimed, leaping off his horse before Miranda even saw what had caught his eye. Kneeling in the mud, he held up a strand of broken wire in his gloved hand. "See this?"

"Did they break through it?" Miranda asked.

"Only if they brought a set of wire cutters," Keith said dryly.

"What do you mean? Are you implying someone cut the fence?"

"Yup," he replied grimly. "These horses didn't break out. Someone intentionally let them out, and I've got a clue about who might have been behind it."

"Who?" she asked. "And why?"

"I didn't want to upset you or your grandmother, but I overheard a conversation between your aunt and uncle the day they arrived. They weren't happy about this situation and seemed inclined to do something about it."

"Like what?" Miranda asked.

"They didn't say, but they mentioned a guy named Marvin. Does the name mean anything to you?"

"Yeah. Marvin McRae worked here for about thirty years 'til Jo-Jo gave him the boot. He was never a very nice man, even when Gramps was around, but they were boyhood pals, so Gramps kept him on as a hand."

"If your grandmother fired him, he's probably got a beef."

"I suspect you're right," Miranda said. "What if something bad happens because of this?"

"The liability is on your shoulders," Keith replied. "I suspect that's exactly what Judith and Robert were hoping for. They were really clever if they hired someone else to do their dirty work. There's no one to point a finger at them."

"I suppose so," Miranda said. "But even if it was Marvin, that doesn't solve the problem of finding and capturing two hundred horses. How are we going to do that?"

"We'll have to see if we can entice some of them to come back." Keith pulled cutters and pliers out of his saddlebag and started pulling down more wire.

"What are you doing?"

"Making a wider gate. Go ahead and tie the horses and help me coil this wire up. We don't want them to get tangled in it when they come back through."

Miranda regarded him skeptically. "You really think they'll just come wandering back?"

"Yup," he replied. "Not all, but some of them will.

They were safe and secure in this pasture, and horses like to be safe and secure. After they realize the grass isn't greener on that mountain, at least not in wintertime, they'll want to come back. And they'll look to enter in the same place they went out. Our job is to make it real easy for them to do just that."

"So we're just going to wait and see?"

He shrugged. "Not much more we can do at this point, other than putting the word out to neighboring ranches to keep an eye out for them. We especially don't want to piss the ranchers off if they find wild horses running through their cow pastures. If that does happen, however, maybe we can get some help corralling some of them."

"We'd better get back and tell Jo-Jo about this," Miranda said. "She's going to want to make some calls."

"I agree that she needs to know they got out," Keith said. "But there's no reason to tell her our suspicions. If Marvin really was acting as a hired gun for your aunt and uncle, that's going to create a really touchy situation for you. Let's be certain before we say anything."

"I agree." Miranda nodded. "She's already had enough stress as it is. But how do you propose getting proof?"

"I'm going to pay Marvin a little visit."

"I don't even know where he lives. How are you going to find him?"

"I'll begin at the places where you always find all manner of skunks and low crawlers—the local watering holes."

―∞―

"Keith! Randa! I'm glad you're back." Jo-Jo met Keith and Miranda on the front porch as they were scraping the mud from their boots. "I just got the strangest call from Donna Knowlton over at the Flying K. She says her sons saw a bunch of mustangs while they were up on the mountain gathering strays. I just can't understand it. How did they get out? And why, when they have plenty of green hay and a thousand acres of good pasture?"

"Mustangs are a bit unpredictable that way," Keith said.

"I guess I know that now, but what are we going to do about it?" Jo-Jo asked.

"Don't fret about a thing," Keith reassured her. "I know these animals pretty well. We'll get them back."

"Keith has a plan," Miranda said. "He thinks some of them will return on their own."

"Some will," he agreed. "As for the rest, our first priority is to find out where they are."

"Will the BLM help?" Jo-Jo asked.

Keith shook his head. "Not likely. Once they deliver the horses, they wash their hands of any more responsibility. I think the easiest way to locate them would be to bring in a helicopter to do a sweep of the mountain. It could even push them back in this direction."

"So I'll have to hire a helicopter? That's likely to cost hundreds if not thousands of dollars. Another expense I can't afford." Jo-Jo shook her head with a sigh of dismay. "Maybe Judith is right and I didn't think this decision through as well as I should have."

Keith and Miranda exchanged a knowing look.

"I'm so sorry, Jo-Jo," Miranda said.

"It's not your fault, child. These things happen." Jo-Jo gave a resigned sigh. "I s'pose we just have to find the best way to deal with it."

"I'll phone Mitch to see what it would take to fly his bird in to gather them," Keith said. "Don't worry about the cost. Mitch'll probably only charge us for the fuel, and I'm happy to cover that."

"Why should you?" Jo-Jo protested. "It's not your responsibility."

"I told you I'd secure the fence," Keith said. "It's my negligence if they broke through it. You said the Knowltons saw some of the horses? Did they say exactly where?"

"No, but she did say the band they spotted were being chased by a pack of wolves."

"Wolves?" Miranda repeated. "I didn't know we had wolves around here."

"We've just never seen any in these parts before now," Jo-Jo said, "but they've been steadily spreading across the state since they were reintroduced to Yellowstone."

"Wyoming's full of them," Keith said. "The only good thing about that is if there's wolves up there, the horses have just one more reason to come back home. I'd almost lay money that we'll have some of them back in the pasture by tomorrow. In the meantime, I'd like to go and talk to the Knowltons. It would be helpful if we could at least pin down the general area where were spotted."

"I'll phone Donna," Jo-Jo said, "and let her know to expect you."

Two hours later, Miranda and Keith left the Flying K with only the vaguest idea of where one band of horses might be. "Dirk wasn't the most helpful person in the world, was he?" Miranda remarked.

"Yeah. He's nothing at all like the guy I remember."

"You knew him before?"

"Not well, but rodeo is a really small world. After

two full summers doing my trick-riding gig in Cody, there weren't too many cowboys I didn't meet at one time or another. As I recall, Dirk Knowlton used to be a helluva rough rider."

"He's rough all right. All I can say is his brother's a whole lot more personable."

Keith felt an uncomfortable churning in his gut. "How would you know?"

"Wade is Jo-Jo's attorney," she said. "I met him when he reviewed the contracts. Jo-Jo even tried to play matchmaker."

"Did she now?" he remarked, careful to keep his tone bland.

"Yeah." She slanted Keith a sly look. "She was quite enthralled with him. Said Wade Knowlton's the most eligible bachelor in all of Madison County."

"And what did you think of him?" The truck gave a slight lurch as he slammed it into third gear.

"Oh, he was a real charmer all right…" She grinned. "But not my type at all."

He glanced her way. "No? Why's that?"

"He was far too staid for me." Her grin spread wider. "Not many people know this, but I tend to go for the more adventurous type—the kind of guy who likes to throw knives and roast snakes. You know, the type who also tells erotic bedtime stories…the one whose kisses make my toes curl and knows the secrets of my body better than I do." She cocked a teasing brow. "Know anybody like that?"

"Oh yeah, sweetheart. I know that guy real well." He reached for her, pulling her close to his side.

"Keith? I understand your reluctance to stay here, but

it makes no sense for you not to be part of the ranch. I hate this idiotic situation. It seems so stupid and point-less. If we didn't have you, we'd have to hire someone else. Why can't we be together *and* work together? Lots of couples do so successfully."

"Because it would look like exactly the scenario that film intimated about me—that I'm just a lothario who preys on horse-loving women."

"But you aren't!" she insisted.

"You know that, and I know that, but what about the rest of the world? How would it appear if I'm living with you and your seventy-two-year-old grandmother, just the three of us in a happy little ménage?"

"Weren't you the one who said other people's opin-ions don't matter? If you don't work here, you'd have to work somewhere close by for us to be together, and then people would probably talk anyway. So what difference does it really make?"

"My good name makes all the difference in the world to me," he said. "That film destroyed my credibility, and I'm still trying to deal with it."

Miranda chewed her lip. "Then we'll just have to find a way to repair the damage."

"Nothing can ever undo the damage."

"So you're just going to let that film stand in our way?"

"No," he said. He still didn't know the answer, but one thing he knew for certain, his future happiness lay in finding it. "We'll figure something out, *Aiwattsi*, I promise, but right now our biggest concern is getting those horses back."

Chapter 29

THE NEXT DAY, KEITH AND MIRANDA STOPPED AT several small hole-in-the-wall bars, making inquiries about Marvin. He had plenty of outstanding tabs, but no one had seen the man…until they asked about him at the Pioneer.

The man behind the bar was big and imposing, with features as worn and weathered as the cracked leather barstools. He zeroed in on Keith, eying him up and down suspiciously. "Haven't see you 'round here b'fore."

"Nope," Keith replied and then sat on a stool, patting the one next to him for Miranda.

The bartender hesitated. His gaze darted pointedly to a sign posted on the wall to the right of the bar. WE RESERVE THE RIGHT TO REFUSE SERVICE TO ANYONE. He then turned back to wiping glasses.

What was his problem? That Keith was a stranger? Or did he have an issue with Indians? Fearing the growing tension, Miranda stepped in. "Hi. I'm Miranda Sutton. Maybe you know my grandparents? Bud and Josephine?"

The bartender's expression suddenly relaxed. "Yeah, Bud was a good 'un. I was sorry to hear he passed on. How's Jo-Jo doing these days?"

"She's well enough," Miranda replied, "but needing help with the ranch. That's why Keith and I are here."

He cocked a bushy brow. "So you ain't just passin' through?"

"No. I'm here to stay," Miranda said. "I'm living at

the ranch now with Jo-Jo. We're turning it into a long-term pasture for wild horses."

"Yeah. I heard some talk about that," he replied. "There's some around here who might not think much of that."

"It's their right to think whatever they like," Miranda replied, "but it's also Jo-Jo's right to do whatever she pleases with her property."

"That so?" His bushy brows met in a scowl. "Them's big words from such a little lady." He finally asked in a gravelly baritone with a hint of humor, "What'll you have?"

"Two beers," Keith answered. "Whatever's on tap."

The bartender grunted acknowledgement and turned to fill the order. A moment later he slammed two foamy mugs onto the bar beside a dish of stale pretzels.

"'Scuse me," Miranda began again, "do you happen to know where we can find Marvin McRae? Have you seen him lately?"

"That depends on why you're looking for him," the bartender replied, his wariness returned.

"Some of the mustangs got loose, and we're needing some help rounding them up."

"Heard some talk about that too," the bartender said.

"From whom? Marvin?" she asked.

"Mebbe."

"So he *was* here?"

"Yeah, just last night, but I didn't wait on him. You might want to talk to Janice. The ol' horn toad was pretty chatty with her." He signaled a redheaded waitress from a table across the room. She dropped off her order and then approached the bar. She glanced at Keith and Miranda, and her eyes widened. "Keith?"

Keith set down his beer, his brows furrowed as if struggling to place her.

"It's all right, I don't expect you to remember me. Janice Combes. My father was—"

"Combes Bucking Bulls," he finished with a grin. "Yeah, I remember you now. It's been a long time."

"Yeah. It has. I've been away for years and just came back."

"Do you know Miranda Sutton?" Keith asked. "She just moved in with her grandmother over at the Circle S in Silver Star."

"So you're the one who took on all those mustangs?" Janice said.

"Yeah," Miranda answered. "You heard about it?"

"Who hasn't?" Janice laughed. "You've become the talk of the county. I also heard some of them already got loose."

"Word does spread like wildfire around here, doesn't it?" Miranda remarked dryly.

"Well, I probably hear more talk than most, working here," Janice said.

"The bartender said Marvin had a few words to say about it?"

"Choice words, more like," Janice answered. "He was on a real rant last night. He's a mean ol' bastard, but he tips well. In fact, last night was the biggest tip I ever got from him. Come to think of it, he threw quite a bit of money around. He also ordered only call brands. Not his usual MO at all."

"What did he have to say about the Circle S?" Keith asked.

"He's still pissed off about getting canned and went on a long tirade about getting payback."

"Did he now?" Keith remarked.

"Yeah, but I didn't pay him too much heed. You know how drunks will go on. I figured he was probably just blowing smoke."

"Maybe not. The horses didn't push through that fence," Keith said. "Somebody cut it. And it sounds like Marvin had as good a reason to do it as anyone."

"The fence was cut?" Janice pursed her mouth. "Well, I reckon that sheds quite a different light on things, doesn't it?"

"Is he a regular here?" Keith asked.

"When he has money, he is. So I expect him back. I'll be off for the next couple of days, but I'd be glad to see what I can coax out of him for you the next time he's in."

"You'd do that for us?" Miranda asked.

"Absolutely. Cutting that fence was despicable. Just leave it to me." She winked. "I'll find out sure enough if he did it."

⚬⚬⚬

The next morning, a number of horses had congregated in the pasture. Once more Keith's prediction had proven true. Throwing her clothes on, Miranda rushed downstairs to the kitchen. "Did you see them, Jo-Jo?"

"Did I see what?"

"The horses! A bunch of them have come back."

Jo-Jo went to the window to peer out. Her lips curved into a smile. "I'll be damned."

"Have you seen Keith yet?"

"Not yet. He's probably out there." Jo-Jo nodded toward the pasture.

Miranda grabbed her jacket and boots.

"No coffee?" Jo-Jo asked.

"No time," Miranda said, rushing out the door. She found Keith saddling Sassy and Sadie.

"What are you doing?" she asked.

"We need to move this band to another enclosure. Otherwise, they'll go right back out again."

"So you're still leaving the fence open?"

"Only for another day or so. If the rest haven't returned by then, they probably won't. We'll need to go look for them. You'd better go grab your hat and some gloves, cowgirl," he said. "We might be out here for a while."

Miranda spent the afternoon corralling horses with Keith. Although they rode harder than she was used to, Miranda easily followed his lead. She wondered more than once what it would be like to run the place together. To build a future together.

They followed the same routine the next couple of days as several more small bands trickled in. On the third day, they got a call from Janice Combes. "Hey, Miranda! It's Janice from the Pioneer. I've got some news for you."

"Oh, yeah? Did you get anything out of Marvin?"

"Matter of fact I did. It took half a bottle of Crown Royal, but he finally spilled the beans. It seems that Miz Sutton's son-in-law paid him a thousand bucks to cut the fence and stampede the horses up the mountain."

"So it really was a grudge," Miranda said.

"Sure enough," Janice replied. "After he cut the fence, he turned Keith's stallion loose just for pure spite 'cause he thinks Keith replaced him. Several people in the bar heard it all. So you've got ample witnesses."

"I don't know how to thank you, Janice. That's everything we needed to know."

"There's more," Janice said. "Dirk and I located a few of the mustangs yesterday when we were bringing stray cattle down from Bulldog Mountain. If you and Keith need any help tracking them, we'd be glad to ride up there with you. Just let us know if you need us."

"Keith's trying to bring in a helicopter, but we may take you up on that," Miranda said. "I can't tell you how much I appreciate the offer, Janice."

"No problem. What are neighbors for?"

"That was Janice?" Keith asked when she hung up the phone.

"Yeah. You were right all along. It was Marvin. Should we notify the police?"

"I'd rather let that be your grandmother's call, since her daughter and son-in-law are involved."

"Yeah, I see what you mean. I doubt she's going to want to press charges. What are we going to do?"

"Let's just hold off doing anything until we get all the horses in," Keith replied. "Mitch said he'd be happy to send Trey up here with the chopper, but he won't be free for at least another week."

"How many are left?" Miranda asked.

"At last count, all but twenty-two have returned."

"Since there's only a few of them still out there, should we try to gather them by horseback?" Miranda asked. "Dirk and Janice offered to help if we need it."

"If we go that route, I'll need Little Bear."

"Little Bear? Why?" Miranda asked. "I thought you retired him."

"I did, but I have a strong hunch we'll never be able

to catch those horses without him. By now Blue Eye thinks those mares are his. He's not going to give them up without a fight." His gaze narrowed. "I suspect it's going to come to a showdown between us."

———∿∿∿———

Having made the decision to go after the horses, Keith made a series of calls. To Miranda's surprise, the trucks and trailers began pulling in the very next morning. Keith's cousin was the first to arrive with Little Bear. Climbing out of the truck cab, she stepped forward, offering a callused hand and a friendly smile. "You must be Miranda. I'm Tonya." She gestured to a redhead who'd accompanied her. "This is Krista Everett. Her family runs a backcountry-hunting outfit outside Dubois. I thought maybe you could use another hand, especially one used to riding rough terrain," she explained.

"Nice to meet you both," Miranda said.

"Do you remember Krista, Keith?" Tonya asked.

"I do," Keith said. "I know your brothers. Jared and Reid, right? What are they doing these days?"

"Jared's running the outfitting business since my Dad semiretired, and Reid just got back stateside from Afghanistan. We're hoping he'll be home by Christmas."

"Is he out of the marines for good?" Keith asked.

"He is. I think Ton and I will both be glad to have him home again."

Miranda wondered what that implied. Was Tonya involved with Krista's brother?

"Nice place you have here," Tonya said, changing the subject.

"Thanks," Miranda replied. "I'll be happy to show you around later. Should we go ahead and unload your horses?"

Just as they were about to do that, another truck pulled up the drive with the West Livestock emblem on the door and Mitch's son Dave behind the wheel. The engine had barely cut off when Donny jumped out with a wide grin. "Hey Keith! Miranda! Thought we'd join the mustang wrangling party."

"The more the merrier," Miranda said with a laugh. "It's great to see you both!"

For the next few hours, Keith was like a general planning his campaign. With map in hand, he circled the area of Bulldog Mountain where the horses were last seen. Since the horses were halfway between the two ranches, he decided to split the wranglers up into two teams—Donny and Krista would join Dirk and Janice in their approach from the south, while he, Tonya, Dave, and Miranda would come in from the north.

They set out early the next morning, prepared for a long, hard ride in near-freezing temps. Keith led the expedition on Little Bear, and Krista brought up the rear behind Miranda, who was thankful for reliable ol' Sadie, who was as sure-footed as a mountain goat.

After almost three hours of riding on treacherous mountain cow paths, Keith picked up a trail of hoofprints and fresh dung. Not long after that he spotted Blue Eye and his stolen harem. Signaling the riders, Keith pulled up. "Let's not go any closer."

Miranda uncapped her camera, zooming in on the stallion and his mares. Blue Eye had taken notice of their presence with perked ears and flared nostrils, standing as a sentinel over his mares. "What do we do now?" Miranda asked in a low tone.

"First we'll give the others our GPS location in the hope they can flank 'em for us. Next, we'll need to try and get those mares moving. If I can separate the stallion, the mares just might cooperate, but I don't think Blue Eye's going to be too amenable to that."

"What if you can't separate them?" Miranda asked.

Keith and Dave exchanged a grim look.

"What are you not telling me?" she demanded.

"If we can't do this any other way, I'll have to shoot him," Keith replied.

Miranda's jaw dropped. "I can't believe you said that! You'd actually *shoot* him? How can you even think it?"

"How can I *not* think it?" Keith argued "He's not going to give up those mares without a fight, and I can't afford for anyone to get hurt in the process. You already knew there was a fifty-fifty chance I'd have to do it anyway. I told you from the beginning that would be his fate if I couldn't make him safe to be around."

"But there's got to be another way!" she protested.

"Look, there's no point in getting all worked up about it," he said. "I have a plan. It's not guaranteed to work, but let's just see what happens, okay?"

"What kind of plan?" Miranda asked.

"I'm going to use Little Bear to draw him away from the mares," Keith said. "While Blue Eye's defending his claim, the rest of you are going to push those mares back toward the ranch."

"But what about Little Bear? Didn't you say stallions will fight to the death? How are you going to stop that?" Miranda asked.

"Dave and I will try and rope them, but if things go bad, we'll have to use the rifle."

"No, Keith. You can't! This whole thing sounds way too dangerous."

He shrugged. "I've roped plenty of mustangs before. You up for it, Dave?"

"Hell yeah." Dave grinned.

"I'm staying with you," Miranda said.

"Fine," Keith replied tersely. "I don't have time to argue about this anymore. Just stay out of the way. This is dangerous, and I don't want you to get hurt."

A moment later, Keith radioed Dirk and Janice with their position and then pulled back just close enough to keep the horses in sight, but still distant enough that Blue Eye wouldn't feel the urge to move his band. Once the other wranglers were in position to support their effort, Keith dismounted and unsaddled his horse.

Miranda's breath caught at Little Bear's instant transformation. With his gaze pinned on his adversary, he raised his head and snorted, his body trembling with nervous energy, much like a warrior preparing for battle. Little Bear pranced, pawed, and jigged as Keith led him in the direction of the herd, murmuring instructions in low tones that only the horse could hear.

With their heads raised and ears pricked, the mares looked on with avid interest as Keith released his horse. Arching his crested neck and raising his tail, Little Bear galloped toward the periphery of the band. Miranda's breath caught in apprehension as Blue Eye spun and charged to meet him. The two horses came together, roaring and rearing.

While the mares watched them engage, Dirk, Janice,

and the others surreptitiously circled the band. At the same time, Keith on the ground and Dave in the saddle approached the combatants, ropes at the ready. Miranda watched with her heart in her throat, terrified for Little Bear and even more for Keith as he moved straight into the battle zone where two pairs of hooves slashed the air.

Swift and sure, Keith repeatedly dodged the danger of lashing heels and snapping jaws as he prepared to make his move. The first cast of Dave's lasso glanced off Blue Eye's shoulder. The second missed completely. The third finally caught Blue Eye's neck. In a flash, Keith moved in, looping a foreleg with his rope. Blue Eye now fought on two fronts, one eye turned to Little Bear, the other to Keith, while wildly kicking, biting, and plunging.

While Tonya, Krista, and Janice led the mares away from the fray, Donny and Dirk caught Little Bear with their lassos. Using ropes, muscle, and sheer will, the four wranglers struggled to separate the battling stallions. While Keith continued the war of wills with Blue Eye, Donny and Dirk overcame Little Bear. Battered and bleeding, the older stallion disengaged and exited the theatre, wearing his battle scars with pride.

With fists clenched at her sides, Miranda watched the final battle for supremacy between Keith and Blue Eye. She was vividly reminded of the pivotal scene in *The Horse Whisperer* when Tom Booker used similar methods to wrangle the bellicose Pilgrim. After what felt like eternity, Keith managed to bring the belligerent Blue Eye to his knees. To her amazement, the horse suddenly quit struggling. With flanks heaving and mouth foaming, Blue Eye gave a great groan of surrender and lay down in defeat.

"I'm sorry it came to this, my brother," Keith said, stroking and caressing the horse's neck. "But there can be only one master." Time suspended as he crooned more words that she couldn't understand. When Keith finally looked up at her, his grim expression had softened. "You see, *Aiwattsi*? It is over. Now, the real work with this horse can begin."

———

Once recovered, Blue Eye seemed perfectly happy to follow the trail of his mares back down the mountain to their pasture. When the last weary wrangler arrived back at the ranch, a feast awaited. Jo-Jo had outdone herself with a spread of food that covered virtually every surface of the kitchen and dining room. The party lasted for several hours before eventually breaking up, with Dirk and Janice driving home, Dave and Donny heading to the bunkhouse, and Tonya and Krista retiring to the guest room in the ranch house.

Once the guests had left, Miranda revealed the truth to Jo-Jo. "You really believe Judith and Robert were behind this?" Jo-Jo asked incredulously.

"It's possible Marvin acted on his own," Miranda said, "but that doesn't explain the source of the cash he's been throwing around."

"Unbelievable." Jo-Jo shook her head. "My own daughter."

"I'm sorry I came between you," Miranda said.

"You didn't, sweetheart. I'm just going to have to set Judith straight once and for all."

"What are you going to do?" Miranda asked.

"I have half a mind to disown her completely," Jo-Jo said, "but since no harm was really done, I'm just going to make it clear she isn't welcome back for Christmas. Or maybe the next one either. Speaking of which...will Keith be spending it with us?"

"We haven't talked about it," Miranda said.

"He isn't still planning to leave, is he?"

"I don't know that either," Miranda said sadly. Jo-Jo laid her hand on hers, her faded eyes seeking Miranda's. "I didn't think he was the right one for you in the beginning, but I'm not so sure anymore. If you really love him, Randa, I think you'd best do whatever it takes to convince Keith to stay."

Miranda left her grandmother and pulled on a jacket, eager for a word alone with Keith. She opened the door and found him waiting for her on the front-porch swing. He silently held the blanket open and welcomed her into his arms. Claiming the quilt and the quiet of the night, she snuggled under his chin.

"I'm guessing you spoke to Jo-Jo?" he said.

"Yes. I told her all about Judith and Robert's role in this sabotage."

"What did she say?" Keith asked.

"She was livid," Miranda said. "She called Judith right away. Of course my aunt said Marvin lied and denied all culpability, but Jo-Jo doesn't believe her. She's almost ready to disown Judith at this point. I hope it all blows over in time, but they won't be welcome back to the ranch for a while. This day seems so surreal to me," she said. "I still can't believe you did what you did with Blue Eye."

"I'm just glad he finally gave in," Keith said. "I truly didn't want to shoot him."

"Would you really have done it?"

"Dunno." He shrugged. "I'm just glad he didn't push me to the point of having to make that decision."

"I got all of it on film, you know. I'm adding it to my documentary. You're the star of it, by the way."

He frowned down at her. "I'm not so sure I want to be in any more films, Miranda. I got third-degree burns the last time around."

"I know you did, and that's exactly why I need to do this. I want to make it up to you, to make things right again."

"What's done can't be undone, *Aiwattsi*."

"Please trust me in this, Keith. I know this could turn things around for you if you would only narrate it for me."

"You want me to narrate it?" He shook his head. "Why?"

"Yes. I want to tell the mustang story through your eyes. You understand them better than anyone. It's almost magical the way you connect with those horses. There's no one else I want. No one else who could bring the same passion and poignancy to this project. Please, Keith," she pleaded. "This means everything to me."

He cupped her chin and gazed into her eyes. "There's no one else I would even consider doing it for. Just let me think about it, okay?"

"Okay," she said softly. "There's something else I've been wanting to talk to you about, but I didn't know how to bring it up."

"What is it, *Aiwattsi*?"

She took a deep breath. "Keith... I've been giving

this a lot of thought. Do you think once everything is set straight again, that maybe we could talk a little bit more about that nonfake engagement?"

"I'd like very much to talk about a nonfake engagement. Maybe even with a nonfake ring wrapped around that skinny little finger"—he reached for her hand and gave it a squeeze—"but we can't have a future together until I have something more to offer you than just my name."

"What if we took you on as a partner? If we let you buy a stake in the ranch, would that ease your mind? I figure you'd then have a vested interest in this place and a reason stay."

"I already have a reason to stay," he said, stroking her cheek with the pad of his callused thumb. "My vested interest is in you, but you need to understand something, Miranda. I don't believe in free rides. I pay my own way."

"If it's the same concerns you voiced before, I might have an answer. What if Jo-Jo were to sell you a few acres? Maybe enough to set up your own independent training facility? Would that work for you?"

Keith drew back with a surprised look. "I don't know. Do you think your grandmother would go for that?"

"Are you kidding? It was Jo-Jo's idea. She's come to think a lot of you, Keith, and wants you to stay here almost as much as I do. I'm sure she'd give you a real fair price and even hold a mortgage if that made it easier for you. It's worth exploring, isn't it?" She regarded him with hope-filled eyes. "If you wanted to, you could even start an internship program for fledgling horse trainers. Interns are really cheap labor. I know this from personal experience."

"If Jo-Jo agreed to do this, I'd pay her fair market value for her land and nothing less."

"But that could be tens of thousands," Miranda said.

"Which would still leave me enough to build an indoor arena," he replied. "If I'm going to do this, it can't be half-assed. I'd need a year-round training facility."

"But, Keith, how could you afford it?"

He gave her a rueful smile. "Maybe you shouldn't judge a book by its cover. I'm not rich, but I'm not poor either, or stupid. I invested a good bit over the years. I've got a decent nest egg. I live simply by choice, *Aiwattsi*, not by necessity, and I have no wish to change that."

"Me either," she said. "I've come to appreciate the simple life. My needs are pretty minimal too. Will you do it? Can we talk to Jo-Jo?"

"Only if we also talk to a lawyer about a prenup."

She blinked. "A what?"

"A prenuptial agreement. I'd want you to consent to one."

"I don't understand. Why?"

"Because I don't want anyone, especially your aunt and uncle, to have any reason to believe I was after you for your grandmother's ranch."

"That's crazy!"

"No, it isn't," he said. "If we move forward with this idea, that has to be part of the bargain."

"I don't like it," she said, "but I suppose I can live with it if you can."

He took her face in his hands and kissed her tenderly. "The only thing I *can't* live with, *Aiwattsi*, is the thought of being without you."

Chapter 30

KEITH DROVE THROUGH THE GATES OF THE RANCH WITH A feeling of peace and harmony he'd never experienced before, a change he suspected had everything to do with the woman by his side.

"Nervous?" she asked, catching his gaze.

"Surprisingly, no," he answered. "What about you?"

"A little," she replied with a wan smile. "I kind of wish you had warned them first. What if they don't like the idea? What if they don't like *me*?"

He reached out to take her hand. "Don't worry. They will, *Aiwattsi*. Just be aware that my people take a little while to warm up to outsiders."

"That's just it." Her lower lip quivered. "I'm afraid they'll always think of me as an outsider."

"Some probably will," he said. "But not my family. Tonya liked you from the very start. Huttsi will too. Kenu is more reserved and harder to read. He may take a while longer, but be patient. He has a strong sense of family. I know he'll come to love you as a daughter."

He parked the truck and gave her a reassuring peck. "If you are uncomfortable in any way, just say the word, and we'll go."

"Thank you for bringing me here, Keith. I know how hard this must be for you."

"It is," he confessed, "but your presence has made it much easier. Come, it's time to meet my family."

Taking her hand, Keith led Miranda around to the back of the house.

"The back door?" she asked with a puzzled look.

He grinned. "My grandmother will be in the kitchen. She always is at this time of day." He followed with a knock and then entered without waiting for a reply.

"Two Wolves!" Huttsi's eyes lit up. "My heart jumps. It has been far too long." Dropping the dough she was working with, she came to him, wrapping flour-covered arms around him.

He hugged her back and planted a kiss on her wrinkled cheek. "Huttsi, there's someone you need to meet." He reached for Miranda, who stood in the doorway, hands clasped in front of her and a nervous smile hovering on her lips. Bringing her close to his side, he completed the introduction. "This is Miranda…my wife."

Huttsi's black eyes widened. "Your *wife*?"

"Yes." He grinned and kissed Miranda's hand. "We got married yesterday. We had originally planned to wait until next year, but neither of us wanted a big wedding, so there seemed no real reason to wait."

Huttsi gave a solemn nod. "So you have finally chosen."

He knew what she meant. He'd decided to live his life outside of the reservation. "Yes. I have chosen."

She looked to Miranda, the corner of her lips curving with approval. "It is good. Go now and find your grandfather."

He hesitated to leave Miranda, who appeared tense enough to break.

"Come, child." Huttsi offered a soft smile and took her by the arm. "I must teach you to make fry bread."

Keith cocked a brow at Miranda in a silent question. She answered with a firm nod. "It's all good, Keith. Go to him."

Once more, Keith found his grandfather at the sweat lodge, this time outside talking with some elders. He regarded Keith without even blinking. "I knew you would come."

"How? Was it a vision?"

Kenu nodded. "Two visions."

"What were these two visions, Kenu?" Keith asked, handing him a pouch of tobacco.

"The first vision was the return of the black wolf and the white wolf. Once more they were engaged in a great battle, but this time as they tumbled together locked in combat, the two bodies merged into one—a gray wolf."

Keith considered Kenu in amazement. How could he know that Keith's struggle was over? That he'd finally come to reconcile his two worlds? "What was the second vision, Kenu?" he asked.

"It was once more the gray wolf, but this time he was bedded down in a great field…with a doe."

Aiwattsi. How did the old man know? He'd said nothing to his family about Miranda. Had Tonya? Even if she had, he hadn't shared his pet name for her with anyone. His wonderment became awe. "I brought you a gift, Kenu."

His grandfather smiled. "Show me this gift…Gray Wolf."

Keith led him to the horse trailer where he unloaded Blue Eye. The horse came quietly off the trailer and eyed the old man with a toss of his head and a snort.

"You have brought back the spirit horse?"

"Yes," Keith replied. "But this time, he, like me, is complete."

Epilogue

Sundance Film Festival, Park City, Utah
One year later

"AND THE WINNER FOR BEST INDEPENDENT AMERICAN Documentary is *Native Whispers*, a moving biopic of a man, a horse, and mutual redemption, produced and directed by Miranda Sutton-Russo."

Miranda's hands shook as she ascended the steps to the podium and microphone. The single note card wavered in her trembling hands. Although she'd penned a brief acceptance speech on the million-to-one chance that she'd actually win, her eyes were now too blurred with tears to make out the words. Letting the card flutter to the stage, she stepped up to the mic to speak the words that were imprinted on her heart.

"Two years ago, I never could have envisioned making this film, or that when I embarked on this journey, this documentary would change so many lives. Five hundred mustangs now have a permanent home on lush pastures in Montana. Almost a hundred others have been trained and now have homes with loving families. Over a dozen at-risk Native American youths have turned their lives around by working with these once wild horses." Her voice cracked as she looked to Keith. "A single man found the redemption he so desperately needed, and in *him* I found my soul mate." He returned a smile filled with pride and love.

Miranda drew a breath and continued, her voice quavering. "But none of this ever would have come to pass without the woman who always believed in me and encouraged my dreams. I only wish she could have seen it all come to fruition." She paused, blinking back the tears that threatened to overcome her and then raised her statuette to the heavens. "I wish to dedicate this award to my incredible grandmother, Josephine Mirabelle Sutton."

About the Author

Victoria Vane is a #1 bestselling, award-winning author of smart and sexy romance. Her works range from comedic romps to emotionally compelling erotic romance and have received over twenty awards and nominations, including a 2016 Red Carpet Finalist for both *Rough Rider* and *Jewel of the East*, 2015 Red Carpet Finalist for Best Contemporary Romance (*Slow Hand*), 2014 RONE Winner for Best Historical Post-Medieval Romance (*Treacherous Temptations*), and *Library Journal* Best E-book Romance of 2012 (The Devil DeVere series). She currently resides in Palm Coast, Florida, with her husband, two sons, a little black dog, and an Arabian horse. Find her online at www.victoriavane.com, on Facebook, or on Twitter @authorvictoriav.